The Nibelung Gold

By Koos Verkaik

Outer Banks Publishing Group
Raleigh/Outer Bank

SECOND EDITION – July 2019

Library of Congress Control Number: 2019944685

ISBN 13: 978-1-7320452-9-3
ISBN-10: 1-7320452-9-1
eISBN : 978-0-4634408-6-5

 1

Wolf wondered what had possessed him to make such an early start. It had been a late night. His head was still spinning from the liquor, his legs were heavy, and when he crossed a bridge the stench rising from the dark canal sickened him.

Although with almost half a million inhabitants, Amsterdam at the end of the nineteenth century had become an overcrowded city. Today there was a serene quiet on this early Sunday morning.

Wolf wore old, worn trousers and a similarly shabby jacket. A felt hat stood on top of his head, balancing on his thick, dark curls. The clothes came from a cupboard in the room he owned at the Oudezijds Voorburgwal in the center of the city.

No one who saw him would guess that he was also the owner of a beautiful house on the bank of the river Vecht, where he lived among the moneybags; a century earlier successful Amsterdam merchants had started to build their impressive country seats there, and Wolf had acquired his by inheritance.

He was on his way to see Jacob Leopold van Beek, who lived in a splendid house along the Prinsengracht, one of the three main canals in Amsterdam that were started in the year 1612 and took 50 years to build.

In spite of their age difference—Wolf was in his early twenties, Jacob well over fifty—the men were good friends, and they shared a passion for everything that had to do with the occult. They had invested money in a unique project: the thorough investigation and documentation of all possibly paranormal events.

Anyone who could demonstrate that a phenomenon like telekinesis existed by moving an object at a distance purely by the power of the mind, would be paid one thousand Dutch guilders Jacob kept in a small box in his desk.

No one had ever managed to do it.

Now, on this early Sunday, a woman who had announced herself in a letter as Wera Keller from Munich would visit Jacob to demonstrate that she had a thorough command of telekinesis. Someone who made the effort to take a train from the south of Germany to North Holland had to be taken seriously.

And so Wolf tried to get rid of his hangover during his walk and just before half-past seven he reached the high, narrow canal house of his friend and partner. Panting heavily, he climbed the stone stairs to the front door and dropped the copper knocker. He heard shuffling footsteps. The door opened. The ponderous body of Jacob filled the space between the doorposts. Two strong hands grabbed Wolf by the shoulders and gave him a shaking.

"What on earth took you so long, Wolf? Oh, I see it by your look. Your eyes are as red as those of a ferret. She's already here. Come inside, quick! She gives me the creeps... I'm really scared to be alone with her."

Jacob stepped aside while he spoke and pulled Wolf inside. In the dark hall, he slipped behind Wolf and started to push him with his hands against his shoulder blades in the direction of the front room. Wolf quickened his pace to stay ahead of the man.

In the room, two walnut desks were placed opposite one another. Above the paneling, there were rows of shelves around all walls. They sagged badly under the weight of brown files containing reports and the upper files touched the high, ornamented ceiling.

The door to the back room was open.

There was Jacob's huge study.

In an armchair near the French windows sat a young woman.

Wolf only noticed her when he had already reached the middle of the study, and there he stopped abruptly.

This was undoubtedly the most beautiful creature he had ever seen. He realized that immediately, just as he understood that it was not by coincidence that he had thought of the woman as a creature instead of a human being. She was a woman first of all - there was no doubt about that. Yet at the same time, there was something beastly about her. When she looked up at him with her dark eyes, he read something in her look that was neither human nor animal; he underwent a strange sensation as if a clever fortune-teller had allowed him to look into two crystal balls at the same time.

She rose to her feet.

Now she looked fragile. Her charm was overwhelming.

She made a simple remark, but with her voice, she molded it into something that was very much like the first line of a grand poem.

"So you must be Mr. Wolf. . ."

As she took a few steps into his direction, he staggered towards her as if all the liquor of yesterday was back in his blood, pumped to his brain by his wildly beating heart.

Her hand felt cool in his. He knew that his own hand was as hot and moist as his forehead.

Jacob plumped down in a chair. The arrival of his friend had given him new courage. He slapped on his knees and said in a loud voice, "Please sit down again, Mrs. Keller. You do the same, Wolf. First, I have a few questions for you, Mrs. Keller."

"Why did you prefer to meet us on a Sunday morning?"

Wera smoothed down her long black dress as she seated herself again in the armchair.

"That way I could be sure that no one else would be present here besides the two of you."

"This is something between the three of us. Is that what you are trying to say?"

"I will convince you of my special powers. I will also tell something about it that is especially meant for Wolf."

Jacob had recovered almost completely. Now, he showed that he was used to dealing with people who were in the possession of the oddest talents. Still, he evaded her glance as often as possible.

"You speak Dutch with a mild accent. Do you have a thorough command of other languages?"

"Only if that happens to be necessary," she answered mysteriously. Jacob nodded.

"Then you just pluck the words out of the air," he guessed.

Her reaction was a smile.

"You have eyes with which you might be able to hypnotize someone. As far as that is concerned, I have to disappoint you. We are not men who let ourselves be led by someone else's will."

Wolf was not so sure of that at the moment. The entire time he had continued to stare at Wera's fine face, her big eyes, and the complex plaiting of her thick, almost black hair.

"What is it that you want from Wolf?"

"Later ..." she answered.

"Very well. Let's waste no time," said Jacob. "We'll start with the test. After that, we can decide if we still want to listen to you, all right?"

He stood up and walked to his desk. He opened a drawer and took out a marble die that was as big as his fist.

"We will not play the game with objects that are so light that even a sigh or a breeze will set them in motion," he said. "One thousand Dutch guilders is quite something. For example, a police officer here in Amsterdam has to work a long, long time for a sum like that - for two years or more."

"The same as a police officer in Munich," Wera assured him with her clear, pleasant singsong tone.

"So you dare to play this particular game with the dice? You will remain at a proper distance and try to move it with the power of your mind?"

"Oh, I will make it roll. You are even allowed to tell me the number that has to appear on the upper side after I have let it come to rest."

Wolf broke out in a cold sweat and restlessly fidgeted on his chair. His thoughts went slowly. It occurred to him that Jacob, the realist, the skeptic, the suspicious investigator, was seldom if ever thrown off balance when he came face to face with someone who claimed to have a paranormal phenomenon. When Jacob had opened the door, however, he had told Wolf immediately that he was scared.

Scared of Wera Keller.

What had she told him when they had been alone together?

"There is something more," he heard Jacob say, who bent down for the second time to open a big drawer.

Jacob took out a peculiar object, which he had made himself. He had taken a mirror out of its frame and replaced it with transparent glass. On both small sides of the frame, he had fixed a support so that he could place the frame on the desktop and use it as a screen.

He placed the die behind it.

"Just taking precautionary measures," he said.

"And how about the money?" asked Wera.

"In a little box in my desk. If you pass the test, I will give you the money straight away. I hope you don't mind that the die is behind glass now..."

Wera stood up.

"Not at all. Investigators take all kinds of measures. And they are absolutely right to do so. I'm happy to abide by your wishes."

With quick fingers, she started to unbutton her dress. Jacob raised his hand.

"You don't have to undress yourself!"

Wera made a wild hissing sound. Jacob kept silent and remained standing at the side of his desk.

"I want to show you that I have nothing to hide. Don't tell me that this procedure is new to you. It is expected from many an experimental subject, and the investigator would often prefer to hold the subject's hands as well."

Wolf tried to concentrate on the die behind the glass. It did not work. When he automatically looked at Wera again, he was overwhelmed with feelings he had never experienced before.

All her clothes lay on the back of the chair. She stood proudly upright, with her hands on her hips. All of a sudden Wolf realized that there was another category above absolute beauty, which could not be described.

Now she spread her arms with the palms of her hands turned upward to show that they were empty; then she spun around on her heels a couple of times. Her voice resonated in all corners of the big room, as she spoke in a melodious tone.

"Choose a number of the die, Mr. Van Beek."

"All right. Five. Yes, I am thinking of five..."

Jacob's voice sounded uncertain.

Suddenly, there was the sound of creaking wood. All the drawers and little doors of Jacob's impressive desk flew open, and the desktop seemed to warp. The skillfully decorated legs came loose from the floor. Then with a loud bang, the desk landed on the parquet again.

The marble die began to move.

First, it slid to and fro with a soft rubbing sound; then it started to turn around and around, faster and faster. It flew up and shot through the glass pane in the frame. Pieces and splinters of glass rained down, while the die skimmed along walls and cupboards like a bird escaped from its cage.

Moving back above the desk, it remained hanging in the air for a while, motionless, denying the law of gravitation, and then it fell straight down. Bouncing on the desktop, it caused pits and scratches. Then it lay still. Wera repeated the number that Jacob had chosen.

"Five."

Wolf jumped to his feet. His shoes crushed glass into grit as he walked up to the desk. Together with Jacob, he stared at the die. The white, red-veined marble of the upper side showed five deep-drilled holes.

Later Wolf would not be able to remember for how long he had stood there staring. What he did remember was Wera was dressed again when he finally straightened his back and turned around. Never had he felt so strange and confused. He became so sick that he staggered back to his chair quickly and sat down. Through the mist before his watery eyes, he saw how Wera walked up to Jacob and reached out her hand. Jacob, who still had not recovered himself and trembled with fear, nodded in silence and took a flat wooden box from a desk drawer. He opened it and paid Wera the promised thousand Dutch guilders.

Wera moved her hand past her head and felt that the braids in her hair had come loose in several places.

"Where can I find a mirror?" she asked.

Jacob led the way to a door and opened it for her. As soon as she had left the room, he walked back and sat down opposite to Wolf. There was an expression of bewilderment on his face. On his skull, which was bald with the exception of a narrow white brim of white hair, trickled thick drops of perspiration. Nervously he plucked at the sideburns that grew along his puffy cheeks almost down to his chin. He rolled his eyes in reaction to the fact that he was searching for words with which he could describe the situation.

"Unbelievable. Impossible."

That was all he finally managed to say.

Wolf stood up again. He had found in the labyrinth of his thoughts a way that would lead to the release of feelings of panic and sickness.

"I am well aware that it is still early," he stammered, "but what I need now is a good swig of brandy."

He walked up to a cupboard and opened it.

"You want some, too?"

"Are you crazy? Of course not!"

Wolf pulled the cork from a half-full bottle and took a pull. After a short hesitation, he took a second and even a third swig. He wiped his lips with the back of his hand, replaced the cork, put the bottle back on the shelf, and closed the cupboard.

"You saw what I saw, Jacob. Otherwise, you would never have given her the thousand guilders."

"It not a hallucination. The broken glass proves it. And all those scratches on the desktop."

"She mentioned to me. That she would tell something about her special powers, and that would have to do with me as well. But she does not know me at all, does she?"

"You have made a number of journeys during the last two years, and you have talked with countless people about paranormal affairs. You have, in spite of your young age, already built up a certain reputation. She knows about our foundation. Remember that she did send us a letter…"

"Her letter…" Suddenly Wolf spoke in a soft voice. "Did she write her address on the back?"

Jacob got up with a sigh. Avoiding the pieces of broken glass, he went to his desk one more time. A few moments later he handed Wolf an envelope.

"See for yourself."

The moment Wolf started to take the letter from the envelope, he heard Wera walk into the corridor. Then a loud banging, followed by a long, drawn-out scream.

Something cracked, something tore; there was a sickening sound that was very much like what one heard when a famished beast of prey had started to tear its victim apart and devour it. There was also a deep growling, which slowly faded away.

Then it was silent.

Both men had stood up. Hoping to draw courage from the firmness of the other, they looked each other in the eye, but all they could read there was fear. Jacob was the first one who went to the door. Wolf put the letter in his pocket, and then he followed with careful steps.

Wera lay stretched out on the floor in the corridor. The magic of her beauty had been cruelly washed away in waves of blood. Her dress now existed of long strips of torn cloth, the black covered with shining red. The flesh under it was scraped down to the bone in several places. Dull eyes stared up from a skinned face. Above her fleshless skull, her plaits lay like a bizarre helmet that had fallen off her head.

Jacob covered his nose and mouth with his hand. Slowly he stepped back into his study.

Wolf knelt down near the body and muttered, "How can something like this happen? And why, oh, why … ?"

What he saw was so revolting, that it was beyond his comprehension; if it had been less shocking, he probably would have been seized by panic or passed out.

But his heart skipped a beat when life came back in a flash in the dark eyes of the mutilated woman, when she lifted up her head, reached out her hand, and caught hold of his wrist.

Gasping for breath, he tried to free himself from this grip. Yet her fingers contracted with such strength that he feared that she would crush his bones. She pulled herself up. The sparkling, dark, vivid eyes were extremely big in their deep sockets. Her cracked lips began to move. Automatically he bent his head closer towards her. He felt drops of blood spatter against his ear, as she said in a pleading tone, "Keep searching for me. Please! Try to save me."

He wanted to say something, but he was frozen in fear.

"Don't forget about the collective!" said Wera.

Her grip slackened. Her head bumped back on the black and white tiles. Again, her eyes grew dull, as if candles had burned behind them that was now extinguished. The lower jaw sunk, revealing blood-covered teeth.

Wolf straightened himself and looked down on her; his stomach contracted and forced the gastric acid up to his gullet. In a half-drunk fantasy, he tried to project the naked beauty he had seen before onto the bloody body on the floor, an attempt to make his final memory of her much nicer than it was.

Then he turned on his heels and entered the big room to find himself a carpet with which he could cover the body of Wera.

Jacob was sitting on the floor with his knees pulled up and his arms wrapped around his legs, his head down.

"Wolf?" he asked with a sob. "Is that you?"

"Yes…"

"Oh, God, boy, was it Wera's voice that I heard there?"

"Yes," repeated Wolf.

"The door! You have closed the door, haven't you? What is happening here? It scares me, it really does. How on earth can someone in that horrible condition be still alive, and able to speak as well?"

"I don't know. She is dead now, that's for sure. She must have made use of her final strength..."

Finally, Jacob dared to look up.

"Aw, come on, stop it! There's no tiny spark of life left in someone who has been cut open from head to toe. The brandy, boy, the brandy. Now I need a good swig as well."

Wolf took the bottle from the cupboard. He did not bother to get any glasses. He sat down on the floor with Jacob, pulled the cork from the bottleneck, and took a pull himself before handing the bottle to his old friend.

Jacob was still sobbing. He drank, coughed, wiped his mouth, and rubbed his tear-stained eyes. Fresh tears ran down from his chubby cheeks.

"What are we supposed to do now, Wolf? I don't even understand what happened here, so how am I to know how to react? Did all our searching for paranormal cases make us raving mad? Are we getting punished, because we have gone too deep in all these unexplainable affairs? Did we conjure up a devil, who…"

He fell silent. The need for a new swig of brandy had suddenly become of more importance than the uttering of suspicions.

Suddenly, Wolf jumped up. He felt instantly sober.

"The floor in the corridor!" he said. "The black and white tiles. Her head rests on a white one."

"What does that have to do with it?"

"There should be blood on it. A whole lot of blood. Now, wait…"

With large strides, he went to the door and opened it.

The corridor was empty.

The tiles were spotless.

"Did she wear a coat when she came in?" he shouted.

"Yes," Jacob yelled. "I helped her out of it myself and hung it on the hallstand."

Wolf ran to it.

With unending patience, Jacob had taught Wolf to observe, to look, to develop a good memory. At a glance, he saw the solid door, the marble walls, a high mirror, a copper umbrella stand, and the hallstand. A coat hung on a hook. On a shelf sat a top hat. Coat and hat belonged to Jacob. Wera's coat was not there. He went back to Jacob immediately.

"She's gone. There is no blood on the floor. The coat is no longer there. But the desktop is damaged, the glass in the frame is broken, and you are missing one thousand Dutch guilders."

"This is sheer madness," said Jacob. "Let's go upstairs. I don't want to stay here any longer. I want to sit down and come to my senses. There is an explanation for everything. And as soon as the fear and perplexity have vanished from my mind, I will find out what actually happened here."

They left the study. Wolf closed the door behind him and followed his friend upstairs to the second story of the big canal house.

 2

"She was a woman of flesh and blood," said Jacob. "No apparition or the product of our fantasy. But Wera Keller was able to show us things that were not there. What an extraordinary experience, Wolf! Tomorrow I will put it all on paper. It will become the most interesting report in our archive."

He sat in an armchair near the marble fireplace in his living room. Wolf stood in front of one of the high windows and looked down on the street, the canal, and the houses on the other side.

"The die sailed through the air," said Wolf. "There was no question of illusion. She had the disposal of an entire packet of special qualities. If I only knew what she was trying to tell me! 'Keep searching for me. Try to save me. Don't forget about the collective...' I don't know how to interpret this."

"Well, I know a bit more about it. She arrived much earlier than agreed, and I let her in. Her beauty made me speechless for a long time. I felt very uncomfortable when we sat down facing each other. Finally, I was able to speak again, and I started to ask her questions. She made a baffling confession. About the collective."

Wolf turned around.

"Go on..."

"I asked her how she could be so sure that she was able to make objects move from a distance, while countless tests had shown that such a thing is impossible. She answered that she was a member of a special society. Talented mediums from all over Europe have united and formed a network that creates unknown possibilities. They combine their powers when they all go into a trance at the same time. The moment she entered my house, the mediums had begun to concentrate on her. A unique experiment, of which we both have seen the results. If she has spoken the truth, we have a deal with a collective that is able to work miracles!"

Wolf nodded.

As an investigator he had learned to separate the wheat from the chaff; he had unmasked many a charlatan, but also met several mediums to whom he had to give the benefit of the doubt. Jacob had taught him what to pay attention to and how to recognize even the most refined tricks.

"What a staggering explanation," he sighed as he sat down. "But it does not make clear to me why she asked me for help. 'Try to save me.' She wanted to tell me more I am sure. But why didn't she do it?"

All Jacob would do now was talk. By searching for explanations, he could make his fear disappear. He wanted to think things over, have a deep discussion, and finally calm down.

"Let's take a look at the possibilities," he said. "Just suppose that there really exists something like a collective of paranormally gifted mediums. We don't know who they are. It is very well possible that you and I have already met some of them. If they all have concentrated on Wera Keller this morning, are they all aware then that she had come to visit us? What if Wera Keller doesn't want to lend her assistance to the collective at all, but follows commands because she has been brought under hypnosis, because she is susceptible to their joint stream of thoughts, because ... "

"Yes, yes, this could all be possible," Wolf interrupted him. "But then I still don't understand what it has to do with me."

"She did not come here to earn that thousand guilders," said Jacob. "Of that, I am very sure. It all revolves around you."

"What?"

"Yes. What? Good question. I have, of course, too little information to understand the exact reason for her visit. However, it remains a fact to me, Wolf, that it has to do with you." Jacob nodded slowly. "I do not doubt it. There are mediums who know about you and who have plans for you."

"What could they expect from me?" wondered Wolf.

Jacob snapped his fingers.

"You will find out soon enough. I think that Wera Keller cast a spell on you. And you will go searching for these particular mediums. I think that you will not rest before you have seen Wera Keller again! How does that sound to you?"

A bizarre thought entered Wolf's mind. He held his breath and caught this idea in one sentence that he kept for himself: *It seems very much that Jacob is all too quick with his conclusions—as if he is influenced by invisible powers from the outside, by the collective meddling of unknown mediums.*

"Wolf? How does that sound to you?" repeated Jacob.

Wolf shrugged his shoulders.

"I'm not sure, Jacob. I will do the same as you. I will take my time, think things over, and write about it tomorrow. Then we can compare our reports. I don't want to draw conclusions right now."

He walked up to Jacob and shook his hand.

"I'll write my report in my room. I'll be back here tomorrow evening. All right?"

"A good idea. Being an investigator, you are prepared for anything, Wolf, but what happened to us today really beats everything. Yes, what we are going to write tomorrow will be the most fantastic reports ever! See you!"

"See you," said Wolf. He left the room, went downstairs and left.

Amsterdam had woken up.

Church bells were ringing.

Coaches rattled over the cobblestones.

Wolf screwed up his eyes against the glaring sunlight and hurried home.

 3

There was a loud knock on the door.

Wolf lay on his bed, face downwards. Leaning on his elbows, he pressed himself up and opened his eyes.

"Wolf!" a voice sounded. "There's someone for you at the door. Someone with a coach. Are you awake?"

"Yes," he called back. "Tell him that I'll come down."

He sunk back on the bed. His head was spinning. He was certain of four different facts: he found himself in his room in Amsterdam, another lodger had knocked on his door, someone was waiting for him outside, and he was as drunk as a lord. He had no idea what time it was and couldn't recall either at what time of the night he had come home. He wondered how he had managed to climb the steep stairs of the house in this condition. Anyhow, he could not remember that he had done so.

He turned back the blanket and sat up.

The sun shone inside and between the curtains.

After he got up with difficulty, he poured water from the jug into the wash basin and started to wash his face.

Everything that had happened in the house of Jacob van Beek had engraved itself on his mind.

On his way home he had run across an acquaintance. Together they had gone somewhere to have a drink. How the rest of the day had passed remained the secret of Brother Booze.

There was blood on the towel after he had dried his face on it. Examining himself in the mirror, he discovered a bloody cut right under his ear. After he had combed his hair, his curls would cover the wound and make it invisible. Less concealable was his left eye, which was swollen and had become blue and red.

He gave his mirror image a significant nod.

"You look terrific," he said.

He slipped into his trousers and searched for his golden pocket watch; it was gone. He fleetingly recalled something about it, but the image that loomed up before his mind's eye vanished before he could fully remember it.

He pulled on a shirt, put on his felt hat, and left the room.

On the dark landing, he saw his neighbor leaning against the door of his room.

"I was just going to knock one more time. But there you are, ready for a nice, brand-new day…"

Wolf grinned at him, buttoning up his shirt and jacket as he ran down the steep stairs. Halfway down he had to stop for a moment and catch the rail to keep his balance. It seemed better to go easy from now on.

The front door was ajar. He opened it wider and saw Abraham de Wild standing on the sidewalk; he was Jacob van Beek's secretary, a lean, older man with long, thin, gray hair and striking, pale blue eyes. Behind Abraham, in the street, stood a coach with a coachman.

Abraham paid no attention to Wolf's battered face and immediately explained the reason for his arrival.

"Mr. Van Beek is dead…"

❀ ❀ ❀

The coach was already on its way to the Prinsengracht when Wolf finally had recovered himself enough to open his mouth although he could only come up with one single word.

"How?"

"He lay on his bed on his back; his hands folded on his chest. It was still early in the evening as he lay there, staring at the ceiling as if he had waited patiently for death coming to pay him a visit."

Abraham produced a big handkerchief and wiped the tears from his cheeks.

"A lamplighter saw that the door of the house was wide open. He became suspicious and went in to take a look. He did not dare to enter the dark corridor and warned the neighbors. They thought it wise to call the police. A police officer went inside and found Mr. van Beek. Then Dr. Coenen arrived, but there was nothing he could do."

"My God," sighed Wolf.

He sat there, leaning forward with his elbows on his knees, and covered his face with his hands.

The coachman pulled the reins. The horse stopped. A man had pushed a heavily loaded handcart almost to the top of an arched bridge. He couldn't get any further and had pulled the cart sideways to prevent it from rolling backward with all the consequences thereof. A "bridge puller" appeared to help him, a man who was always there to earn a few coins and use a long rope with an iron hook to bring a cart with merchandise over the canal.

In the coach, the secretary now sat in the same position as Wolf.

He had said enough.

He could not speak another word.

As though turned into stone, they sat there next to each other, surrounded by the bustle of Amsterdam on a Monday morning.

❀ ❀ ❀

Wolf knew that he would not have been able to walk the few miles to the house at the Prinsengracht as he had done yesterday.

Inside, he sat down on a chair in the front room and closed his eyes. Abraham had taken place at one of the walnut desks. Opposite to him sat Lodewijk Dekker, a high-ranking police officer from Section Prinsengracht near the Vijzelstraats section of the city. The two housemaids who worked here from Monday to Saturday, Maria Sterk and Hilde Hertog, had just been questioned by him. They both had cried and dried their tears on their snow-white aprons.

"You can go now," said Dekker.

With one hand, he shoved his saber to one side along his belt, so that it would not hinder him when he leaned backward. With the thumb and forefinger of his other hand, he smoothed down his mustache. Then he gave a short nod in the direction of Wolf.

"It seems that the young man has fallen asleep. He came in on staggering feet. Overcome with grief. But my eyes don't fool me; he's still drunk from last night. Can you tell me who he is?"

Wolf kept his eyes closed and listened.

"Willem Hendrik Wolf. Everyone calls him Wolf. He drinks to excess. All day . . . and all night."

Abraham leaned forward and said in a softer voice, "But I am always willing to forgive him, Mr. Dekker. As a matter of fact, I would go through fire and water for him. He's such a wonderful person ... "

The policeman raised his eyebrows.

"Is he related to the dead man? And it looks like he has been in a fight recently."

"His father, Julius, was a businessman. Jacob van Beek was his associate. Together they made a fortune in overseas trade. In those days it was whispered that one of every ten ships that put into the Amsterdam port, no matter if it came from the Baltic, from England, the Dutch East Indies, or America, had sailed for Wolf's and van Beek's firm. Julius Wolf and his wife Suzanna died of cholera in 1866, when the epidemic made its appearance, as you probably will recall."

"Let's hope and pray it has been the last one as well," responded Dekker.

"Willem here was still very young then and was the only heir. He is very rich - loaded! But he prefers to go out and have fun in the poor working-class areas like the Jordaan, where he has his friends, and he keeps far from the business world."

Wolf felt certain memories coming back to him. The secretary had mentioned the Jordaan. That was where he had ended up last night. Somewhere there he had taken his watch from his pocket to look at the time. Someone had noticed and probably had stolen it.

"No poor devil can show a golden watch that he has earned by honest work. Someone would take it from him," he thought.

Suddenly he was in the middle of a fight. His lifesaver appeared to have been one of his best friends, Johan Simons. It dawned on him that he had promised something to Johan, but he could not remember what it was.

"Wolf was partly raised by Jacob van Beek, who finally considered him to be his very own son," said the secretary. Lowering his voice, he added, "Confidentially, I have always kept an eye on him myself and taught him intensively after he gave up his studies. I know as no one else that he's a man of many talents."

A tear rolled down from Wolf's black eye.

The policeman gestured at the file-filled shelves.

"It is well known that Mr. van Beek went deeply into affairs of the occult and other wild events."

"As a man who was financially independent, he could fully concentrate on his favorite pursuits. Behind the world of every day is the world of the elusive, and some people are able to show us a glimpse of it. That intrigued him greatly."

"I understand," said Dekker, who knew that rich people had a great interest in the occult; tables danced everywhere, and ghosts spoke in many a darkened room.

"I take care of Mr. van Beek's accountancy, and I also assist him at his research. I work out reports and am in correspondence with people from all over Europe and America."

Abraham paused, shocked by his own words.

"Oh! I talk about him as if he's still alive." Only with much effort did he manage to recover himself.

He looked across at the files now and pointed toward them with a trembling finger: "Everything's in the right place. Arranged in order of subject and date. Clairvoyance, spiritism, magnetism, faith healing, levitation, automatic writing, telepathy. Special files for special subjects like ectoplasm of bilocation . . . Wolf knows all the files. He is co-financier of this large-scale project and hunts for new phenomena himself throughout all of Europe."

"So that's the way the rich spend their time," sighed the policeman. "By the way, the officer who was here yesterday till late night told me about a strange situation in the study of Mr. van Beek."

The secretary rose to his feet immediately.

"The study is right next to this room. Please come with me."

As soon as the men had turned their backs to him, Wolf stood up as well and followed them with staggering steps.

He remained standing in the doorway leaning against the post.

"I have told the housemaids not to clean here," he heard the secretary say. "By order of Officer Meijer, who was here yesterday evening."

Dekker shivered as if he suddenly felt cold.

"There's a very special atmosphere here," he said. "Sinister. That's the first word that comes to my mind."

"I agree. Yes, I agree," said Abraham thoughtfully. "I have no explanation for it for I never had a strange feeling here before. Do you see those fragments of glass on the floor? And there, on the desktop, pieces of broken glass in a frame. Plus a marble die. Allow me to tell you why Mr. van Beek kept that die here in his study."

Briefly and to the point, he explained about the test that would prove if someone was able or not to move an object by the power of the mind. He took the police officer with him to the desk where he opened a drawer to show him the little box.

"As you can see for yourself, this box fits exactly in a hole, and there it rests on a false bottom. If you didn't know that it existed, you would never find it. It stood on the scratched desktop, with its cover open. I've put it back in the drawer. In this, he kept the nice sum of one thousand guilders. As you can see for yourself, the box is empty now. The housemaids are honest through and through. Even if they knew the money was here, they would never have put a finger on it. But Mr. van Beek himself and I were the only ones who knew that the money was here and what it was meant for."

"And of course, I knew that as well," said Wolf.

His voice sounded flat.

"Ah," said Dekker, turning around, "you are awake. I really hope that you are sober enough now to join in the conversation. And perhaps you are willing to answer some of my questions afterward."

Wolf nodded.

He had put a hand in his pocket and felt with his fingertips along the rims of Wera Keller's letter. He would hide it from the policeman and would not say a word about what had happened here on Sunday morning.

It was all too fantastic.

Even the secretary would probably not believe him.

Not to speak of a matter-of-fact police officer.

"I don't think that Wolf can help you with anything," remarked Abraham.

Dekker heaved a sigh and raised his hands to give expression to a feeling of total helplessness.

"Someone had been inside here," he said. "Just imagine that van Beek played a game with the die just by himself. He let it roll over the desktop. From pure frustration, he threw the die through the frame and broke the glass. He'd already taken the thousand guilders from the box, because he had decided to buy something with it, or perhaps he had to pay someone with it. All right? What remains, then, is the puzzle about the front door standing wide open. You can only unbolt it from the inside. Someone slipped outside, while van Beek lay dead on his bed... Or does someone want to make me believe that he had opened the door himself, as hospitable as he could be, and then went upstairs to his bedroom to die?"

Wolf nodded for the second time. The policeman was right. Jacob locked the door every night. With a key and two bolts.

Hilde Hertog showed up behind him.

"Mr. de Wild," she said, "there is a visitor. Dr. Coenen is here again. The coroner is here as well and asks for Mr. Dekker."

The secretary and the policeman walked past Wolf. Voices sounded in the corridor, and then there were footsteps on the stairs.

Wolf doubted if he should walk up to the cupboard for a good swig of brandy. Instead, he went to the fireplace. He took the letter from his pocket and set fire to it with a match. He only let it go when he had almost burned his fingers; then he took a poker and mixed the blackened remains with the ashes in the fireplace.

He was aware of the fact that he had a secret now that he could share with no one.

Today his old friend and he would have written a report about the events of that Sunday.

Now it would always remain a question what Jacob would have put to paper.

 4

From the house, at the Prinsengracht, it was not a long walk to the Jordaan. Wolf and the police officer went there together. Wolf was silent. He had seen the dead man lying on his bed, and he could not dispel that image from his mind.

The policeman talked constantly.

"Dr. Coenen and the coroner do not agree with each other. The doctor thinks Jacob felt sick and went upstairs, where he lay down on the bed with his clothes on. After some time he began to feel better. He rolled onto his back and fell asleep. Then, all of a sudden, his heart simply stopped beating. Daalberg, the coroner, counters these arguments forcefully. He says that someone who has to deal with a cardiac arrest is not dead immediately and would not remain lying there so quiet and relaxed. He suspects that something snapped in his brain, which made it impossible for him to move a muscle. It is as if God pronounced the word *dead*, upon which His sentence was executed instantly. I myself have thought about a quick-working poison. That possibility will be examined. I have also asked both gentlemen if it is possible that van Beek died in another room of the house and was carried upstairs by someone. They said that such could very well be right, but there was no occasion at all to take that into account. I prefer to examine things down to the last detail. That is why I am coming with you to search for the young man who can tell me where you were Sunday night. I'm not accusing you of anything, you hear? I will also find out what the housemaids did on Sunday and what secretary Abraham de Wild was doing."

They went through streets and alleyways, past old houses, stores, and pubs that had fallen into disrepair. Most people had left their overcrowded houses. There was a brisk trade on the streets, everyone loudly singing the praises of their wares: rags, fish, chestnuts, eggs, fruit, rubbish. There were beggars, hoboes, and street musicians. Pickpockets ducked away as soon as they spotted the man in uniform.

"Where are you going to?" asked Dekker in an impatient voice. "Where does that friend of yours live?" He seldom came here. This was the department of his colleagues from the police station at the Lauriersgracht.

Wolf opened his mouth for the first time.

"Johan Simons has no roof over his head. If he's out somewhere on the streets, we'll run across him sooner or later."

Not much later he spotted Johan standing at a street corner on an upturned box. He was short of stature and broad-shouldered, had bright blue eyes, and wore shabby clothes and a hat. With pompous gestures, he praised another man's goods. Green soap. With his melodious voice and clever ideas, he always managed to get the attention of an inquisitive audience; the merchants were eager to make use of his service. At the end of his argument, he made a favorable-sounding offer, and immediately a beautiful, well-dressed woman stepped up to the merchant and bought a box of soap.

Other women quickly followed her example.

Wolf knew exactly what had happened here. The beautiful woman was in on it. Her enthusiastic behavior urged others to buy.

Johan noticed Wolf and saw the policeman standing next to him. He jumped from his box, walked past the handcart of the soap merchant and came up to him.

"Wolf. A brown eye and a black one. What a nice combination," he laughed. "And now you only dare to come here when you're under police protection?"

Lodewijk Dekker got down to business right away.

"I want to have a talk with you."

Johan's reaction was quick as well. He produced the golden pocket watch and showed it on the flat of his hand. He ignored the policeman and looked hard at Wolf.

"Is this what it's all about? If you want to get back what you have given me in a drunken fit, you only have to ask for it. You don't need a policeman for something like that, do you? I really don't know you this way, Wolf..."

Before Wolf was able to react, the police officer asked, "Did he give you that watch?"

"Well, yes," said Johan, as he put the watch back in his pocket again. "So it is mine. I'm going to sell it, and then I'll squander the money. Oh yeah, I'll go through my money in one wild night." He looked at Dekker with piercing eyes, firm, defiantly.

Dekker said, "Now tell me, Johan, why did he give it to you?"

Johan shook his head and burst out laughing.

"I really don't know what's going on here..."

"What happened yesterday?"

Dekker's voice sounded sharp and with authority.

"Wolf and I have known each other for a long time. Yesterday afternoon he was sitting down on the sidewalk, leaning against a wall— he was drunk. He had been drinking beer with someone. He heard the church bells of the Oude Wester and took out his watch. Someone tried to snatch it away from him. He jumped up and got into a fight with the thief. Well, that thief gave him that black eye and a cut right under his ear. I rushed to rescue my friend. Together we beat that man up— oh, how we hit him! After that, we stayed together and went for a proper drink. We had a beer. Lots of it. And then we switched over to brandy. Wolf was so happy that I helped him that he gave me the watch."

"Isn't that odd?"

Johan shook his head. Wolf shrugged his shoulders and grinned.

"No, not at all," said Johan. "Wolf is a mystery to me. He always has plenty of money, and he gives it away just like that. I wouldn't be surprised if someone told me that he was rich. Thanks to him I manage to survive time after time."

"How late were you drinking?"

Johan roared with laughter.

"What do you think? Till I was no longer able to tell the minute hand of the clock from the hour hand. It must have been far after midnight. But tell me, officer, what is it exactly you want me to say?"

"Never mind," said Dekker.

He patted Wolf on the back.

"Everything's all right, Wolf, everything's all right. I wish you strength. And please, don't drink that much today."

He turned on his heels and disappeared into the crowd.

Johan moved to get back to his box.

"Wait a minute," said Wolf hesitantly. "I think I made a promise to you."

Johan stopped.

"That's right, damn right indeed! A better life. But it isn't the first time you did so. Every time you're as drunk as a lord, you start to talk about a better life for me. A life full of adventure."

The moment he heard this, Wolf remembered.

"Then it's high time that I make my promises good. Come with me, Johan. We'll talk about this and get us something to drink."

 5

The persistent morning mist still hung over the cemetery when the hearse, drawn by two black horses, arrived. A soft breeze blew patches of fog over the tombstones. The hearse stopped, and the bearers took out the coffin. A long procession fell in behind.

Wolf experienced these moments as an anxious dream.

Stupefied, hardly able to think, he shuffled down a gravel path along the graves.

He heard the voices of different speakers without understanding a single word.

When he made a short speech himself, his own voice sounded strange to his ears.

Farewell, good old friend, he thought.

The coffin was lowered with ropes. Wolf threw a shovelful of earth on it. When he straightened his back again, he saw something miraculous happen at the other side of the grave. The people stepped aside in silence in order to give way to a veiled woman, who held a small, complicated, plaited wreath of beautiful flowers in her hand. The curious thing about it was, that she had approached the people quietly from behind; no one could see or hear her, and yet they gave way to her as though by instinct.

She stopped at the edge of the grave.

She made a bow and threw the colorful wreath on the coffin. Then she lifted up the veil with the back of her hand, showed her face, looked at him. It gave him a shock. He recognized her immediately. Wera Keller. She sent him a bewitching smile.

Her lips moved:

"Help me..."

Both words, formed in silence, struck deep into his mind.

The veil fell, and the woman turned on her heels and walked away. The ranks closed again, and Wolf could no longer see her.

He was seized with different and even conflicting emotions at the same time. Fascination, admiration, love, fear, desperation, and a fast-growing feeling of anger. He was angry with himself because he had not been able to react alertly. He should have jumped over the grave and grabbed her. But her look had paralyzed him, and when he finally managed to recover himself, she had already disappeared.

6

Jacob van Beek left a fabulous fortune. He remembered different people in his will. A part of the money was allocated to the poor of the city. Maria Sterk and Hilda Hertog received a yearly allowance for as long as they lived. Abraham de Wild got a sum of money at once plus a yearly allowance. The rest of the money, the house, and its contents went to Wolf.

Wolf asked Abraham if he would become his secretary. De Wild and his wife could, if they wanted so, move into the house at the Prinsengracht. The investigation and documentation of paranormal events could go on. De Wild reacted with enthusiasm and asked, in his turn, if both housemaids would stay on.

Wolf left everything entirely in de Wild's hands and together with Johan he went to his country estate at the river Vecht and prepared himself for long journeys.

His elder friend Jacob had been right when he had made a prediction on the day of his death:

"I think that Wera Keller cast a spell on you. And you will go searching for these particular mediums. I have the idea that you will not rest before you have seen Wera Keller again! Well, how does that sound to you?"

It sounded frightening.

 7

Two years later Wolf found himself in Prague.

From a sun-drenched garden, he looked at the back of a stately house.

No one knew that yesterday, at twilight, just before the lamplighters would come, he had stood on the lookout at the front of the same building. There he had watched how Johan had climbed up quickly, making use of every irregularity in the big, rough stones of the outer wall. Luck was on their side. There were no passengers or carriages in sight, and the civic guards seemed to be busy elsewhere. Johan had sneaked inside via a window of the upper story; he was still hiding somewhere in the big house.

This was Wolf's approved method of seeing through walls.

Here lived a famous medium who was internationally known as Martha from Prague.

Before she had started her séance that afternoon, she had given orders to close the heavy curtains in her study to keep out the summer sunlight. Ghosts loved the darkness, as did the charlatans who claimed to be able to conjure them up.

In the garden, her visitors had gathered. They sat down on cast-iron chairs, under big umbrellas, and drank tea.

Only Wolf was walking to and fro and did not seem to suffer from the hot summer sun.

He had become someone now who could make or break reputations in the field of spiritism. A one-man inquisition, hunting for the truth, who made the inexplicable explicable, or gave it the benefit of the doubt until he finally saw through the trick. After he had discovered that certain phenomena and materializations seemed to be real, his heart overflowed with enthusiasm.

His name fitted perfectly to his character; like a wolf, with unflagging zeal, he followed every track that had led to the solution of complex riddles. His wealth gave him the status of a nobleman, and everywhere he went the doors opened wide for him.

"Mrs. Martha from Prague invites you all to come inside," sounded a voice from the house.

Everyone rose to their feet and entered the house through the French doors.

Wolf observed how the servant, the man who had called them inside, had a short conversation with everyone and collected the money one had to pay to attend the séance; crowns rained on the man's silver platter.

He passed Wolf by.

Wolf never paid for his presence at séances.

The tea service was taken away, and inside a strong fruit, liquor was poured into ornate glasses.

Martha from Prague entered the room to welcome everyone.

"I am happy to see you all," she said in a clear voice.

She was big and heavy. A sleeveless, silken gown fluttered around her as she walked straight up to Wolf.

"Mr. Wolf, it is a special honor to me to receive you here in my home," she spoke, in a mixture of German and English words, with a Czech accent. "You are far away from home. I recognize you from a drawn portrait in a newspaper. Once I even saw a photograph of you. I hope you understand what I'm saying..."

He made a short bow as they shook hands. He spoke slowly, giving her the time to interpret his words.

"Oh yes, I understand you very well." He spoke German—during his journeys he had learned to express himself in different languages. "It was about time to pay a visit to this country—so famous for the beer that has been brewed here since time immemorial. Now I finally have the chance to taste it myself."

Martha van Prague searched for the right words to react to his noncommittal but friendly remark. Even before she had found them, it was Wolf who went on:

"It is said that you talk in many languages when you are in a trance."

A shiver ran down his spine as his thoughts suddenly turned to Wera Keller, about whom Jacob had said, two years ago, that she was able to pluck the words out of the air any time she needed them...

Martha's eyes began to sparkle. She smiled and nodded enthusiastically.

"Even dead languages. Recently I even spoke Old Egyptian."

"What are you going to show us today?"

The other guests had come standing around them and listened with interest. Martha raised her glass. Looking around she said, again in a combination of English and German, but now also using Czech, "I will, as usual, do my utmost to help you all. I will try to pass through the messages that come from the other side of the grave as clearly as possible. Since I have such a noble visitor, I want you all to be a witness to a particular phenomenon: the materializing of a ghost."

Her listeners reacted with a pleasant surprise.

"He will step into soft clay. Later I will fill the footprints with plaster. That way I will obtain a perfect cast from a person who has not been among the living for a long, long time."

She raised her glass one more time.

"Today, someone will go home with the plaster feet of a ghost!"

A stroke of luck for anyone who collected curiosities—and actually everyone in the highest circles was doing that.

Martha seemed self-confident. If she had been intimidated by the presence of the young man from Amsterdam, she did not show it. She drank to his health and then mingled with her other guests, who dispersed again in the big room.

When everywhere in the house the clocks struck three times, Martha said that it was time to begin.

She led the way.

The hall was darkened.

Her guests followed her upstairs over creaking steps, up to a flickering point of light on the next floor. Everyone had a feeling of being observed by invisible monstrosities that could jump forward any time from hidden niches. Even Wolf underwent these terrifying sensations. To him, the world was one big freak show, with the most amazing surprises on every corner.

The study was dominated by a huge, oak table with twenty chairs around it. An oil lamp, hanging down from the ceiling, spread a soft light. There was also light coming from a fireplace, wherein burning logs drove up to the heat of this summer day.

Martha sat down at the head of the table. After everyone had found a seat, she folded her hands in her lap and closed her eyes. Her chin sank. A deep sigh ended in unintelligible mumbling. Slowly her face turned pale. On her arms and cheeks appeared spots that moved to and fro, as if the ink was welling under an almost transparent skin. Wolf watched it and wondered if it had to do with the shining of the oil lamp, in combination with the flickering flames in the fireplace.

Martha sank forward and clutched the edge of the table. The thick tabletop was full of scratches and grooves and gave away the high age of the piece of furniture. Right in front of Martha on the table stood a strange object. It was a gigantic, fantastic horn of an unknown, exotic animal, fastened to a walnut pedestal with silver rings and pins.

The horn was hollow.

Martha moved her left ear closer to it and listened carefully for a while. Then she brought her mouth to the opening and leaned with her forearms on the tabletop.

She spread her fingers.

"Regina?" she asked.

A deep male voice seemed to come straight from the horn, while Martha's lips noticeably moved.

"Apage sanatas!"

Wolf, grateful for the lessons Abraham de Wild had given him, suspected he was the only one who understood it. It was Latin, and he translated it aloud in German, supposing that he helped the others this way.

"Go away from me, Satan!"

"Who are you?" asked Martha in a flat voice. "Make yourself known or disappear. I am searching for Regina."

Wolf did not understand Czech but was familiar enough with séances to know that she was looking for an acquaintance in the world of the dead, with whom she had built up a special bond during earlier contacts.

Now there was howling as from a wounded animal. The voice came through, hissing and panting:

"Inter arma silent leges."

"There are no laws during the war," translated Wolf.

"Did you die in battle?"

"Aut vincere, aut mori," panted the voice. *"Cui bono … ?"*

"Winning or dying. For whose sake?"

Martha's voice was full of emotion. Her face, however, remained without expression.

The heavy pedestal of the horn began to move. Horrified, the people shrank back, making the backs of their chairs creak. The bizarre work of art rose from the tabletop, hardly high enough for one to slide a coin between the underside of the pedestal and the table; it started to rattle and hum and moved to all sides. It revolved on its axle, like a crazy spinning top, by which action the sharp point of the horn became a deadly weapon.

"Let it stop, please, let it stop!" cried, someone.

From the horn came bloodcurdling sounds, which shot from the spinning horn as though flung outside by a wild hurricane.

Then, as suddenly as the work of art had set in motion, it stopped and stood still right in front of the face of the medium.

"Martha, it's me . . . Regina," said a voice that seemed to come from all corners of the room at the same time.

Cautiously, the guests shoved their chairs closer to the table again and carefully listened to the conversation Martha now had with her acquaintance from the realm of the dead. Martha leaned backward, with her head against the chair rest, and now it was clear to everyone that Regina spoke via her; Regina's spirit had taken possession of Martha's body. Each person, in turn, was given a chance to ask questions about departed dear ones. Every now and then another voice sounded from Martha's mouth, in response to a request from one of the guests about a certain person.

Wolf did not understand it but knew the procedure. He knew what would happen. During hundreds of earlier séances, it had been exactly like this. The guests asked questions, were surprised by the right answers, were moved, cried, sobbed, shivered, sighed.

Slowly but surely everyone entered a trance, carried away by the medium. The temperature in the room rose to an almost unbearable height. The strong liqueur they had drunk in the room downstairs went to everyone's head.

Wolf looked around.

The study was excessively furnished. In a corner stood a big wooden desk. There were ferns in stone pots everywhere. One wall was hidden from view by a huge bookcase. Another wall was bare and consisted of horizontally fixed planks. Against it stood a long marble tub, filled with smoothed out, moist clay.

"Mr. Wolf, do you have any questions? Regina is still here," Martha said suddenly again in a combination of German and English.

"Yes," he answered curtly and immediately took a small memorandum book and a pencil from his pocket. "Which language will be the best for me to use?"

"You can ask me anything you want," he heard Martha say in the voice of Regina, in German without an accent.

This was the moment he had been waiting for.

This was the moment he had come to Prague for.

He opened the memorandum book on an empty page. Everything he came to hear now, he would write down in pencil. Later, in a place where he had more light, he should trace the letters in ink.

Wolf had occupied himself with a special experiment, inspired by what Wera Keller had told to his old friend Jacob van Beek. He had impaneled his own collection of mediums. In short, it came down to this: He wanted to find out if special powers were ignited when a group of mediums started to work together.

This intriguing thought had lodged in his brain.

He only needed more indications.

"Hello, Regina," he said. "Perhaps you can help me..."

All eyes were turned towards Wolf. Everyone was curious about what he was going to ask. Then, suddenly and unaccountably, a strong gust of wind went through the room. Something exploded in the fireplace. Sparks shot to all sides, while thick smoke was sucked up through the chimney.

Although all the windows were closed, the heavy curtains started to fly. Now there was a small chink between the curtains. A harsh beam of light, wherein the dust was dancing, shone precisely on the horn. Martha blinked her eyes. She was foaming at the mouth.

"My uncle Martin died recently." Wolf's voice sounded imperturbably calm. "On January the seventh of this year, to be exact, at a quarter past nine in the evening. He was the brother of my mother, who died a long time ago. This is the first time that I ask about him. Regina, do you know who I'm talking about? Can you find Martin for me? His surname is Loots. Born and died in Amsterdam."

"Several spirits force themselves upon me," sounded Regina's voice. "Oh, it's a true cacophony of voices, I cannot understand anyone individually. I have to open my mind to impressions. They come from all sides together. Wait . . . wait... What is the matter with a walking stick? A walking stick with a decorated grip."

Wolf looked up in surprise.

"He made use of a cane during the last period of his life. A hardwood cane. With an ivory grip. From the Dutch East Indies. It was a present from my father, his brother-in-law. It was sent to Amsterdam on one of the countless ships..."

"There was something wrong with his legs. He dragged himself along, didn't he?"

"Yes. Can you see him? Is he there with you?"

"I cannot reach him. I have to make use of the help of intermediaries. Oh yes, he is there, but too far away to be able to see him. Martin. Martin Loots... He eagerly wants you to know that he is all right. There is something about a horse that makes him curious. Could that be a black horse?"

"His favorite horse! It is well taken care of. I have seen that personally."

"If you only knew how grateful he is for that. And now . . . I lose all contact. A last farewell. Goodbye. What Martin needs now is a long period of rest. He found it so difficult to leave the world of the living. In a later stadium, he will try to talk to you personally."

Wolf nodded. He closed the memorandum book and put it back in his pocket. He had made not a single note.

There was a short silence.

Then all hell broke loose.

Martha raised her hands up to the ceiling. Her head jerked up, and she breathed in through her mouth, making rasping, guttural sounds. Her eyes, protruding and twisted, looked like huge mothballs. The windowpanes rattled in their grooves, lamps swung wildly to and fro. The heavy desk began to move. Books fell from their shelves. The contents of several cupboards started to shake, jingle, and thump.

The horn spun over the tabletop again, at a terrifying speed.

As Martha let her breath escape through her nostrils, her guests were subject to fantastic visions—they had a feeling as if an ice-cold winter storm raged over a snow-covered plain. The next moment the shivering people became aware again of the almost unbearable heat in the room.

"There! There! Look!" someone shouted.

Near the wall, an unidentifiable entity had appeared. A vague specter, a whirling shadow, a floating, fast-changing form, it slid along the planks. Strange, soggy sounds came from the marble tub, and a revolting scent filled the air.

Everyone had seen the apparition.

Silence fell the moment that it disappeared.

Martha's eyes turned back into their natural position. Her pupils were so big that the irises were almost invisible in the half-dark.

The door opened, and a servant entered. He quickly went to the windows, opened the curtains and the windows brusquely. There came no cooling draft from the outside.

The people blinked their eyes. It was a bizarre experience for everyone to shiver with fear in the heat of this room.

"Please come downstairs with me," the servant suggested. "Nice, cool drinks are ready there for you."

The guests rose to their feet immediately. There was panic in their eyes, and they were heavily perspiring. Several of them heaved deep sighs.

"Away from here," whispered someone.

Walking past the marble tub, one could clearly see a number of small but deep prints in the evil-smelling clay. At the head of the stairs, suddenly everyone seemed to be in a hurry. Each wanted to be the first to reach the ground floor. It was as if they expected ghosts and devils to come pouring out of the study to catch the ones who were not fast enough and drag them away to the eternity of a dark hereafter.

 8

The servant closed the door. Only Wolf and Martha had stayed behind in the study.

Martha's eyes were clear. There was a cold radiating from her that cut right through the atmosphere in the room and made Wolf shiver for a moment.

"I hope everything went to your entire satisfaction," said Martha.

He replied evasively, "Some mediums hardly have any memories of what is said or what has happened during a séance."

"I mostly remember everything, although I cannot speak many of the languages I have such thorough command when I am in a trance."

She walked across the room.

"First I will make some plaster casts. They dry quickly. If I do it now, I will be able to give them to my guests."

On a sideboard stood a bowl of water. She took a bag of plaster from a drawer and put a large portion of it in the bowl. She picked up a spoon and started to mix, but looked up in surprise at a loud knocking sound; it seemed to come from behind the planks on the wall. Wolf remained sitting motionless. The knocking changed into a banging. Suddenly, four planks began to move. A hatch that had been invisible slowly opened and a small hand appeared. The hand groped about and slid over the edge of the tub. With great power, the hand pushed into the mud and then pulled back into the hatch.

Before the hatch closed without a sound, there came a voice:

"When the curtains are drawn, it is almost impossible to see the planks move, Wolf!"

Martha started to stammer. All of a sudden she looked very uncertain and, in spite of her massive figure, even vulnerable.

On the other side of the planks, there was a bumping noise.

There were voices and sounds of a struggle.

Martha had left the stirring spoon in the bowl and covered her face with her hands. Now she peeked between her spread fingers as the door was pushed open. A broad-shouldered young man, dressed in a gray suit, stepped inside. His hat stood on the back of his head. He had an arm wrapped around the waist of a little woman who was as lean as a rake. With his other hand, he held her right wrist. Her right hand was brown from the mud.

"The mysterious apparition happens to be a good friend of Mrs. Martha," said the man, speaking Dutch. "She slips easily through the opening in the wall, and in her long, white gown she is like a swift, elusive ghost. Take a look at her bare feet. They are just as dirty as her hands."

As soon as the young man let the fragile woman go, she slipped past him and ran out of the room. Martha shrank back and made repelling gestures to Johan as if she were seeing a real phantom for the first time in her life. Then she fell down on the floor and remained lying there, staring up at the ceiling with glassy eyes.

Wolf ignored her.

"Nice work, Johan," he said.

He went up to the wall and pushed against the planks. The hatch opened. Then he went to the table and lifted the pedestal of the horn. It was much lighter than he had expected. He turned it upside down and discovered it was hollow; inside, he saw a complex mechanism that was very much like clockwork with a windable spring. Turning the object upside down had caused the mechanism to come into operation. Gearwheels came down and started to turn, and the machine rattled and hummed as it had done before. Wolf put the piece of art on its side and let the wheels turn until the spring had run down.

With the nail of a finger, he followed one of the countless scratches on the tabletop; now he knew how they had come into being.

Martha sat up and started to cough.

"I am so sorry, Mr. Wolf," she said, in a cracking voice. She had to do her utmost to find the right words in German or English. "Please keep in mind that people expect more and more of a medium."

Wolf turned towards her.

"My mother was an only child; there has never been a brother by the name of Martin. And so there never was a walking stick with an ivory grip from the Indies, and I never had to take care of a black horse either."

She did not understand him. He had spoken too fast, and her knowledge of German was lacking. She scrambled to her feet with difficulty and with a frightened look at Johan she sat down on a chair at the table. Wolf sat down as well, and Johan leaned his back against the wooden wall.

"My assistant came inside without anyone seeing him," explained Wolf. "If you only knew how much deceit we have discovered that way together on our journeys..."

"I know you are right, so right..." sighed Martha. "But please—this is not what you think, this is something different. As I already said, people expect you to do more and more. In fact, they expect miracles. I beg you, don't disgrace me. For I do have my gifts, my specialties, my contacts beyond the grave, my intuition—"

"There are some questions I would like to ask you. What I will do after that depends on your answers. There is a chance that I will keep silent about this incident, but there's also the possibility that you'll be left with your reputation in shreds. It is all about just a few questions. Three, to be precise. Please, try to relax and go into a trance..."

"Do you want me to conjure up a particular spirit?"

"No. Not at all. Now, please open up your mind to me."

Martha leaned backward, stretched her arms on the tabletop, and stared up at the ceiling.

A servant opened the door. Johan whispered to him to keep his mouth shut, walked up to him, pushed him back, and closed the door.

Martha moved her head to one side. Her mouth fell open, and she stared out in front of her with a glazed expression.

"Now, you just tell me this: Who is Wera Keller?"

The medium swallowed. Her eyebrows sank, she screwed up her eyes.

"I don't know anyone by that name. Wera Keller . . . I'm sorry, the name does not call up any associations."

"Is there something like a league of mediums? Have you ever heard about that?"

She compressed her lips. Softly, almost imperceptibly, she shook her head.

"Negative. I know no league of mediums."

"Very well. Here comes my last question for you: Do you have any information for me? A remark, a warning, an indication, a bit of advice, anything?"

Now the medium began to nod.

"I . . . I think so. Wait. There is this word. In the distance. In the dark. Now I can see it, I am able to read it. Yes. Now the letters don't move any longer. I cannot tell you where they come from, they're just there and . . . and now they burn into my mind. They are hurting me . . .

❀ ❀ ❀

Drops of perspiration formed on her face. Her cheeks flushed red. She drew back her hands as if the tabletop were red-hot iron.

"The word," urged Wolf. "The word!"

She nodded for the second time.

And then she said:

"Nibelung!"

Wolf took the memorandum book and the pencil from his pocket made some short notes and stood up. He leaned towards her and whispered in her ear, "I thank you very much, Mrs. Martha, from Prague. You just saved yourself a lot of trouble. Everything that happened here will remain between you and me. Do you understand what I'm saying? Everything."

Martha sat up and blinked her eyes.

"I beg your pardon?"

Wolf repeated what he had said. Martha reached out her hand and said, "Thank you, Mr. Wolf, thank you so much."

Wolf and Johan left the study and went downstairs. Via the hall and the front door, they left the big house, and not much later they walked in the hot summer sun along the river Moldau, in the direction of the Charles Bridge.

 9

Johan knew Wolf's character through and through. Any moment now he expected him to explode with fury, after another disappointing visit to a medium. The mood of the wealthy young man from Amsterdam could darken unexpectedly, and on those occasions, it was wise to stay as far away from him as possible.

Johan had quickly executed the order to rent a saddled horse and, breathing a sigh of relief, he now watched Wolf riding off in the scorching heat.

"Go searching for the coolness of a tavern," Wolf had said. "Drink a couple of beers and eat something. We'll meet again in the foyer of the hotel. I need some time to think about the next steps I'll have to take."

The horse galloped over the cobblestone of the streets. People jumped aside and swore at the reckless rider. Two horses pulling a carriage spooked, and one of them reared up. Wolf paid no attention. He followed the Moldau and left the city without looking back once.

Only after the horse had begun to sweat excessively and was no longer able to keep up the wild gallop, did he stop and dismount.

Wolf himself panted heavily, but his frustration had eased off.

Now he turned around and was surprised to see how far behind he had left the city. Prague was largely unfamiliar to him. He only recognized the spires of the big St. Vitus Cathedral and of the Tyn Church in the wide square where his hotel stood. How he had hoped to be able to finish his investigations in Prague! Well, only a few little clues were needed to make his plan complete.

He led the horse by the reins and began to walk along the bank of the Moldau. He thought the situation over.

On his journeys, through Europe, he had contacted countless mediums. Seventy-nine of them—twenty-three men and fifty-six women—had convinced him of the authenticity of their gifts and had provided him with useful information.

They had at their disposal enormous spiritual powers.

He had noted their cryptic descriptions and puzzling advice in his memorandum book. In a larger notebook, he had it all carefully worked out. Many a day and night he had spent searching for similarities and order in the different remarks and the finding of truth behind vague indications.

He had drawn connective lines and schemes; tried to master all the details; and often had felt confused, tired, helpless, and desperate.

But every single medium had helped him a bit further on his way.

And all he needed now was one little piece to make the puzzle complete.

On a certain day, at a certain moment, on a certain spot, something special would happen, just because he would be present right there at that crucial time... It was an ambitious experiment, for all the mediums would co-operate with him. They waited, as agreed, for a telegram from Wolf. At a certain point in time, they all would go into a trance and concentrate on an event that would take place at the described spot. A combining of powers from Europe's most talented mediums should make something special happen.

Together they would spin this magical web.

Independently of each other, the mediums had foreseen a special event. Together they would do their utmost to set something to work, and the result could be anything: an apparition, a materialization—or maybe something quite different.

This was the only way for Wolf to find out if Wera Keller had told the truth about the power of a collective.

In his home in the country seat, Wolf kept more than eighty golden watches, set with diamonds. On the backside he engraved, as a reminder, the exact point of time of the operation.

Every medium would receive such a watch.

He was eager to know what would happen when he stood there, on that special spot. If his calculations were right, it would happen on November the sixth of this year, at half-past two in the afternoon.

The final thing he needed to know was where to find the right place. Meanwhile, time was pressing. A new indication might lead to a solution. He had hoped that Martha from Prague would come up with that solution, yet she hadn't disappointed him totally.

Nibelung.

She had not been the first medium who had pronounced this word. He had to make inquiries into that.

Wolf tied the horse to the branch of a bush and walked down to the river by himself. The silent water was low and reflected the blue sky. He sat down on a big stone and took a silver case from his pocket. He removed a thin, ivory toothpick and put it down on a smaller stone in front of him. His hand shook nervously as he held it right above the toothpick. He forced himself to concentrate. This was a game he played often, and it always calmed him down. He would be happy to give away an enormous amount of money if he were able to get the toothpick to come loose from the stone and float free above the Moldau—by the power of his mind only.

He looked at the small object for a long, long time, but it didn't move.

He wondered again if Wera Keller had been able to move the die thanks to a combination of powers of her mediums. He wanted to find out the truth. As he put the toothpick back into its case, he suddenly frowned.

It was as if his mind had registered something.

A vibration, a sign, a thought.

He jumped to his feet immediately and looked around.

In the distance, he saw a coach stop in front of an inn. The building was almost hidden behind high trees, and he probably wouldn't have noticed it at all if he hadn't seen the coach first. Impulsively, he decided to go there. He wanted to taste Czech beer and quench his thirst.

But that was not the real reason why he loosened his horse and mounted. An unexplainable flash of intuition forced him to pay a visit to the inn.

Wolf was able, by his sensitive nature, to pick something from the air that blew past other people.

Within a few minutes, he had reached the building.

The still-sweating horse let itself be led easily to a place in the shade under the trees. Wolf tied the horse to a post next to a water trough filled to the brim. The coach he had seen had probably gone to the back side of the building, where stables were situated and where it was able to change horses.

Wolf walked up to the door.

The doorpost was decorated with skillfully cut wooden hands that, by the special position of the fingers, symbolized different spells; it was forbidden to evil spirits or people with dishonest intentions to enter this inn.

If the hands, which were fixed to the door with rusty, iron nails, were the same age as the building itself, the inn must have been there for over a century.

Wolf went inside.

In a big, dusky, cool room he shuffled through the straw that was spread over the floor of tamped earth. Not much later he was sitting at a wooden table and drinking a big glass of beer. While he wiped his mouth with the back of his hand, he looked around at the other guests. It was rather quiet. A coachman was standing at the bar, a couple was sitting at a table, and some men were in conversation with the innkeeper.

Then he noticed two people who were sitting by a window.

A young woman was shuffling cards while the man opposite her watched inquisitively.

Wolf stood up immediately and walked over to them. He knew countless games of cards, from the breathtaking poker played by the professional gamblers during long train journeys to the complicated actions of fortune-tellers. The woman in the inn belonged to the latter category. With swift fingers, she placed cards on the table in four sections of eight. Then she touched card after card with her finger and gave an explanation.

The man across from her nodded each time, to make clear to her that he understood what she was telling him.

Wolf recognized cards with symbols of the tarot, subdivided into four groups: goblets, pentagrams, bars, and swords. He saw pictures of the magician, the devil, the hanged man, the knight, the jester, the sun, the moon, the hermit, and the emperor. He also saw signs of the zodiac and images he had never seen before on tarot cards. It was obvious that this fortune-teller made use of her own cards and her own methods.

The number of cards surprised him.

Next to her right hand were two huge piles.

She was still talking, pointing at different pictures and then taking new cards from the piles and putting them on top of the others on the table.

The man opposite to her nodded and became enthusiastic; he started to grin and rubbed his hands contentedly. When she made a waving gesture with her hand, to make clear to him that the session was over, he stood up. He grabbed in his pocket, produced some coins, and put them on the table. After having made a bow for her, he turned on his heels and walked away.

The young woman didn't touch the money.

Now she looked up at Wolf with dark, knowing eyes.

Her look fascinated him.

And he knew right away what he thought of her:

A devilish beauty…

"Please take a seat," she said in perfect Dutch. "I have a strong feeling that I can help you."

Surprised, he complied with her request. He put his glass of beer on the table.

"How do you know that I'm a Dutchman? And with what would you be able to help me?"

Her full lips curled up in a smile, and she shook her head. Her long, light brown curls danced up and down.

"You are radiating it! Just like you can name a rose nothing but a rose and a dog nothing but a dog, you are a Dutchman from top to toe."

"My name is Wolf. Who are you? Where do you come from?"

"The world is my home, and I speak many languages. Today I call myself Emma; I might have another name tomorrow, and then I will find myself in some other place."

"Do you name yourself Wera, every now and then? Wera Keller?"

He had his doubts. Emma was extremely pretty, but in his memory, Wera had been a thousand times more beautiful.

"That's a nice name. But I've never made use of it. Do you stay in Prague?"

Wolf nodded.

"A magical city," said Emma. "During the ages so many alchemists have tried their luck there, that one could wonder why all the roofs are not made of solid gold. You have gone there yourself to gain experience of spiritualistic origin, haven't you? Well? Am I right or not?"

He was too flabbergasted to come back with a quick answer. Instead, he took a swig of his beer.

The cards were still on the table. She pointed at the four sections, the same way she had done when the other man was sitting opposite to her and told him what they represented. Her finger slid up and down:

"Life, death, prosperity, misfortune . . . four important subjects, four different bases that show their own, specific combinations of cards. You know all about it, Wolf, I can feel that. I can tell it from your attitude, from the way you look. You try to set a poker face, Dutchman, but I read the lines in your face just as easily as I read my cards lying here in front of me. And as a matter of fact, there are not so many lines to discover, for you are young, and your skin is smooth..."

"Anyway, you know how to surprise me and believe me, and it takes quite something to do so," reacted Wolf.

Another smile passed over her pretty face.

"Only a moment ago I was telling that man all the things he longed to hear. Before I read the cards for him, he was uncertain about lots of different things. Now he looks at the future with confidence, and that will undoubtedly be to his advantage."

"That's an easy way to make some money."

She laughed for the third time, but this time her laughter seemed to pose a threat—like the hissing sound of a snake that warns of a strike.

"I will leave the coins right here for the poor devil who will come and sit down here at this table after I have left."

"In a manner of speaking, you mean?" asked Wolf, who was beginning to feel rather uncomfortable.

"If you stay here a bit longer, you will see for yourself that the money is meant for someone who needs it more than I do."

"What are you doing here, if it is not to earn money?"

She picked up the cards one by one, and without looking up at him she answered, "It is very well possible, Wolf, that I sat here waiting for you. Knowing, of course, that you would show up."

Wolf emptied his glass and beckoned to the innkeeper.

"What are you having?"

"Nothing, thank you."

Wolf ordered another glass of beer.

"Now then," he said, "here I am. And what's going to happen now?"

"I will shuffle the cards and put them down."

Not waiting for his reaction, she started to do just that. He looked at her long, slender fingers. Eight golden rings, set with jewels, proved that she really was not short of small coin at all. And she was not afraid to visit this remote inn all by herself and flaunt her wealth with her rings.

The innkeeper put a glass of beer on the table, picked up the empty glass, and walked away again over the rustling straw.

Emma had started to study the cards.

One of the eight cards in the upper right corner, the section of death, showed the horrifying figure of the devil. There were pictures of different animals—a hare, a wild boar, and a toad. In the upper left corner, where life was judged, lay, among others, a jester, a sword with a blood-red point, and a half-moon in a black night.

It all looks very sad to me, thought Wolf.

In other circumstances, he would have calmly wiped the floor with any fortune-teller, but now his nerves were on edge, and he felt very curious about what Emma was going to say.

She put a row of ten cards on the table, under the four groups of eight, and she touched them all with her fingertips as if this short contact gave her an impression of their deepest meaning. Then she nodded.

"Much is clear, Wolf. No, it does not look sad at all. Don't be influenced by cards you don't like. Remember, death can come to you like a release, and the jester is the symbol of uncomplicated joy, or the free word, sarcasm, acuteness, humor, plain truth... Blood on the sword does not have to be your own blood, and sometimes it is better to find the earthly toad on your way than the bird of prey, floating in the air, symbolizing an unattainable wish."

She looked up from her cards and stared him in the face.

"Wolf . . . you know that the cards are no more than guides, don't you? They give us something to hold on to; they give us the possibility to concentrate."

He evaded her glance, picked up his glass, and took a swallow.

Then he said, "Like the crystal ball is a tool that brings the seer into the right state of mind to open his spirit to special impressions."

"Exactly. You know much about it. I see that you have been surrounded by wealth and luxury from the day you were born. You've had everything you wanted. Always. And property went from father to son. Money was simply thrown into your lap. A rich man, that's what you are. Well, intellectually you are not poor either. Wolf, you are a desperate wanderer, you are looking for something with all your might. Instead of staying at home safely, in Holland, you have been obstinate and gone on a long, long journey, trying to find something that is actually elusive..."

She pointed at the pictures of a goat and a hobo.

"Still, you have managed to come far. That is remarkable..."

She pointed at the image of a castle in the row of ten cards at the bottom.

Suddenly she looked at him, and her mysterious eyes scared him. It was as if she had the power to make his spirit drown in the depth of her dark look.

"Today you will get what is yours, Wolf. Here! Here is that card you need so bad. Don't lose it. To me, this card is of no use at all. For you, it is of great value."

She had taken a card from the middle of one of the high piles to her right. With the back facing upward she shoved it towards him over the tabletop.

"Only turn it over after I have gone."

She stood up immediately, collected her cards, made a light bow to him, and said, "I wish you luck on your long, hard road, Wolf... What I see is much blood, pain, and death. And there is gold, shining gold! You little know what you've begun..."

Then Emma turned on her heels and walked to the door. The harsh sunlight shone inside when she opened it. Wolf rose to his feet as well and let the card slip into his pocket without looking at the front side. He went to the bar and ordered his third glass of beer. Picking it up, he turned around and leaned against the bar.

The door opened again, and a young man dressed in rags stepped inside. He looked tired and sweaty. He stumbled to the place where Emma had sat by the window. His mouth fell open when he saw the coins on the table, and immediately he shoved them to the edge and caught them in his hand. Wolf raised his glass up to him and gave him a significant nod.

This could have been a plant, thought Wolf, who had taught himself always to be suspicious.

Then, all of a sudden, a miraculous metamorphosis was enacted; the ragged tramp had now become a proud young man with bright eyes and a self-confident smile. He had the looks of a nobleman. He no longer sweated, and his clothes seemed cleaner and less torn and worn out than before. It seemed doubtful to Wolf that changes like this could come into being just thanks to the finding of a few coins.

A shiver ran down his spine.

There was an unprecedented, powerful form of magic going on here.

Wolf put down his half-full glass, paid the innkeeper, and walked outside.

He wanted to inspect the front side of the card in the sunlight. But once outside, his attention was drawn to something quite different. The coach he had seen before and that had made him decide to visit the inn now passed him by at breakneck speed. The two big, snorting, jet black horses pulling it had broken into a gallop, and he heard the cracking of a whip.

He loosened his own horse as quickly as he could, swung into the saddle, and set off in pursuit. Ahead, the rattling coach turned into a forest path. The high, spiked wheels raised dust and sand, and Wolf covered his eyes with his right forearm. He had no chance of catching up with the coach. But then, suddenly, the black horses slowed down, as if someone were giving him the opportunity to come closer. Spurring his horse on, he pulled up next to the coach and looked up at the driver—or where the driver should be.

"Impossible!" he cried out.

There was no one on the box. The benches were empty.

He discovered a high pile of logs, some of which had rolled down and blocked his side of the path. It was too late to stop the horse, and he urged it to jump. But the horse refused and stumbled over the logs. Wolf landed in the middle of the path.

The coach disappeared in a big cloud of dust.

Wolf scrambled to his feet, his face twisted with pain. The sand grazed his skin when he wiped his sweating face with the back of his hand. The horse was standing at the side of the path, and it seemed that it was not hurt. He carefully walked up to it and heaved a sigh of relief when he managed to grab the reins.

Just before he mounted, he got an idea. He led the horse back to the inn and tied it up to the post again. He walked up to the door. It was clear that the magical wooden hands on the doorpost hadn't kept the evil spirits outside. He opened the door, stepped inside, and looked at the table by the window. The young man in rags who had been transformed into a proud nobleman had gone.

Wolf went outside again and untied the horse. He shoved his foot in the stirrup and slowly pulled himself up. He clacked his tongue. Limping slightly, the horse started on its way back to the city. Wolf took the card out of his pocket. The backside showed, as all of Emma´s cards, a black, devilish mask with gray horns and brilliant yellow eyes, in a dark blue background. He turned the card around. To his disappointment, it was blank.

At that moment he wanted to throw the card away, but then he noticed that thin black lines had appeared in all four corners. Slowly they crept along, twisting to all sides and crossing each other. In a spontaneous way, a clear drawing came into being.

He let the horse slow to a stop so he could examine it more carefully.

The left side of the card showed a huge stone foundation. On top of it appeared the statue of a sitting lion. On the right side was a high, round building that looked very much like a lighthouse to him. And there was water. In the background, he saw vague stripes that could very well be distant mountains or hills. Between the lion and the lighthouse, far away, floated a big steamer.

"The scene of action!" Wolf cried out. "That is where it will happen. There the encounter will take place. On the sixth of November, at half-past two in the afternoon. I have to verify all the facts, check everything over and over again, and then inform the mediums."

But first, he had to find out where he could find the spot that was drawn on the card. He burst out laughing. Finally, it looked as if he would be able to carry out his plan. Letting the card slip into his pocket, he put spurs to the horse.

"Easy, easy," he sighed. "We've already exerted ourselves more than enough today."

But he was too restless and excited to keep calm. The closer he came to Prague, the more he spurred the horse to go faster. He only stopped to ask people if they recognized the picture on the card.

No one could tell him where he could find this place.

Please, he thought, *oh, please, don't let this just be a part of my fantasy!*

 **10**

That night Wolf's bed remained undisturbed. Sitting at the small desk in his hotel room, he had made notes and done some new calculations. Later, he had carefully copied the scene on the card onto a piece of paper. He was not a talented artist in any way, but he managed to make a useful copy. He rested briefly, and then studied his notes again and once more combined everything the different mediums had told him.

The result remained the same: this year, November the sixth, at half-past two.

Now there was something else he had to check.

Martha from Prague had seen letters branded into her mind that formed a word:

Nibelung.

That same word had been whispered to him during séances by four other mediums. He looked up their names.

Hubertus de Keijser from Antwerp, Belgium.

John P. Dawson from Exeter, in the English county of Devon.

Diane Schäfer from Cologne, Germany.

Heike Baumann from a little village not far from Vienna, Austria.

There was one evident resemblance among the five mediums. None of them belonged to the group of seventy-nine men and women he had chosen for his experiment. The seventy-nine mediums had proved themselves; these five others had made a poor show.

Martha from Prague had made a young woman play ghost and had her make footprints in wet clay; the "magical" horn on her table proved to be operated by ingenious clockwork.

Hubertus de Keijser worked together with his wife Cornelia. She received the guests and held a conversation with them, in the course of which she wormed information out of them that could be useful later. Later, Hubertus would go into a trance and contact the world of the dead, and Cornelia would pass the questions of her guests on to him. Wolf soon realized that everything she said held a code. The number of words she used per sentence, the order of the words, and other tricks made it possible for Hubertus to understand which answers he had to give.

John P. Dawson was a true magician with wooden objects. He piled up skillfully decorated pieces of hardwood: birds with spread wings on dogs, cats, and all kind of wild animals, and on top a huge butterfly. He then made the tower of animals collapse. The butterfly came down first, followed by the birds, and finally, all the mammalians fell, one by one. All Dawson had to do was to point at the wooden animals from a great distance.

Wolf had walked through the park-like garden at the back of Dawson's house and spotted a stone statue in the middle of a round pond. The brook water was led through the pond via two opposite pipes. The statue, a beautiful mermaid, moved her head up and down, she rolled her eyes, and water spouted from her mouth and from the shells she held in her hands.

A gardener told Wolf that the statue was made under the leadership of Dawson and that the head and eyes moved by the power of the streaming water. Anyone who could create something like that was undoubtedly able to make wooden objects move as well.

Finally, Wolf found out the truth.

Channels were bored in the wooden objects at an oblique angle and partly filled with a thick, viscous oil. The holes were invisibly covered with little wooden stoppers. The oil crept down slowly through the channels and then threw the objects off balance and made them fall to the ground.

Diane Schäfer was a talented medium who claimed to live on air; she hadn't taken any food for many years and only every now and then took a few sips of water that came from a well drilled into the igneous rocks of the Eifel region of Germany. Johan sneaked into her house one night and was able to report to Wolf the next day how he had seen Diane feast upon a hot meal and had drunk big glasses of Rhine wine.

Heike Baumann was a girl of only twelve. Everywhere she went, the furniture started to move, the lamps swung to and fro from the ceiling, and crockery fell from the cupboards. But a priest had seen Heike smash a couple of dinner plates to pieces, after which she asserted never having touched them at all.

When Wolf visited her, she was in a malicious mood. She was storming and raging, falling on the floor and rolling to and fro. She foamed at the mouth. And then, all if a sudden, she sat up, looked at Wolf with big, fearful eyes and snapped at him:

"Nibelung!"

Later she claimed she could not remember having said that at all.

Wolf could see through the charlatans.

He knew all about false bottoms, invisible henchmen, tricks to make ghosts appear on photographs, swift fingers of conjurers who raised their status by providing their shows with paranormal-looking acts, ventriloquists who conjured up ghosts, men who caught rifle bullets with their teeth, fortune-tellers for whom half a word from their customers was enough to understand what they longed to hear. .

❀ ❀ ❀

He knew all their tricks.

But Martha from Prague, Hubertus de Keijser, John P. Dawson, Diane Schäfer, and Heike Baumann were no charlatans!

As far as that was concerned, it was little Heike who put that perfectly into words after she had come to rest and sat down together with Wolf in a room:

"No one wants to believe me. That makes me so furious. And that's why I sometimes throw things around if it doesn't happen spontaneously."

Martha from Prague also made clear to him what it was all about in her case:

"People nowadays expect more and more from a medium."

A long time ago he had written to Abraham de Wild and asked him to find out what the word meant. It was likely that Abraham already had discovered one and another interpretation, but Wolf hadn't been in Amsterdam for months. Fairly soon he would pay a visit to Abraham in the house at the Prinsengracht, or maybe he would ask him to come to his country seat home near the river Vecht.

It was already getting light outside when Wolf closed his notebook. He leaned forward and, with his head resting on his arms, fell asleep.

 # 11

The next morning Wolf sent Johan out with the new drawing.

"Show the picture to everyone you meet. Go from street to street, from district to district. Let the drawing go from hand to hand when you visit an inn somewhere to have a meal and quench your thirst. I hope you will come back with good news."

He hardly took time to have breakfast in the restaurant of the hotel. He was satisfied with a few bites of bread and a cup of coffee. Then he went outside, with the playing card in his hand.

There was already much activity on the square. There were market stalls where mainly food was sold, carriages rattled over the cobbles, people swarmed among the wares. In front of the Tyn he saw an artist at work; the painter had put down his easel and was sitting on a stool, busy making a rough sketch on a wooden panel. The outlines of the church, with its towers and many spires, was almost done. Wolf went up to him to have a chat. The artist spoke reasonable English and German.

"The church was burned down in 1819," said the man. "It was fully rebuilt again in 1835. The citizens of Prague themselves have raised the money to make this possible. I always sell a painting of the Tyn on the very day I made it. As soon as the sketch is ready, I will proceed with oil colors."

Wolf asked him about the price.

The man looked him up and down with the eye of a businessman instead of the gaze of an artist.

He came up with a fancy price.

Wolf nodded and showed him the playing card.

"Later you can paint that church as often as you like. Paint a copy of this drawing as accurately as possible on a new panel. Work fast and precisely. I'll pay you twice the price you just mentioned. I can make an advance right away if you wish. Well, what do you say?"

The man reached out his hand.

"My name is Michael. Today I'll be at your service completely. Believe me, you can trust me—I will not run away halfway through the work, and I would like to receive the full payment in advance."

"You can trust me as well," said Wolf in a scornful way, but he decided not to bargain and paid Michael the promised money.

Then he explained what the idea was.

"All right, I understand," said Michael. "I will make the sketch as quickly as I can. No doubt soon someone will recognize the place."

Michael took the panel from the easel and put up another one. The first one had stood with the long side up; the second stood with the long side horizontal. Wolf stayed around to keep a constant eye on the playing card that he mustn't lose and fathom the reactions of the people who passed along.

The painter worked hard. The panel had already been coated with a white layer of paint, and now he rendered the sketch in black and gray. The lion and the tower were already recognizable. Then he started to work with oil paint.

"I'll have to guess about the colors," he remarked. "The lion is most probably made of metal, and the tower seems to be mainly white."

The water appeared. The steamer floated between the lion and the tower, and in the background, the hills became vaguely visible.

"Do you recognize the location of this scene?" Wolf regularly asked passersby.

He addressed the people in different languages.

There was no one who could help him.

Around about noon his feet began to hurt, and he began to feel drowsy. Still, he did not think of leaving his post. He ordered a boy to get something to eat and to drink and promised him a good tip. The boy could have run off with the money, but he came back with the food and a bottle of red wine.

Wolf doubled his tip.

Michael stood up and said, "Sit down on my stool for a while. I can work just as good when I'm standing on my feet."

Sitting down, Wolf shared the food and drink with Michael and continued to observe the people passing by. Michael worked on while he ate. Every now and then he took the wine bottle from Wolf to take a good swig. In the meantime, the painting had become a true work of art.

Late in the afternoon, when Wolf had almost given up all hope, fortune finally smiled at him.

The painting was almost finished. A well-dressed, middle-aged couple stopped. The man pointed, smiled, and said something in German.

Wolf, who had almost dozed off in spite of himself, suddenly was wide awake. He walked up to them and asked, "Do you recognize the picture on the panel?"

"But of course, of course!" said the man. "I can tell because we live not far away from there. What a crazy idea to paint the harbor of Lindau here in the most beautiful square of Prague!"

"Lindau..." Wolf pronounced the word slowly. When he said it for the second time, it sounded questioning: "Lindau?"

"A town in the southwest of German Bavaria," explained the man. "Situated on an isle at Lake Constance. Just take a look. Here you see the lion, the symbol of Bavaria. And there's the lighthouse. Both have been built recently, in 1856. Lindau was the first town that made use of iron steamers, and not long ago the town also became reachable by train. And here . . ."

The man pointed at the subtle line pattern the painter had placed in the background.

"That is Switzerland, on the other side of Lake Constance. Oh, how odd it is to see a painting like this made here."

"It is completed," said Michael with a sigh.

Wolf took it from the easel, with his fingers against the sides to guard against touching the wet paint, and held it out to the woman.

"For you," said Wolf. "Just to prove that little miracles actually exist."

"A little miracle, but what a big surprise," reacted the women. She carefully took the painting.

The couple, still confused, thanked Wolf kindly and went on.

Johan returned from his wander through the town. He gave the drawing back to Wolf and said, putting on a disappointed face, "There was simply no one who could give me a useful clue. One thing I know for sure, and that is that you won't find the lion and the lighthouse in the neighborhood of Prague."

Wolf said goodbye to the painter.

"Let's go to the restaurant in the hotel, Johan. It's time for a proper dinner. After that, I will go to bed immediately, for I'm ready to drop with sleep. Tomorrow we'll leave Prague. I have to find out which trains will take us to German Lindau as fast as possible. The drawing on the playing card shows us the harbor of that town! I want to take a look there. And then we'll go back to Holland, where I'll get all my notes together and check them one more time to see if all I figured out really fits. Then I'll send messages to all mediums who are willing to cooperate with me. That will be seventy-nine telegrams altogether and just as many golden watches..."

He put the self-made drawing and the playing card in his pocket.

Johan had spent no money on eating or drinking.

He hadn't allowed himself the time to visit an inn and had only drunk water from a pump and from a well.

"If you only knew how hungry I am," he sighed. "Terrific, that you know now what's on the playing card. By the way, along the way, I found something for you in a bookstall."

Once in the restaurant, Johan took a book from his pocket and handed it to Wolf.

It was a small, old, tattered book, printed and published in Germany.

The binding was torn, and some of the sections had come loose.

The cover showed a knight in combat with a dragon.

Wolf read the title aloud:

"*The Nibelung Treasure...*"

12

Wolf finally found time to pore over the book when he traveled from Prague to Munich by train. He had found a quiet place at the back of a carriage. In Munich, he would change to another train that would bring him to Lindau. He had to concentrate hard to understand every line, for reading in a strange language was quite different from being able to speak it.

It turned out to be a novelized version of a thirteenth-century epic, but he read it in the same way he digested the contents of paranormal reports—he followed the main lines, making notes every now and then.

The story led back in time, to the first half of the fifth century.

In the tale, the hero, Siegfried, asked Gunther, the king of Burgundy, for the hand of his sister Kriemhilde. In those days the reputation of Siegfried was generally known. He had taken away a priceless treasure from the Nibelung, marvelous dwarf people, and even defeated a dragon. The blood of the dragon had made him immortal. The king granted Siegfried's request, but first, he had a special task in store for him. Siegfried had to travel with him to the Iceland princess Brunhilde and help convince the king to marry her. The two men accomplished their goal and returned with Brunhilde to Burgundy, where both couples were married.

Unfortunately, some years later, a hell of a row between Kriemhilde and Brunhilde regarding the respective social ranks of Siegfried and Gunther.

Brunhilde gave orders to kill Siegfried.

Siegfried, it turned out, was not immortal after all, for there was a weak spot between his shoulder blades. When he bathed in the blood of the dragon, the leaf of a linden tree had covered that spot. Upon Siegfried's death, Kriemhilde married the king of the Huns, who appears to have been none other than the feared Attila.

She took revenge on the murder of her husband in a ruthless, bloody way.

The story was full of magic and miracles.

Wolf was spellbound by the dwarf people who called themselves Nibelung, after their King Nibelung, whose name meant "son of the mist."

So Nibelung were creatures of the mist.

Wolf put the book away. Later, when he read it for the second time, he would concentrate more on the details.

"Ah, the Nibelung . . ." a voice sounded suddenly.

Wolf looked up and saw a man who had come to sit opposite him; he was of small stature and wore a snowy white suit and a high hat. He had a hairless, smooth, round, pale, expressionless face like an earthworm and looked at Wolf with lackluster eyes. Without waiting for a reaction, the man continued.

"It would have to do with the Burgundian monarchs. But the original story is much older." He raised both his hands, and his bloodless lips curled up in a smile. "But what does it matter? It's just a beautiful story. Even Attila the Hun appears in it! Four hundred years after his death someone described him as the scourge of God, and that always remained his most striking nickname. It is said that the killing, plundering Huns moved faster on their horses than the rumors had indicated. Cruel times they were ... cruel times indeed!"

"You are a Dutchman," remarked Wolf.

"Everything you want, everything you say," answered the man, and Wolf was immediately on the alert.

The train sped forward over the iron track through Germany, and as Munich came closer—the town, Wolf realized with a shiver, where Wera Keller had come from.

"They were magical times as well, weren't they?" asked Wolf, who wanted to keep the conversation going so he could observe the man and learn more about him.

"But of course, of course!" the man called out. The enthusiastic tone of his voice made his expressionless face look extra bizarre. "Let me give you an example. Kriemhilde's hot-water trial! Wasn't she married to Etzel, who is actually no one other than Attila himself? A female slave accused her of adultery. And so poor Kriemhilde had to put her hand into a kettle filled with boiling water, to pick up a stone from the bottom. She did it. She had no pain. Her hand was undamaged when she showed the stone triumphantly to the hundreds of witnesses who had gathered around her. That way she proved her innocence..."

Johan, who had gotten up to stretch his legs, entered the carriage and sat down next to Wolf.

"Johan, this is Mr..."

Wolf gestured to the man opposite to him. The man took off his hat to Johan. His head was bald and smooth.

"Gerardus Klijn, how do you do?"

"Where do you come from?" asked Wolf.

Strange enough, the answer sounded like a question:

"Amsterdam?"

"Well, isn't that a coincidence?" remarked Wolf. "That's where we come from, too. On which street do you live?"

Klijn had put on his high hat again. He leaned forward with his elbows on his knees and smacked his lips. White foam came from his mouth. Suddenly he sat up straight, bumping against the back of his seat. His hat sank over his forehead. It was as if he had an inner conflict. Nervously he rubbed his legs with his fingertips. He panted in cadence with the train.

"The street," repeated Wolf.

The little man nodded and held his head to one side as if he caught a sound with one ear.

"It is not light, but it isn't dark yet either. Twilight. That's the word I was looking for. And there I go, where I walk . . . through Amsterdam. Two years ago. The Prinsengracht."

Wolf sat up. He heard Johan heave a short sigh. The little man was panting again. Johan wanted to say something, but Wolf gestured with his hand to make clear to him that he should hold his tongue.

"There's a door wide open. A man steps outside to look around for the very last time. It is a farewell. He takes his leave of Amsterdam. Of life." He nodded decidedly and repeated: "He takes leave of life. Death had already crossed the threshold and waited for him upstairs in the bedroom. He knew it, and he remained calm. He couldn't escape it.

"How did he know?" asked Wolf.

Suddenly, Gerardus Klijn seized himself by the throat and started to make gurgling sounds.

Passengers who sat farther down in the luxuriantly furnished carriage looked anxiously their way.

A waiter who had just come in with a carafe of wine, two glasses, and food for a couple from Pilsen put his silver on a small table and ran to the back of the carriage.

Wolf grabbed Gerardus by the wrists and pulled his hands away from his throat. The waiter, thinking that the men were having a quarrel, wanted to butt in. Johan jumped to his feet and said in a calm voice, "You stay out of this."

Wolf gave the little man such a shaking that his hat fell from his head.

"Answer me! Answer me!" he shouted.

Now that everyone in the carriage was alarmed, he saw no reason why he shouldn't use the volume of his voice to scare the man and force him to speak. Again Gerardus was foaming at the mouth. It had the smell of gastric acid. His eyes, small as currants, danced up and down in the white of his face.

"Whispering..." The word sounded soft.

But Wolf had heard it and thought he understood.

"Whispering by whom? The collective?"

"The collective ..." repeated Gerardus.

"Why?" Wolf now sounded even louder than a moment ago. "Why? Now tell me!"

But at that moment Gerardus' body slackened. He slid down from his chair and dangled his wrists. Wolf lifted Gerardus up. The little man swung to and fro like a marionette, his feet trailing above the thick carpet that covered the floor of the carriage. Then Wolf put him back in his seat. With his shaking knees and drooping shoulders, the little man resembled a white larva fallen from the beak of a bird.

The waiter put a hand on his shoulder.

"Does he speak German?" he asked Johan, who was standing right next to him.

Johan shrugged his shoulders.

"If he is what I think he is, he'll speak all possible languages," said Wolf.

The waiter, who did not understand this remark, addressed himself to Gerardus Klijn and asked him in German to come with him.

"Allow me to pour you a drink. A schnapps will do you good."

Wolf and Johan sat down, ignoring the looks of the people who were sitting in front of them and twisting around in their chairs to stare at them.

"You look rather upset," said Johan. "This touched you deeply, didn't it?"

"Yes, you might say so," responded Wolf. "And it did scare me as well. I just need some time to find my right mind again and try to find out what actually has happened here."

"It seems to me that his knowledge is beyond everything. Yes, that is very scary indeed!"

Wolf did not react. He kept silent for a long time and thought things over.

The train reduced speed and finally stopped at the crowded station of Regensburg—the last big town before Munich. The waiter appeared, and now his face was as white as that of Gerardus had been. He brought two glasses of schnapps with him on his salver. He walked up to the back of the carriage and stammered, "Please, gentlemen, this is for you... And I honestly confess that I've taken a glass myself, too. I poured it out for your fellow countryman and ... eh, do you mind if I sit down for a while?"

Wolf and Johan took the schnapps from him. The waiter sat down on the seat where Gerardus had sat.

"You'll probably not believe it," said the waiter, as he stared out of the window, oblivious to the rush of travelers, luggage porters, and railwaymen. "Your countryman vanished without a trace. Just like that. Not when the train stopped. It was earlier. I was filling his glass, and when I turned around—he was gone! No one can disappear in just a second. Then we arrived at the station, and the doors opened.

Impossible to find out where he has gone. Who'll believe me when I say that he vanished into thin air?"

"I," said Wolf.

Johan gave his glass back to the waiter.

"Drink up, man. Now do us a favor and ask the entire train crew who remembers this man. And then bring us another schnapps." He looked at Wolf. "You do agree, don't you? Do you want to order some food as well?"

"It's all right this way," said Wolf. "I would like to know as well if other people have seen him, besides the nosy travelers in our carriage. I don't even want to think of food." He handed the waiter his empty glass. "But more schnapps is always welcome."

Shortly after the train had left the station again, the waiter appeared for the third time.

"Is there something like a phantom traveler?" he asked himself aloud. "There's no one who remembers seeing this man, although I gave a clear description of him. A man as white as death, of small stature, a high hat on a bald head... See him once, and you'll never forget him, isn't that so?"

"Phantom travelers do exist," said Johan. He pointed over his shoulder with his thumb to Wolf. "He knows all about these strange affairs of the occult, and slowly but surely I'm learning everything about it as well. So believe me, phantom travelers are just as real as phantom trains...and I'm sure you've heard about phantom trains, haven't you?"

Wolf didn't join in the conversation; he closed his eyes and tried to marshal the facts.

After two years he still didn't know what to think of Wera Keller. And now two other meetings had taken place with people who apparently were able to appear and disappear when they wished to do so. The fortune-teller who called herself Emma and the unreal, larva-like Gerardus Klijn could appear and disappear. All three of them were people of flesh and blood; he was convinced of that. But they possessed capabilities he would label as inhuman. More than once it had occurred to him that countless marvelous events could be explained as phenomena sprung from someone's own mind.

He was convinced that numberless hits scored by mediums during their sessions could be explained by the capability of these people to look inside the minds of those who consulted them. They were able to catch their streams of thought and put them into words; the raising of spirits from the realm of the dead was nothing but a symbolic aid, something to hold on to for both medium and client, something they mutually believed in. But with Wera, Emma, and Gerardus it was different...

 13

Wolf and Johan spent the night in Munich. While Wolf went through his notes once again and wrote a report about what had happened on the train, he had sent Johan out to make inquiries about Wera Keller. There was little chance that Johan would get to know more about her in this big city, but at least it was worth trying.

Wolf was still wide awake when Johan knocked on his door in the middle of the night.

"There was no one who had heard of her, Wolf. I have done what I could, but it is simply impossible to talk to the entire population of Munich in a few hours' time while your beer glass gets refilled all along..."

He came inside, staggering on his feet.

"I understand. And I think you'd better go to sleep now."

"In a while. There's something I'd like to discuss with you."

Wolf looked at him and raised his eyebrows.

"When you're going to perform that experiment in November, I really want to be there. In fact, we've never talked about that at all. You're not planning to do such a thing all by yourself, are you?"

"You can be there. As a spectator. And to support me, of course. I really would appreciate that. I don't think that your presence will have any influence on what is going to happen."

"No, but I'd love to be a witness of these events."

"Very well then! Off you go. I bet you'll sleep like a log."

Johan turned on his heels and headed for his room on the other side of the corridor. All of a sudden there was a loud bump, followed by the sound of breaking glass. Wolf jumped to his feet.

"What was that?"

He ran past Johan into the corridor. On both sides, the doors were rattling. The lamps on the ceiling swung to and fro. But most of the noise was coming from downstairs; it was as if all hell had broken loose in the foyer! Wolf stormed down the stairs, with Johan on his heels. He felt an irritating pressure on his eardrums as if the air around him had been compressed. The canvas of a painting hanging on the wall along the stairs started to flap, its wooden frame creaked, and the paint blew away in clouds of fine particles.

In the foyer, a crystal chandelier had come down and fallen to pieces. A chilly wind blew inside through the windows, whose panes had broken. The night porter crouched on the floor on his knees, bent deeply forward, protecting his head with his hands. Other hotel guests, all dressed in nightclothes, ran down from another staircase. The heavy front desk was trembling, and armchairs and coffee tables turned around and around in a bizarre ballet. A second chandelier came loose from the ceiling and crashed to the floor.

Then, unexpectedly, it was silent.

There was total chaos in the foyer. The night porter stood up slowly and looked at the havoc. More and more hotel guests came down. Soon they were speaking and screaming at the same time.

Wolf focused his attention on Johan, who stood there leaning against a wall. He had to think of Heike Baumann, the little girl, the twelve-year-old from Austria, and her ability to move furniture and make windows rattle.

"Johan, is it you who sets all these horrible powers free? Are you responsible for this?"

Johan shook his head in surprise.

"Of course not... That is to say, not that I know... I should be able to feel a thing like that, shouldn't I?"

"I don't know," said Wolf. "We'd better go back to our rooms. There's no reason for anyone present here to think that you might be the cause of all this."

"Me included," muttered Johan, as he followed Wolf upstairs with staggering feet.

Wolf did not get a wink of sleep that night.

Next morning, no one had an explanation for what had happened. The havoc in the foyer was cleared away. Wolf asked questions of the hotel staff. Later, on the train to Lindau, he wrote a report about it, and then he closed his eyes and fell asleep.

 # 14

When he finally arrived in Lindau, Wolf felt like a pilgrim who had reached his final destination after a long and hard journey. There was a crush of people at the new station, and the city was also crowded, but he did not seem to notice it at all. He went his own way and let himself be guided by something he called his inner voice; it was not a real, audible voice, but it was not intuition or instinct either. It was a knowledge that had penetrated into his mind from the outside.

This feeling was new to him.

It gave him a pleasant sensation.

While Johan took a coach to ferry their suitcases to a hotel, Wolf walked to the harbor. Suddenly he found himself standing there in front of the lion and the lighthouse. Everything was exactly like he had seen on the drawing. Even the steamer was there, far in the distance on Lake Constance.

He took out the playing card.

He wasn't even surprised when he saw the lines of the drawing slowly vanish, the same way as he had seen them appear in Prague.

The card was empty again.

Wolf nodded with enthusiasm.

This was how it had to be.

"Here it will happen," he said to himself. "In November..."

15

Wolf's secretary Abraham de Wild had gone to Wolf's splendid country seat home on the river Vecht. As always when he was there, his thoughts went back to the time when Wolf's father Julius had lived here.

Now he had come at the behest of the son.

He was heartily welcomed by Leonard Pol, the caretaker who had lived for years and years with his wife Cornelia next to the coach house.

He found Wolf in a big room on the first story of the stately building. The French windows were open and gave out onto a view of the well-kept ornamental garden, the vegetable gardens, and the summerhouse at the waterside.

A large map of Europe was hanging on the wall. There were pins on seventy-nine different places. They showed the places where the mediums lived who would take part in the experiment. The pins were connected with red woolen threads, strung in the order of the time when Wolf had visited them. In that way, a whimsical web had come into being, and Wolf stood there looking at it. But he immediately turned around and walked up to the secretary when he saw him entering the room. He spread his arms and smiled.

"Abraham! There you are! Good to see you again."

The men embraced. Then they stepped back to take a look at each other. Abraham had become visibly older. Not much was left of his long, gray hair.

"Good to see you, too—safe and sound," laughed the secretary.

They sat down. There were only two chairs and a writing desk. Pieces of paper hung down from the four walls, and even the floor was covered with papers. Wolf had copied all his notes on them. Some of the sheets contained only the oracular language of mediums; others showed graphs, drawings, ideas, or worked up theories.

Both men had much to tell. They listened carefully to each other. Cornelia Pol came in to bring them something to drink and asked the secretary if he was hungry.

"I'll eat later," said the secretary. "I stopped on my way at an inn."

After Cornelia had left the room again, Wolf started to talk about the book of the Nibelung that Johan had found in Prague.

"I went into that matter," said Abraham. "I correspond with so many people, that the answers came in quickly after I sent round some questions. The story is older. Much older. It is an ancient Germanic heroic legend, and we can only make a guess at its origin. Wait, I have written down one thing and another." He took some sheets of paper from his pocket and started to unfold them. "Here... the hero Siegfried is Sigurd in Old Norse and Sivrit in Middle High German. The Nibelung are a race of dwarfs, and they are in the possession of a treasure that represents fabulous wealth. The treasure is guarded by the dragon Fafnir. The old god Wodan, who is called Odin in the Scandinavian countries, gives Siegfried the stallion Grane, a descendant of his own magical horse Sleipnir. A blacksmith for whom Siegfried once worked gives him the sword Gram.

"With this weapon Siegfried rides out, heading for adventure. He kills the dragon, becomes immortal, wins the treasure.

"What happens then differs from one storyteller to another, from one author to the other. In the course of time, the story has changed many, many times. It is rather peculiar that one version claims that the name Nibelung descends to the ones who managed to get possession of the treasure. In that way, Siegfried came to be a Nibelung.

"It is curious that different mediums spontaneously have mentioned that word Nibelung..."

He gave the papers to Wolf.

"Just read this when you have the time. Then you will see for yourself that I have studied the matter comprehensively."

Then he rose to his feet and walked up to the map on the wall, carefully avoiding the papers on the floor.

"The web of the mediums," he said. "That's what you call it, isn't it? You have met the most important mediums."

"The very best of them."

The secretary rubbed his pointed chin and screwed up his pale blue eyes.

"I'm just wondering . . ." he pondered, "where on the map you should prick the pins of Wera Keller's supposed mediums. I mean, shouldn't they be the very same as many of your own pins? In other words, Wolf, did you—without realizing it—visit a number of mediums from Wera's collective?"

Wolf had stood next to him.

His breath had been taken clean away.

He had never thought of this.

"Now that you say it . . ." he stammered.

In his head he heard Wera's begging voice again: "Keep searching for me. Please! Try to save me." And then: "Don't forget about the collective!"

He stared outside. A little man in a white suit was rowing his boat to the bank of the river. In front of him sat a woman dressed in a long, flowered dress. He was wearing a high hat, she a broad-brimmed straw hat. Wolf took a spyglass from the windowsill and went to the balcony. He extended the spyglass, looked through it, and focused the lens. With growing astonishment he saw the rowboat slide up onto the steep edge of his garden; the man jumped out and used a long rope to moor the boat. He reached out his hand and helped the woman to step out. He himself jumped in again and produced a picnic hamper.

"Do they think there's no one at home here?" asked Wolf aloud.

Abraham, who had remained inside, couldn't hear him.

The woman walked farther into the garden and suddenly looked up at him. Her face became visible now from under the brim of her hat. Her mouth fell open. She reached out her arms. The spyglass fell from Wolf's hands onto the stone floor of the balcony. The front glass came off and rolled away.

"Wera!" he cried.

Abraham stepped onto the balcony. He was just in time to see Wolf climb over the balustrade and let himself fall. Wolf landed on his feet and fought off the pain that shot through his ankles.

"Wera!" he shouted for the second time.

He had recognized her right away and knew that the man in white had to be the larva-like Gerardus Klijn.

"Help me!"

These two words entered his mind like thunderbolts, the same way they had two years ago when Wera had formed the words with her lips at the grave of Jacob van Beek.

"Here I am! Wera! Here I am!"

He ran through the big garden as fast as he could, his eyes pinned to her; her beauty was stunning, unearthly, almost grotesque. And now, finally, he was with her again. He reached out his arms to her.

But as he took another step toward her, she covered her face with her hands, and her voice sounded in his brain:

"They're taking me back!"

She vanished immediately.

A split second later Gerardus Klijn had disappeared as well.

Panting heavily, on the verge of panic, Wolf stood there in his garden and stared at the two objects that proved he had not been hallucinating: the rowboat and the picnic hamper.

Abraham had run downstairs and now came racing into the garden.

"Did you see what I saw?" asked Wolf in a voice that betrayed his fear of a denying answer.

"A man and a woman," said the secretary.

"Right. Wera Keller and Gerardus Klijn."

"Well, I don't know that, of course; I've never seen them before. But where are they? Good heavens, what's happening here?"

"They vanished into thin air."

"Impossible."

Abraham walked past a bed of low box bushes and went to the waterside. He looked out over the river. In the rowboat lay a parasol. He turned around and opened the picnic basket on the boat. It contained food and wine, knives and forks, napkins, plates, and glasses.

He repeated with a sigh, "Impossible. Two people cannot disappear just like that. Unless they both fell into the water and drowned..."

He returned to the water's edge, and his eyes searched the river as if he really expected to discover two drowning persons.

"We'd better go back inside," said Wolf with a deep sigh.

The men headed back towards the house.

"I would give anything for it if I could hear what Wolf senior and Van Beek would think about all this," said Abraham.

The French doors on the ground floor were closed. They walked around the house to the front door, the way Abraham had come outside earlier. The door was still ajar. Abraham grabbed the knob, and the door opened suddenly with such force that the man stumbled backward.

Wolf passed him and made to step inside, but an ice-cold gust of wind almost blew him off his feet.

In the hall, all kinds of things were happening at the same time. A mirror came loose from the wall and fell into pieces on the floor. A marble statue, a goddess from Greek mythology, jumped up and down as if she had come to life until she turned over and came down so hard that her head broke from her neck. The head spun around through the hall in circles until it bumped against a wall and fell apart in big fragments. Two antique chairs were pushed together by an invisible power with such force that the backs broke. A cupboard came into movement and danced over the floor.

Wolf clenched his fists, hit the air, and shouted, "Stop it! Stop it!"

Suddenly it was quiet. Nothing was moving anymore.

Abraham stumbled inside.

"I've never seen anything like this," he gasped.

Wolf cried, "Johan! Where are you? I only realized what you just … "

He fell abruptly silent. The corners of his mouth slid down, and he shook his head slowly.

"This is something I hadn't expected in the least," he said, now in a soft voice.

"What do you mean?" the secretary wanted to know.

"All the time I thought that it was Johan who generated these powers. But he's not here at all, he's gone to Amsterdam. It all revolves around me, Abraham. My God, what's happening to me?"

Abraham left the hall. He hurried through the garden to the coach house to ask Leonard and Cornelia Pol to come and clean away the havoc. He knew very well that he did this mainly as an excuse to get away from the big house for a while, away from Wolf...

16

November gave an early warning for a long, cold winter. Bavaria was all white. The snow fell from a solid gray sky. There was no wind. The two horses that had brought the coach up to Lake Constance were shielded from the cold with thick blankets. Johan jumped down from the box and opened the door of the coach. Wolf stepped out.

"Shall I bring the coach closer to the lake?" asked Johan.

"No, this is far enough."

Abraham, who remained in the coach, pushed down the window and stared outside. The snow was falling straight down and vaguely revealed the outlines of the lion and the lighthouse. The calm water disappeared between them in patches of fog. He could imagine how crowded it could get here on warm, sunny days when the steamers came and went and people lazed about or sat outside. Now Lindau seemed to be asleep. This time of the year the harbor was deserted. Johan sat down opposite to him, taking the place where Wolf had sat. Abraham took a watch from his pocket.

"Twenty-five past two, Wolf. Only five minutes to go..."

"I go."

"Strength. Johan will come to help you right away if you are in danger."

"I count on that."

Wolf heaved a deep sigh. The horses snorted, and it looked as if they were belching smoke. The animals were restless and scraped their hoofs through the snow. It was as if the sensitive horses could perceive something of the tension that was built up by the power of thoughts of the seventy-nine mediums who had gone into a trance and weaved their mental web.

Wolf put his hands into his pockets and walked up to the harbor.

If this mental web actually existed, then he was the symbolic spider, and it would be no more than five minutes before he would know what he was going to catch.

The most important indication that something was bound to happen, he found in the cold silence that surrounded him. It was unnatural that there was no one here. No human being showed himself, no bird made itself heard; it was as if all that lived intuitively kept away from this so magical place.

Wolf stopped at the waterside. There were no boats. He let his gaze travel over the left pier that bent diagonally further on and was bordered by the monument of the lion. The right pier was exactly the same and ended by the lighthouse. The entry to the harbor was between the lion and the lighthouse, and right there the water suddenly started to bubble. Wolf saw it immediately and held his breath.

It's going to happen, he thought.

There was an unpleasant pressure right above his eyes. He underwent the strange sensation of being torn away from reality as if he only now was alerted to the fact that his surroundings always had given him a mental anchorage, and this same anchorage now no longer existed.

There was no gravity any longer. Wolf felt that he was no longer standing with his feet in the snow. He was floating above the ground. The water at the entry of the harbor now began to move; a whirlpool came into existence. Soon the water splashed in all directions, while the center of the whirlpool became deeper and deeper. Waves dashed against the lion and the lighthouse.

A violent storm, making a sound like a terrifying sigh, swept all snow from the air and hit Wolf so hard that he rose into the air, turning over and over.

The next moment he had disappeared.

"I must go there!" cried Johan, flinging open the door of the coach.

Abraham put a hand on his arm.

"Wait a while..."

Both men had seen with their very own eyes how Wolf went up, came down again, and then vanished into thin air.

Less than half a minute later a vague image of Wolf appeared behind the heavy falls of snow, like the blurred projection of a magic lantern.

The figure rose slowly to its feet.

Now Wolf looked more like his old self again.

He looked around and shook the snow from his hair.

"He has lost his hat," remarked Abraham, who stared at him intently.

"And he is holding something in his hand," said Johan, whose eyes were sharper than those of the old secretary. "An object. I cannot see what it is. Shall I go to him now?"

"No, don't be so impatient. Maybe it's not over yet. He will come to us in a while. That was the plan..."

Wolf had turned his hand with the palm upward. There was something dangling down from his forefinger.

"An ornament?" guessed Johan. He stuck his head out of the open window of the coach—then he whistled softly between his teeth and guessed one more time: "Gold?"

"Listen! Listen!" cried Abraham. "Do you hear that? Horse's hooves and rattling wheels. Another coach is approaching. I think you'd better go now, Johan. See to it that nothing happens to Wolf!"

Johan was already outside. In his hurry to reach his friend as soon as possible, he did not reckon with the frozen layer under the fresh snow. He slipped and landed hard on his hands and knees.

Right in front of Wolf, a black coach had come to a standstill. The two horses were sweating, and they breathed heavily through their nostrils. A man jumped down from the box, and a second one opened a door and jumped outside. They wore wide capes, hats, and boots. Each held a short wooden club in his hand.

Abraham grasped his cane by the tip so that the copper grip could function as a deadly weapon.

"Wolf!" he cried, as he stepped out and ran past Johan, who tried to scramble to his feet again.

Wolf was quite unaware of anything. He stared at the ornament, a neck ring, that swung to and fro from his outstretched finger. The man who had jumped down from the box was the first to reach him. He lashed out with the club and hit Wolf in the back of the neck. Wolf opened his mouth, made a retching sound, and fell face down. The other attacker snatched the ornament away from him. As they turned to run back to the coach, Abraham arrived on the scene and swung his cane like a wild man. Surprised by his brutal behavior they stood still; the copper grip whistled past their hair. Johan popped up next to Abraham. Now it was two against two. Johan was not armed, but to his advantage, he was a hardened fighter who had gained practical experience in the streets of the Amsterdam Jordaan.

"The ornament!" hissed Johan, understanding how important it was to get it. "Break their bones, Abraham. They've got it hidden under one of these capes!"

Abraham took a step forward and swung his cane once again. Johan dove for the feet of one of the men caught hold of him firmly and brought him down. At the same moment, a club struck the back of his head. He yelled with pain and let go of his adversary. Two hands seized hold of him and pushed his face deep into the snow. There was a flaming stab, right on the spot where the club had hit him.

They're using a knife, it flashed through his mind, *and now they're going to finish me off.*

He heard Abraham cry for help. It seemed to him that the voice was shouting from far, far away. Grasping for breath, he inhaled snow instead of air. The hands let go of him. He pushed himself up. He stared down and saw the impression of his own face in the snow, red-rimmed by the blood that had trickled down through his hair and along his cheeks from the wound on the back of his head. His arms gave out, and he collapsed back onto the ground, rolling over on his back.

Abraham plumped down next to him.

Not much later his cane was thrown down on the ground.

Horses snorted. Wheels rattled. The black coach disappeared.

"Johan! Abraham!"

Wolf spoke in a concerned voice.

The secretary was the first to scramble to his feet. He put a hand on his left shoulder.

"It feels as if they have broken my collar bone," he sighed. "But I think it is only bruised. And how about you, Wolf?"

"It's my neck that hurts so much. I can hardly move my head."

As fast as their painful limbs allowed them, they knelt down near the bleeding Johan, who was lying motionless in the snow.

"Is he dead?" wondered Wolf aloud.

It was Johan himself who reacted with a forced smile:

"It's apparently not my time yet."

Wolf and the secretary lifted him up carefully and brought him to the coach. The secretary wrapped a shawl around Johan's head. Wolf looked around for his hat, but it was nowhere to be seen. He climbed up on the box and set the horses into motion. As fast as he dared to let them go over the icy roads, he drove them into the town. The streets were deserted. Finally, he saw someone on a sidewalk. He pulled the horses up immediately.

"Excuse me, sir. Where can I find a doctor? I'm in a hurry. There's a wounded man inside the coach."

"Dr. Weser lives not far away from here," said the man. "Just follow me!"

He started to run. Wolf urged the horses into motion again.

The man went around a corner and ran across a square. Around a corner one more time, and into a side street. Then he stopped and pointed at a door.

"There. Dr. Weser."

Wolf thanked him and jumped down from the box. Together with the secretary, he lifted his friend from the coach. The man had been helpful again and had already knocked on the door. The door opened. Wolf made a decision.

"Abraham, bring Johan inside. We'll meet again later at our hotel. I want to take a look around the harbor."

The secretary supported Johan; his own body hurt too much to argue with Wolf.

"Very well, then! I'll stay with Johan. Take good care of yourself."

"All the best, Johan," said Wolf, and then he hurried away.

 # 17

Wolf was disillusioned. With his hands deep in the pockets of his coat, he walked down the street. For two years on end, he had made preparations for what should have been the most interesting day of his life. Now a terrible pain flamed from his neck to his head, and he felt sick.

No matter how deeply he thought things over, he could not remember what exactly had happened.

He had stood there at the harbor and seen how the water started to bubble. A strange feeling had come over him. He had been lifted up by invisible powers and then, all of a sudden, he stood there again—staring at a golden object in his hand. Something hard hit him in the neck. He passed out, recovered consciousness, scrambled up, and saw his companions lying in the snow.

There was a gap between the moment he went up into the air and the moment that he was looking at the ornament—an emptiness like a bottomless pit, an unbridgeable ravine, a revelation apparently up for grabs, but actually out of reach.

This irritated him tremendously.

He shook the snow from his hair.

I must try to find my hat, he thought, as if this was of great importance now.

Looking around, he didn't know where he was. The first time he visited Lindau, he had focused on the harbor. He didn't know the streets of the city. The square looked familiar, but hadn't he been here just a minute ago? A wall of big buildings was covered with paintings of biblical figures. The colors were bright, and there was a shining gold leaf. The snow had stuck to the wall in countless places, which made it seem as if the figures went through a wintry landscape.

Wolf stopped and looked at it.

The pictures radiated a certain enchantment, which calmed him down.

Then he went on and intuitively turned into an alley, where his lower legs disappeared into the snow up to his calves; great amounts of snow had come down from the high, gabled roofs.

He reached the other end of the alley, and there was the harbor again—right in front of him!

There was no sight of his hat. The steady snow had already covered up all tracks from the coaches. With his foot, he wiped away the upper layer of snow on the spot where he thought that Johan had lain. The blood underneath it appeared. It had mixed with the snow and seemed to be frozen.

Staring at the gray water of the lake, he tried to recall what exactly had happened to him, hoping that small detail would come back to him that would lead to a complete remembrance.

But nothing like that happened.

What about the mediums? Were they still in a trance, and was the collective power of their thoughts still being transmitted to him?

He was not sure about that either.

He walked on until he had reached the edge of the quay. The lion and the lighthouse were only vaguely visible through the falling snow.

Wolf shrugged his shoulders in despair, which caused a new, shooting pain in his neck. Impulsively he raised his right hand in order to touch the painful spot with his fingertips. In a flash, he saw something glisten around his wrist.

He lowered his hand immediately and stared with amazement at a beautiful bracelet. Only now, when he saw it, did he become aware of its weight.

It's gold, he thought. *Pure gold!*

He looked up in fright when he heard a horse snort.

The sound came from nearby.

A man dressed in a wide cape approached on a black horse. The animal's hooves hardly made any sound in the soft snow.

The man looked at him from under the brim of a black hat. Suddenly he set spurs to the horse.

It's about the bracelet went through Wolf's head.

He was certain about that, for he knew only too well that he held the bracelet in his hand, the bracelet that one had taken away from him with brute force.

It was too late to run away. No doubt the horse would catch up with him and run him down.

A low, iron railing separated him from the water below. Without a moment's thought, Wolf bent forward, wiped the snow off the railing, climbed over it, turned around, caught hold of the iron and let himself down.

As he hung from the railing above the water, the horse rushed past; the rider bent to one side and made a vain effort to catch him as the horse thundered on by.

Immediately Wolf climbed up again, threw himself over the railing, scrambled to his feet, and started to run as fast as he could. It was not easy for the rider to turn his horse around fast on the slippery sheet of ice under the snow, and that gave Wolf a good start. He managed to reach the alley through which he had come to the harbor a moment ago.

Halfway down he stopped and turned on his heels.

The horse was rearing up at the entrance of the alley.

The rider did not dare to send the animal at full gallop through the piled up snow.

18

Wolf was the first one who reached the hotel. He hung his coat on the hallstand near the desk and entered the spacious foyer, where he dropped down into a comfortable armchair. He ordered a glass of brandy. After having checked to make sure no one paid attention to him, he shoved the bracelet down along his wrist until it became visible from under the sleeve of his jacket. He was really bewildered now he looked at it closely; it was a skillfully made object.

It was an open bracelet that could be bent open to take it off and pinched around the wrist after being put on. The gold was twisted so that it looked like a screw thread. Both sides ended in curls. This was the breathtaking masterpiece of an inspired goldsmith. Wolf had no idea how it had got there around his wrist, just as he did not know where the neck ring had come from. What he did realize was that someone knew that he was in the possession of the bracelet— someone who would do anything to take it away from him. He hid the bracelet again under the sleeve of his jacket. Sipping his brandy, he waited for his two companions.

They arrived two hours later.

It was already late in the afternoon, and Wolf suggested they go to the restaurant in the hotel to have dinner. They chose a table in a quiet corner and placed their orders.

Johan was in bad shape. The doctor had cut off part of his hair and swathed his head in bandages.

He apologized profusely to Wolf:

"You do everything for me. You took me away from my poverty and let me lead a life of luxury. And all I had to do in return was give you a feeling of safety. I'm your bodyguard. Before I had the chance to knock up one of those men, I was already stretched my full length on the ground. First I was hit by that club, then there was that sharp knife... I'm so sorry, Wolf. I wanted to catch him, to strangle him! But I failed. Well, I brought the coach back and inquired with the stable keeper about a black coach, black horses, and men dressed in capes. He could not help me. I am a good-for-nothing, a millstone around your neck!"

Wolf shrugged his shoulders, and his face twisted as another stab of pain went through him.

He said, "Don't worry, Johan. We're best friends. You did your very best."

Abraham seemed to have recovered from the shock of the earlier encounter and started to tell Wolf what he had seen from his seat in the coach.

"For years on end I had to deal with the most fantastic affairs—on paper, that is! I opened, read, and answered letters that were meant for you and Jacob van Beek. Every now and then I was present at a séance. But this is the very first time a wonder was enacted in my presence, right before my eyes. You disappeared, Wolf! All of a sudden you weren't there anymore. An invisible hand wiped you from the quay and flung you into the great nothing. Before I had the time to come to my senses, you were there again—just like that. That is to say, first, you seemed rather vague, like a gray, sketchy outline on a white sheet. Then you were your old self again, and you held that object in your hand. Shining like gold. Was it gold?"

Wolf shoved up the sleeve of his jacket.

"Probably just as real and pure as this one."

He bent the bracelet open and took it from his wrist.

Abraham had already reached out his hand.

"Let me see that …"

While Abraham studied the object, Wolf told about the attacker on the horse.

Thereupon the others explained one more time what they had seen there in the snow-covered harbor. Wolf put on the bracelet again and hid it under the sleeve of his jacket.

Dinner was served.

"From now on we have to be on our guard," said Johan. "I really couldn't give an explanation for the unexpected presence of these golden objects. What I do know is that there are people who wouldn't hesitate to commit murder to get hold of them. They already have stolen one of the two away from you. And you will be in great danger as long as the second golden object is in your possession."

"Well, I think so, too," said the secretary. "No matter what has happened, Wolf, you are in an extremely dangerous situation right now. And we have no idea where that danger is coming from. We cannot even understand what has happened. Yes, Johan and I know what we have seen with our very eyes! How on earth is it possible that you disappeared and came back again with two valuable golden ornaments? And now look at us, as we sit here! We can hardly move from the pain. Who were our attackers?"

"Everything went so fast that I cannot even remember their faces," said Johan. "We will have to arm ourselves. A club, a pistol if necessary. It is obvious that they'll have another try to get hold of the bracelet, Wolf."

"We'd better sleep on it," said Wolf. "We can sit here together the whole night and speculate on what really happened, but believe me— we will not find out the truth. What we need now is rest. That's the most important."

Abraham looked tired. He nodded slowly.

"I think you're right. Tomorrow we'll probably be able to come up with new indications."

"And tomorrow all three of us will have aching muscles," predicted Wolf. "How humiliating it is to get such a beating and realize that your defense doesn't amount to anything."

Johan put down his fork and knife on his still-full plate and wiped his mouth on a napkin.

"That is true," he said. "But believe me, that will change. From now on I will let myself be surprised by nothing and nobody!"

The night passed quietly.

But early in the morning more than twenty windows of the hotel simultaneously burst with a loud crack, while the chandeliers in the foyer swung to and fro, and chairs and tables danced in the deserted dining room. A cupboard fell over in the empty room next to Wolf's.

Wolf sat up in his bed and stared at the chink between the curtains, where the still-dim light of the morning was visible.

It was time to get up and leave Lindau.

They went back to Munich by train.

Johan would make new inquiries about Wera Keller. This time he would be able to do so more thoroughly. Abraham was in possession of the golden bracelet now and would go out searching for anyone who could tell him anything about it. He had given Wolf the address of someone with whom he corresponded about affairs of the occult and paranormal phenomena—a certain Hans-Erich Krohn, a doctor with great interest in the unknown possibilities of the human mind.

Wolf put up at Der Bayerische Hof, a big hotel in the center of the city, and ordered Johan to bring a letter to Dr. Krohn. Johan came back with the message that the doctor was willing to receive Wolf the next afternoon.

 **19**

Hans-Erich Krohn was a corpulent man of small stature with little, piercing eyes, a short-cut gray beard, a bald head, and chubby cheeks. He wore metal-rimmed spectacles with round lenses.

He did not receive Wolf in his consulting room but led the way upstairs to the first story, where he opened a door to a big room at the back of the house. Inside were two leather armchairs, a coffee table, and a bookcase. The fire was smoldering in the hearth, and Krohn put some logs on it.

"I hope that Abraham de Wild will pay me a visit as well, now that he's here in Munich," he said. His voice sounded calm and deep. "And it is no problem for me to come to Der Bayerische Hof. I would love to have dinner with him there. Please, please, sit down..."

The armchair was big and soft. Wolf sank into the cushions.

"The correspondence between Abraham and me is an exchange of special facts. I am fascinated by the mutual influence of body and mind. Every day I'm confronted with the physical defects of my patients. The more I read and hear about the mental side of our existence, the more I come to the conclusion that many physical complaints have their origins in mental problems."

The doctor himself hadn't sat down yet, and now he spread his arms and moved his body to and fro.

"When body and mind are in balance, there is automatically a sense of well-being, a feeling of great happiness." His left arm went down, his right arm went up. "When something changes in the mind, it will have its influence on the body." His left arm went up, his right arm went down. "And if something is the matter with the body . . . well, I think you understand what I mean, don't you?"

"I think so," said Wolf.

"Abraham also wrote to me often about his personal circumstances. I have understood that he is in your service. You are a rich man, very rich indeed; you travel all over Europe and follow up the inquiries of your father and his friend Jacob van Beek. Is that right?"

"Yes, that's right," said Wolf.

"You need mental help. All kinds of things happen that you cannot explain. Objects come into movement spontaneously everywhere you go. You wrote it short and to the point in your letter that was brought to me. I will be happy to oblige you if only to prove my friendship to Abraham. Besides, you really have aroused my interest. So I suggest that you relax and tell me your life story. All I will do myself is keep my mouth shut and listen to you."

Wolf started to talk right away.

He found it easy to pour out his heart to this stranger.

He kept on talking for over half an hour. His head rested against the soft leather, and he hardly felt the pain in his neck that way.

"Well, I can imagine you cannot make head nor tail of this," he ended. "And if you don't believe a word of it, I will understand that, too."

"This is all very interesting," sighed Krohn. "We have to deal with special powers here that can't be explained easily. Among my friends, there are neurologists and psychologists, but also mediums and investigators of the fantastic like yourself. I understand that everything you just told me is confidential, but even if I were allowed to talk about it with these friends, they would not be able to give reasonable explanations either. That is to say, not for everything. For certain things..."

He stood up.

"What are you having?"

"I would like a glass of brandy."

"Do you often drink alcohol?"

"Well... to tell you the truth... yes."

"Cut down on it drastically. I'm not saying that because it can damage your liver in a serious way. From excessive indulgence in alcohol, you will become hypersensitive and susceptible to impressions. Fears get washed away but come back unexpectedly with redoubled intensity. Am I right or not?"

"Yes."

"Every now and then everything around you begins to move. At home and in hotels, like you just told me. It is not a unique phenomenon, as we both know very well—you are just as well informed about these things as I am. Do you also know in whose surroundings such outbursts mostly take place?"

"I guess you mean immature people. Children, in fact."

"Exactly. Even though we don't know yet which particular powers are involved here, we do know that everything slowly but surely ends when someone who effects this gets older. In your case, it should already have been over."

"It never happened to me when I was young."

"How remarkable!"

Krohn opened a sideboard and took out a bottle of wine.

"We'll have wine. That's not such strong stuff. So these outbursts of violence around you are of recent occurrence?"

"Very recent, to be honest."

Krohn uncorked the bottle and filled two glasses.

"You have performed an interesting experiment. You let yourself be guided by a great number of mediums, you combined the information they gave to you, and in that way, you fixed a place where something special was bound to happen on a certain day, at a certain time. At the same moment, all the mediums went into a deep trance, and then something happened to you. Abraham and your friend Johan saw how you disappeared. Not much later they saw you come back again. I would have thought immediately of hallucination where both spectators are concerned, and as for the gap in your memory, maybe you saw a vision that was too shocking to remember, and so you hid it in the dark depths of your mind. But then we still have these golden objects, and they throw these nice theories out of gear. Are you sure that you didn't buy them somewhere yourself, or that someone hasn't given them to you?"

"Oh no, I'm absolutely sure about that. I've never seen either object before."

"Someone could have slipped them into your pocket unnoticed."

Wolf shook his head and then slowly shrugged his shoulders. He took a sip from his glass.

Krohn continued:

"Let's look at the case from a psychological angle, Mr. Wolf." He sat down again, leaned far forward to take up his glass from the coffee table, and then leaned backward with a smile. "Oh, how I love to analyze! First, give me, if you wish, a short description of your young life."

Wolf did so.

As Krohn listened, he leaned with his elbows on the arms of his easy chair and tapped his fingertips against each other. After Wolf had finished his story, he raised a forefinger.

"All right, all right. Everything's clear. There's that little boy, the little Wolf. His father has made a fortune, together with his friend, uh …

❀ ❀ ❀

"Jacob. Jacob van Beek."

"Right. And then he is going to do something completely different. Also with Jacob van Beek. They are going to play a game that is very popular among the rich people—that is to say, they dare to go much farther. They don't only visit séances in the parlors of well-to-do friends; no, they make archives of all special happenings in the paranormal field. Then your father and mother get very ill. They die of cholera in ..."

"In 1866."

"Now the little Wolf is all on his own, isn't he? He receives this fabulous legacy. Money, a splendid country seat at the riverside. Jacob van Beek constitutes himself as his protector, a substitute father, educator... He implicates Wolf in his fantastic inquiries into supernatural affairs. Wolf gets involved, he is fascinated. In the meantime, he becomes aware of the fact that he is extremely rich and doesn't have to do anything he doesn't like. It appears that he has two different personalities. That nice young man living in his country house is rather different from the street urchin who roams about the city and drinks constantly."

Wolf sat up straight in his chair, prepared to make a strong protest, but Krohn raised both his hands.

"It's my turn to talk. In these modern times, we slowly but surely begin to have another view of matters. Can a medium actually talk with the dead? Have the dead nothing better to do than use a medium to tell that they are well? Is there a life after death? More and more scientists begin to suspect that it all has to do with the special powers of the human brain. The medium should be able to read the mind of those who consult him."

He slapped his bald skull with the flat of his hand.

"It's all in there. The brain is the most marvelous part of the human body; it is a unique organ with unknown potentialities. Some people hardly use their brains—others are able to design a palace, invent a steam engine, or compose music for a grand orchestra. Some people can read the future, gauge another man's thoughts, find underground wells, and so on and so on. I think you can find countless other examples in your own files in Amsterdam. And then there are these people who can show something to others that are actually not there..."

He fell silent and looked at Wolf while he bent forward to take up his glass from the coffee table.

"Do we understand each other?"

"I'm not sure what you're driving at," said Wolf.

"Well, then let me explain it to you. I don't think it impossible that you are able to do more, wittingly or unwittingly, than making cupboards move or breaking windows from a distance. Now try to imagine that Wera Keller was a product of your fantasy, who came into existence by the special powers of your mind. Mr. Wolf, I am a man who says what he thinks. All things have their origin, their reason. The young, spoiled Wolf never strived for any goal. Wealth was attended by apathy, maybe also by boredom—and then there were those exorbitant drinking bouts. Paying a visit to the different mediums gave you a reason to travel. And then, two years ago, you suddenly found that aim in life. You started to assemble the mediums, hoping to create something grand, something unique with their help. And what was it again, Mr. Wolf, that happened two years ago?"

"I met Wera Keller," answered Wolf immediately. "Keep in mind, Dr. Krohn, that Jacob van Beek saw her as well. She was with him at home, and there she made the die fly, and there ... "

"Wait a minute!" interrupted Krohn. "There are no witnesses to that. That very same day Jacob van Beek was found lying on his bed ... dead! That's what you told me yourself a minute ago. You also told me that a policeman had his doubts about the death of the man whom we safely might call your guardian."

"That's right. Lodewijk Dekker, the police officer, set up an inquiry. Without any results, by the way..."

Krohn did not pay attention to that remark, but continued:

"You happened to be Jacob van Beek's most important heir as well. How he passed away remains a mystery. Not much later you started traveling, and you began to have puzzling visions, and finally, all hell broke loose at different places where you found yourself."

Wolf's mouth fell open.

"What are you insinuating, Dr. Krohn? Are you saying that I am responsible for the death of Jacob van Beek? Are you talking about murder?"

"Please, don't take this as an accusation. All I did was think aloud. I was just analyzing..."

"A man or an apparition actually, in the train from Prague to Munich gave an explanation for the death of Jacob Leopold van Beek. His name was Gerardus Klijn, and he was talking about a whispering of the collective. Then he disappeared. Just like that... But everyone saw him, even the waiter of the train can tell everything about his strange behavior—"

Krohn burst out laughing.

"We are talking here about the remark of an apparition, a phantom, aren't we? Is that correct? Yes? And just a moment ago expressed the presumption that you yourself might have conjured up phantoms like Wera Keller. Don't you understand the seriousness of your own situation, Mr. Wolf?"

He rose to his feet and fetched the wine bottle to fill up Wolf's glass.

"I've had enough wine," sighed Wolf. "I stop drinking. Right now."

Wolf was beginning to feel rather uncomfortable here. He felt drops of sweat trickle down his temples. On the verge of panic, he tried to find the right words that would free him from these accusations, as an incantation could nullify a curse.

"The golden ornaments!" he cried out all of a sudden, and then he heaved a deep sigh.

"What about it?"

"Abraham has the bracelet. How can you explain the fact that it was suddenly there, around my wrist, after I had disappeared at the harbor of Lindau and had come back again?"

Krohn filled up his own glass and sat down again.

"A man such as you can buy himself as many ornaments as he wants. I do not assert that you did so with these two ornaments; all I do is suggest the possibility."

"We were attacked. Johan is the worse having been stabbed with a knife. Abraham and I received some hard blows. They snatched away the neck ring from me!"

"A daring robbery—that's the first thing that comes into my mind. You described a desolated harbor. The ideal place for thieves to strike. Show a robber gold on a lonely spot, and he will do anything to get it."

"I'm totally confused now, Dr. Krohn," said Wolf with a sigh.

"Well, I really like to shake up someone's mind thoroughly every now and then," reacted Krohn. "All your thoughts flutter around now like leaves in the wind. Soon the storm in your head will die down, and then it is time to come to your senses. If you stay in Munich long enough, and you haven't become afraid of me and haven't started to hate me either, we might organize a second session. At that time I would suggest quite another method. I have made a study of the works of Franz Anton Mesmer, who experimented at the end of the eighteenth century with animal magnetism and somnambulism. The word *mesmerism* is derived directly from his name; for several decades now we have preferred to use the word *hypnosis*. I suppose you are familiar with that. We get better results with it all the time. During a second visit, I would like to bring you under hypnosis and ask you questions. It would be great if Abraham could come with you then. How I would like to meet him! Very well then, I will wait for a new message from you..."

Wolf stood up, understanding that this was the end of the conversation.

"That's agreed," said Wolf.

With uncertain steps, he followed the man downstairs to the front door. There he shook hands with the doctor and went outside. He shivered when the wind blew snowflakes into his sweaty face.

"See you again!" he heard Dr. Krohn say. "I wish you a pleasant time in wintry Munich. Please say hello from me to Abraham."

He waved his hand without looking back.

20

Wolf's thoughts couldn't be compared with swirling leaves; steam trains thundered through his head, phantom trains without engineers, on their way to a city by the name of Big Panic.

He had walked into a pub where everyone was drinking huge glasses of beer. He himself had ordered brandy, and now he had been sitting there for quite a while, his hands folded, staring at the still-full glass, as if he begged in silence for the help of a higher power to see that it wasn't poisoned. He paid no attention to the people around him, who eyed him suspiciously.

Dr. Krohn had treated him the same way he had often treated the mediums: in a manner that was friendly but at the same time hard and ruthless. The doctor had turned the tables, and Wolf did not know how to react.

It was true that it was mostly confused children who set everything around them into movement and caused terrible havoc without actually touching anything when they went off into a fit of rage. Otherwise, as far as he was concerned, all his experiences were totally different from those of these kids. He even had the feeling that what happened to him was unique.

He reached out for the glass, saw how his fingers trembled and drew back his hand immediately.

He had hung up his wet coat and sat down close to the fireplace when he came in; slowly he began to feel warm.

Oh, please, please, he thought, *don't let it come to a new outburst here. Nothing here must start to move, shove, fall, break.*

Slowly he sank forward. Now he leaned with his elbows on the tabletop and stared with big eyes into the amber liquor in the glass. It made him calm down. It cleared his mind. As if heavy thoughts actually had weight, he felt himself getting lighter now as they began to disappear. His ears were no longer susceptible to the noise in the pub.

A shock went through him. He kicked automatically with his feet so that the soles of his shoes scraped the floor. The next moment he found himself, to his surprise, in front of the door of the inn in the neighborhood of Prague, where he had met the fortune-teller who had called herself Emma. It was cold. He stood ankle-deep in the snow. The fingers of the old wooden hands that were nailed to the doorpost seemed to wave him in. He wanted to open the door, but it was locked. Wolf was struck by fear. In wild panic, he started to kick and bang against the door. He screamed, "Help me! Please, someone, help me!"

Then, all of a sudden, he was back in the pub in Munich.

He fluttered his eyelids and looked around. Not one of the guests was still sitting at a table. The people had formed a wide circle around him and stared at him with their mouths wide open.

"There!" pointed a woman. "There he is again!"

Wolf took up the glass of brandy and brought it to his lips. He emptied the entire contents.

Then he rose to his feet, shoved his chair backward, and walked around the table. People moved out of his way as he hurriedly moved towards the hallstand.

"Demon!" shouted someone, and it was immediately repeated by many others:

"Demon! Demon!"

Shouting together gave them courage, and the people started to press on to him. Someone began to push him.

"Demon!"

A fist hit his already painful neck. But then he was outside. He started to run, buttoning up his coat and putting up his collar. He knew that the danger was not past yet when he heard quick footsteps behind him. His neck hurt too much to turn his head while he was running. He stopped and spun around on his left heel.

A man in a black cape came up to him.

Wolf started to run again.

"Wait! Wait a minute!" he heard the man say in German with a strong Bavarian accent. "I mean no harm. I just want to have a word with you."

Wolf did not react.

"It is of great importance," urged the man.

The voice sounded from nearby, and Wolf ran as fast as he could. A new fit of panic lent wings to his feet. He went through streets and alleyways, got lost during his flight, slipped on smooth sidewalks, scrambled to his feet again, ran down people. Only when he got a feeling as if his lungs were beginning to freeze did he give up.

He stopped. Panting heavily, he waited for the man in the black cape to pop up next to him or behind him and tap him on the back. He sat down on the windowsill of a shop. People passed him by without paying any attention to him.

A coachman pulled up at the side of the road, jumped from the box, and opened the door for his fare. Wolf stumbled up to him, waited until the passenger had left, and then asked the coachman, "Could you bring me to my hotel? Der Bayerische Hof…"

The coachman looked him up and down and raised his eyebrows.

"Is this supposed to be some kind of a joke, sir?" he asked.

Wolf felt a sudden fright. He didn't know how to react. Was the coachman going to tell him now that this town wasn't Munich and that he wasn't even in Germany?

The coachman thought he understood why Wolf kept silent.

"Ah, I'm sorry, sir. You're not from here, of course. Looking at you, you must have been searching for a long time." He pointed to a building on the left side of the street. "All you have to do is go around that corner. Then you'll see the hotel right away. It isn't worth a ride, you understand?"

"Oh," said Wolf between two deep breaths. "Thank you very much..."

He began to walk again. A few minutes later he had reached the hotel, and right up to his suite. He took off his coat, flopped down into a chair, and tried to relax, but did not manage to calm down. He stood up to get himself a bottle of liquor and a glass. He filled his glass, took a pull, and sat down again.

The liquor had a tranquilizing effect on him, and now he started to think, paradoxically enough, about drinking less in the future or even stopping it entirely.

Dr. Krohn had scared him with his crazy analysis, but that meant nothing compared to the fear that struck him when he thought about what had happened to him in the warmth of the packed pub.

"A hallucination of the worst kind," he sighed. "And it will get even worse if it turns out to be no hallucination at all, and nothing but the unexplainable truth!"

Wolf felt sick.

Liquor would not make him feel better.

Still, he drank.

21

When Johan came back he looked for Wolf in his suite. Immediately he could tell that something had happened.

"How I wished to bring you good news," he said. "No trace of a woman by the name of Wera Keller. How about your visit to Dr. Krohn?"

"Later, later," responded Wolf. "First I have to marshal the facts for myself. Suffice it to say that he has come up with things I would never have thought about myself."

Fifteen minutes later Abraham knocked on the door. He happened to be in a merry mood and immediately gave the bracelet back to Wolf, who slipped it back on his wrist.

"A museum piece," he said in a decided tone. "A valuable ornament. Undoubtedly very old and of Germanic origin. Imagine, Wolf, an object of one thousand years or even older fell into your hands!"

He sat down and told how he had gone from antique dealer to antique dealer that day, without finding someone who was actually able to help him.

"Then I met someone who began to think that it might be something very special. He gave me the address of a retired museum director, a certain Edmund Reuter. I went to that address by coach and was lucky; the old man was at home. At first, he wouldn't let me in, but he became very enthusiastic when I showed him the bracelet, and he invited me into his study. For a long time, he sat there examining the bracelet, and he even used a magnifying glass in order to see more of the details. Wait, I have made some notes."

Abraham took a piece of paper out of his pocket and unfolded it.

"Edmund Reuter. Knows much about the Germanic in general and about the Vikings in particular. Vikings captured a lot on their raids. But this ornament is a masterly example of their own fine art; it is made by a Germanic goldsmith. It is of pure gold. Now it seems to be a fact that the Vikings often buried their valuables. A hole in the ground was the safe of ancient times—that's what Reuter said. Nowadays they often get dug up. They captured gold or obtained it by trade. Vikings had the much sought after amber. Many stories are going around about Viking treasures."

"The Nibelung?" asked Wolf, who had listened with interest and was glad that Abraham distracted his mind from everything that had happened to him this day.

"Well, I don't know about that," said Abraham, without looking up from the paper. "He didn't mention anything about it. Other stories. What a Viking put into the ground would later come into his possession again—after his death, in Valhalla! That might be a reason why one digs up so many valuables nowadays. Not only in Scandinavia, but everywhere the Vikings went on their marauding expeditions. Small treasures can be explained as an offering to the gods. In hard times they hid their silver and gold, and they did the same when there was talk of mutual war. In spite of many such findings, your bracelet is something very special. Most of the time one finds coins or rings, and often the objects are of silver. A bracelet of solid gold, so cleverly forged, is a curiosity."

He folded up the paper again.

"Of course, the man wanted to know how I came by the bracelet. I mentioned your name and said that it is an heirloom from your father. Then he wanted to know why I made inquiries about it in Munich. I said that you are traveling constantly and that I often come with you and have been trying to find out something about the history of the bracelet everywhere I go. He was satisfied with my answer. It is a valuable object. He would like to buy it from you. That is to say when you are willing to sell it. He asked me to tell you that he has the money for it..."

He had to laugh. Wolf laughed along with him and began to feel relieved.

"Let's go downstairs, friends," he said. "We'll continue our conversation in the restaurant. I'm getting hungry."

During dinner, Wolf dared to tell his friends frankly about his visit to Dr. Hans-Erich Krohn.

"Are you intending to visit him one more time and let yourself be put under hypnosis?" asked Abraham.

"Yes. If only to convince him that it is all quite different from what he is thinking," said Wolf.

"Then I will be happy to come along with you."

"He asked about you—he looks forward to meeting you."

Then Wolf told them how he had sat in the pub, where he suddenly had the strong and strange impression that he was standing in front of the door of the inn near Prague. Abraham and Johan remained silent, not knowing how to react to this.

Wolf concentrated on his food. When he reached out for his glass of wine, the bracelet became visible from under the sleeve of his jacket.

Abraham pointed at it:

"Old Edmund Reuter said something more about that." He tapped with his fingers on his forehead. "How stupid of me. I forgot the notes on the back of the paper. Now, where is it?" While going through his pockets, he remembered that he had folded it up again. And then he had probably put it down somewhere. "It must be on the occasional table in your suite," he said. "Shall I go and get it?"

Wolf pushed back his chair and rose to his feet.

"Let me do it," he said. "I'll be back in a minute."

Wolf left the restaurant and went through the big foyer, then up the broad stairs to the second story. Entering the corridor, he noticed immediately that the door of his suite was open.

Instead of going back to the foyer and notifying someone on the hotel staff, he carefully walked without making a sound over the thick carpet. He knew very well what he was doing, but he was full of frustration and bottled-up anger and was ready to get into a fight with anyone. He was eager to live it up and use his fists.

Every step closer to the door made him more reckless.

He rushed into the room and surprised a man who sat down on his knees on the floor searching through one of Wolf's trunks. The man was big, wore inconspicuous clothes, and had short, dark hair. The moment he caught sight of Wolf, he jumped to his feet, but Wolf hit him on the jaw, and he stumbled back and then pitched forward over the open trunk. Wolf pressed his knee against the man's back and pushed his fist against his face.

"Don't you move an inch," he said. "The next blow will be a much harder one. All you will do is give answers to all my questions. Understood?"

The man moved his head up and down carefully.

Just as Wolf started to ask his first question, someone took hold of him roughly from behind and lifted him up. With an astonishing force, he was smashed to one side. Stumbling over his feet, he went to the left and slammed against the wall. His attacker, a large blond man, was standing in front of him and started to work him over. The man on the trunk scrambled to his feet and came forward, clenching his fists.

"Let's do this together," he said. "You hit him first, then me, then you again, then me ... every time a terrible blow..."

He came standing next to the other man and looked at Wolf, who stood there leaning against the wall and wiping the blood from his mouth.

Now it's going to happen, thought Wolf. *They're going to beat the hell out of me... And why? Why?*

He covered his face with his hands and waited for the next blows to come.

Two times there was the nauseating sound of a hard object hitting flesh and bone, and two times there was a loud scream. Wolf looked between his fingers, saw both attackers fall to the floor, and saw that Johan was standing behind them. He held Abraham's cane in his hand.

"I only hit them with the wood," said Johan. "If I had used the metal knob, they would be as dead as doornails right now. But this way, I hope they will be able to tell us what this is all about."

"Thanks," sighed Wolf. "For a moment I thought I wasn't going to survive."

As Johan knelt down near the men to see what shape they were in, he said, "It is my task to protect you. And I am only too happy that I could make up for what I did wrong in Lindau. Besides, I'm pretty sure you would have survived anyway; they didn't come here to kill you."

Johan had hit the men hard, and now they sat up with great difficulty, their faces twisted with pain. Johan pointed at the wall.

"Go and sit there, with your backs against that wall—and remember how fast I can pound with this cane!"

"Please," said the blond man, "let us be. We will answer all your questions as well as we can."

His right arm hung down limply along his side. Wolf wondered if Johan had broken his upper arm. The other man carefully touched his left collarbone and stared to moan.

"What were you up to?" Wolf asked.

"We were asked to steal a golden bracelet," said the blond man. "And if we were able to find you, we had instructions to kidnap you."

"And where would you have taken me to?"

The dark-haired man did not speak a word. The other man swallowed. Johan held the cane in both hands and swung it to and fro.

"We were to put you in a coach and take you to the crowded Marienplatz," said the blond man. "Another coach would be standing there waiting for you."

"What time?"

"Between now and two hours from now."

"Who gave you the order?"

"The man in the coach will be waiting. Joachim Vulpe. Please believe me, he is an intermediary. He knows no more than I do about the exact meaning of the robbery and the kidnapping. We are well paid. And Joachim Vulpe will be paid much more."

"How did you manage to get inside here?"

"We checked in. We have a room here."

"Has one of you been in Lindau lately?"

"Lindau? No. No, honestly..."

The dark-haired man moaned, and his hand slipped under his jacket and again up to his collarbone. He stood up very slowly, with his backsliding along the wall. His mouth was open. He raised his head and stared up to the ceiling with glassy eyes.

"I think you'd better sit down again," warned Johan.

It seems as if he is about to pass out, thought Wolf.

The man produced a knife with a blade as broad as a hand and as long as a forearm. Suddenly his look was hard and calculating.

"This could become a damn bloody fight," he said, swinging his weapon up and down. "This knife is sharp enough to behead a horse."

Wolf and Johan shrank back, and the two men began to walk with short steps in the direction of the door.

"Let us go, then we'll all stay alive for while," was the last thing the dark-haired man said.

As soon as the two men had reached the corridor, Johan rushed to the door and closed it.

Wolf took a deep breath. Then he picked up the folded piece of paper from the occasional table.

"That's what I came for."

"And now?" Johan wanted to know. "To the Marienplatz?"

"No. Too dangerous. If there actually exists a man by the name of Joachim Vulpe, we do not know what he looks like, while he seems to know who you and I are. His coach will not be the only one standing there in that big square. We know his name, and that is important to us. We can make inquiries about him and try to find him. Come on, we'd better go back to the restaurant."

 22

The corridor was deserted. Diagonally across from Wolf's suite was the room that was shared by Johan and Abraham. A copper bin stood next to the door, containing an umbrella. Johan pointed at it as they passed.

"That's where Abraham always puts his cane. Looking back, I would say that it's a good habit. I have used it and will keep it with me now. Tomorrow I will buy one for myself. It is a terrific weapon. Are you in pain, Wolf?"

"It might have been worse. It is not the first time I bumped against a wall. When I was drunk, for instance."

They both had to grin.

They went downstairs.

In spite of the circumstances, they were in a merry mood when they entered the restaurant and saw how Abraham de Wild was bolting down his food.

They sat down. Abraham looked up in surprise.

"Johan, what are you doing with my cane in a restaurant? What happened?"

After Wolf had informed him, he gave Abraham the piece of paper.

"Very wise of you not to go to the Marienplatz immediately," said Abraham, while he unfolded the paper and turned it around. "If you had done so, you would have made it all too easy for the person who has his eye on you. It would give him a second chance to try and kidnap you. Well, let me see ... what more has Edmund Reuter told me? Ah, very much, actually. I have noted down the most important facts. The bracelet doesn't have to be a Viking ornament by definition. If it is older, it could have been made by someone from the big Germanic tribes, a Frank, a Saxon, a Burgundian. Reuter dwelled during the migration of Germanic peoples, started by the Huns who had already marched at the end of the fourth century and went from the south of Russia to Hungary. The Germanic tribes started to move about at that time - Goths, Vandals, Angles, Saxons, Burgundians ... "

Wolf thought of Attila the Hun and the mythical Nibelung.

Abraham studied his notes and continued:

"Where skillfulness like metalworking is concerned, the Germanic people seemed to have made a late start; the Celts, for instance, were far ahead. But as soon as they had acquired a taste for it, they developed their own style and soon excelled in forging gold and silver. Golden ornaments have been found, dating from the migration of Germanic peoples. The most beautiful works of professional skill come from the fifth and sixth centuries. It is very important to know the origin our your bracelet..."

"It was on the bottom of Lake Constance," said Wolf in a sarcastic voice.

"Don't make fun about that," reacted Abraham. "Reuter has told me something very special about that. In general, we can say that all peoples from ancient times had a bond with wells, pools, rivers, and lakes. They were places to make offerings to the gods—a habit that has survived all times. Even these days we throw coins into a pond and make a wish. Reuter mentioned a specific case from the past and really, it's unbelievable! One hundred years before Christ, a Roman general, a certain Caepio, found himself in the neighborhood of Tolosa—later

Toulouse—in France. There he managed to fish up a fabulous treasure from the holy lakes. And we're not talking about a handful of silver rings and a helmet filled with golden buckles and coins. There was gold, and there was silver. The gold alone would have weighed more than fifty tons! Did you hear what I said, Wolf? We're talking about over fifty thousand kilos of gold here!"

Wolf put down his fork and knife, folded his hands behind in his neck, and looked dreamily up to the chandelier above the table.

"And then the general bought himself the entire city of Tolosa, chased away all men and children, closed the gates, and lived long and happily ever after," he said, followed by a deep sigh.

He did not finish his meal. The food had become cold. Suddenly he felt very tired.

"I will keep watch tonight," said Johan. "On the couch in your suite. Then you'll be able to have a good sleep. It wouldn't surprise me if they made another attempt to kidnap you. From now on I will be more on my guard than ever, you can depend on that. I will not budge from your side."

"Thanks," said Wolf, rubbing his eyes. Then he turned to Abraham.

"Tomorrow morning I will write a report about what happened on the sixth of November. You'd better return to Amsterdam quickly now and go to work again. I will send the report along with you, and you must get it printed and send a copy to all seventy-nine mediums. I hope Dr. Krohn has time to receive me tomorrow. If you leave the day after tomorrow, you can come with me and meet the doctor and be there when he hypnotizes me and asks me questions."

"That's agreed. I really look forward to that."

The three men stood up and left the restaurant.

"What a strange idea to think that someone sits in a coach at the Marienplatz right now, waiting for me to turn up," said Wolf. "And I am getting more and more curious about that Joachim Vulpe and the people who have given him orders."

As the men returned to their room, Johan walked behind Wolf, the cane clenched in both hands.

"Sooner or later we will stand face to face with him," he said. "We are going to track him down, aren't we?"

"We will," said Wolf. "We will find him..."

23

Dr. Krohn had no time to receive them during the day. The three Dutchmen were invited to come at night, after eight o'clock. The doctor was delighted to see Abraham finally in the flesh and wanted to start a conversation with him immediately. They were all still standing in the hall, and all of a sudden something happened to divert his attention. The glass of a mirror hanging on the wall cracked.

Then, somewhere else in the big house, several doors slammed. The wooden steps of the stairs creaked as if someone came down with large leaps and then went up again.

The doctor turned to Wolf. He pointed to a door and said, "Now please, try to control yourself. Just think of all the valuable things I keep there in my consulting room, my instruments, my stock of medicines. It will cost me a fortune if that all gets smashed. You must understand that. I think you are very nervous right now. Don't you worry, don't worry about a thing..."

He led the way to a big living room. There his guests were introduced to his wife Michaela, who soon excused herself and left the room.

Wolf sat down, leaned backward, and tried to come to his right mind.

Only now did the doctor have time to pay attention to Abraham. They discussed their intensive correspondence about paranormal and occult phenomena, Amsterdam and Munich, and finally Wolf's bizarre adventures.

"I was there myself in Lindau when it happened," said Abraham. "Johan Simons saw it, too. Wolf disappeared before our very eyes, and a few moments later he was back again, holding a golden ornament in his hand."

Krohn nodded thoughtfully.

"The incredible power of the human mind," he said. "Ah, we actually know so little about it. Isn't it fantastic, my dear friend, that someone is able to show something to someone else that is not there at all? Only by thinking about it with great concentration?"

"Well, this is quite a special case, and I think that other factors are involved," protested Abraham. "I know for sure that Wolf didn't buy these ornaments himself, just as I'm sure that they are real and not a product of fantasy."

The doctor raised his eyebrows.

"Of course those ornaments are real. But how can you be so sure that they weren't bought? Have you been together with Wolf all the time? Wasn't he traveling for over two years, while you found yourself in Amsterdam? So how on earth can you say that you know such things for sure?"

"I've never had any doubts about Wolf's integrity."

"Of course not. You are his secretary, his most close cooperator, the administrator of his fortune; you live with your family in his house at the Prinsengracht. I would find it rather odd if you told me that you didn't trust Wolf."

Michaela came back and shoved an armchair up to the middle of the room.

"My wife will assist me," said the doctor. "She is a sharp observer and always remembers very well what exactly has happened. She always accompanies me when I am invited to be present at a séance. Two will notice more than one."

The conversation went on for a while, and the doctor served drinks. Then he invited Wolf to sit down in the armchair. The porcelain in a cupboard began to shake, and four chairs scooted over the wooden floor and dashed against the dinner table when Wolf folded his hands and closed his eyes.

Then it became quiet.

Krohn asked Wolf to open up his eyes again.

"Look at me. We're going on a journey, you and I, Wolf—a journey through your mind. Follow my instructions, answer my questions, and it will all go nice and smoothly. Now watch my hands."

He moved his hands to the left and the right with spread fingers. Michaela stood next to Wolf and put a hand on his forehead. Wolf blinked his eyes and his mouth fell open. Not much later he began to smile and sprawled in his chair.

"What's your name?" asked Krohn.

"Wolf. Willem Hendrik Wolf."

"The name of your parents?"

"Julius and Suzanna."

Krohn sat down on a low stool, opposite to Wolf.

"Are you happy?"

"Sometimes I am, sometimes I'm not."

"Do you miss your parents?"

"Yes."

"Could you show them to us? Make them visible, let them walk together through the room?"

"How would I be able to do a thing like that?"

Krohn looked meaningfully at his wife. His raised eyebrows meant, *Is he really under hypnosis?* She put a hand on Wolf's forehead and nodded: *Yes, he is under hypnosis.* Krohn leaned forward on his stool and thought things over.

Then he said, "Did you see Jacob van Beek as a second father?"

Wolf smiled. "Certainly."

"Do you have anything to do with his death?"

The porcelain in the cupboard started to tinkle again. Michaela pressed her fingertips against Wolf's temples. The sound stopped. But Wolf remained restless. He moved his head to and fro and licked his lips.

"Abraham came to me and informed me, 'Jacob is dead.' I stood there, outside, on the street, in the early morning, and I felt so ashamed because I had this terrible, hammering hangover."

"All right, Wolf, all right. Come with me, let's go to Lindau. Do you see it? There is snow. And it is cold. Very cold."

"Cold, yes. Lots of snow…"

"Where did you buy the ornaments? The neck ring and the bracelet?"

"I didn't buy them."

"You have special powers. You can make someone believe that you disappear before his very eyes."

"I don't force anything on anyone."

"Do you think that you actually disappeared there at the harbor? That you vanished into thin air and returned not much later with the ornaments?"

"That's how it happened."

"Can you explain that?"

"No."

"What happened in the short time that you seemed to have left the harbor?"

"I don't know. I simply don't remember."

"Then try to remember. Think. A tiny clue, a small detail..."

Wolf seemed to get angry.

"Wherever I went, I left my hat there."

"Is that so important to you?"

"But of course! I wore it every day. I was attached to it. It was an old felt hat and worth nothing, but I would do almost anything to get it back again."

The doctor turned to Abraham and Johan.

"What do you know about that hat?" he asked in a soft voice.

Johan said, "He was wearing it before he disappeared. When he returned, the hat was gone."

Krohn looked at his wife again.

"This is all so confusing... I need some time to think. See to it that he remains calm."

Michaela tapped her fingers softly on Wolf's temples. He seemed to relax again, and soon his breath was deep and regular.

"How I wish that some of my friends were here right now," said Krohn, still in a soft voice, to Abraham. He stood up and began to pace up and down. "Some of them have studied the human mind more thoroughly than I and could advise me about my next steps." Suddenly he stopped. Then he shook his head. "No, no, that would be all too absurd."

Michaela, a slender woman with lead gray eyes and a pale face, wanted to know what he was thinking of. He shrugged his shoulders, and then he nodded.

"I'm going to give it a try."

"What?" she urged.

He did not answer but sat down on the stool again.

"Wolf," he said, his voice vibrating with emotion, "show us how you disappear. Do you hear me? This is an order. You disappear from this room and come back after a short time."

Silence fell.

Michaela took a step backward and put her hands on her hips. Krohn straightened his back and moved uneasily on his stool. Wolf's cheeks turned red, and drops of perspiration formed on his forehead. He leaned back heavily in the chair, and his nails scratched over the leather of the armrests.

Then all of a sudden he disappeared.

Michaela screamed. Krohn jumped up, knocking the stool over. Abraham and Johan stared with open mouths at the empty chair.

"Impossible, impossible," panted Krohn. "He's making a fool of me. What's happening? It seems as if we are the ones who have been hypnotized. How on earth did he do that?"

With small, careful steps he went up to the armchair. He gave a cry and shrank back when Wolf suddenly was sitting there again.

"Michaela! Wake him up!"

His wife stroked her fingers over Wolf's face and whispered something in his ear. Wolf sat up straight and looked around in surprise.

"Where have you been?" asked Krohn in a loud voice. "Do you dare to claim that you've actually left this room? What have you seen?"

"My God," sighed Wolf. "Give me some time, I'll have to get my breath back first. I . . . I saw a little house on a mountain slope. I walked up to it and noticed that the lower part of it was of stone. The superstructure was of wood. The most striking was the ink black front door—"

"This is crazy!" cried Michaela. "Do you hear that, Hans-Erich? Do you recognize it?"

"Go on," urged Krohn, without reacting to what his wife had just said.

"Black shutters," said Wolf. He screwed up his eyes as if he could think better that way. "A high chimney made out of different colored pieces of rock. Gray and white pieces, brown ones, black ones. I was intending to knock on the door and ask someone where I was. The next moment I was sitting here again."

"Did you see roses? Was the rose garden in bloom?" Michaela wanted to know.

Wolf rubbed his eyes.

He looked as if he'd had a long sleep and had woken up with a start.

"Madam, blooming roses? It is winter! There was as much snow there as here in Munich!"

"You bring up deep memories as if you draw water from a well in a bucket," said Krohn, as he sank down slowly onto his stool. "And now I'm talking about another man's memories, about another man's well. Michaela and I often talk about a little house that is very dear to us. We would like to live there, later, when we're old and gray. You just gave us a perfect description of it. It really exists. The present owners are friends of ours, and we have their promise that they will sell it to us only. It is in east Bavaria, not far from Vohenstrauss. And it is true, my friend painted all the doors and shutters black. You couldn't know anything about this; I never mentioned the house in my letters to Abraham. But Michaela and I talked about it right before you arrived. You are able, just like so many mediums, to read someone's mind. And you are also able when under hypnosis, to make people believe that you can disappear just like that."

Michaela looked at Wolf's hands. She noticed that they were red. She touched them, and then she said, "Hans-Erich, his hands are cold as ice. He must have been outside ..."

Excited as he was, the doctor stood up again.

Abraham and Johan still sat there staring with their mouths wide open, as if they were sitting in the front row of a theater watching an impressive play.

"All right," said Krohn, more to himself than to someone else in the room. "All right. Let's play another game. Are you prepared, Wolf, to go under hypnosis one more time?"

Wolf nodded cooperatively, even enthusiastically.

"Of course I will. I want to know precisely what is the matter with me. What are you intending to do?"

"Distance," said Krohn. "We'll see if you really are able to bridge distances via paranormal ways—or at least make someone believe that you are able to pop up at a certain spot."

He bent towards Michaela and whispered in her ear. She nodded. Together they again brought Wolf under hypnosis. Then he beckoned Abraham.

"You come along with me. Johan and Michaela will remain here— later they can tell us if they have seen him disappear again. We'll go to another room and wait there and see if he pays us a visit."

He led the way to the room on the first story, where he had received Wolf on his first visit. It was cold there, the fire was out, but the doctor took a handkerchief from his pocket and wiped the sweat from his bald forehead. He pointed at the two armchairs.

"Sit down, Abraham. You know from our correspondence that I am a skeptical man. Even the expression 'It has to be seen to be believed' does not always go for me. Still, it seems to me that there is something special going on with Wolf. We all know the phenomena of poltergeists, who make a lot of noise and bring objects into movement. In all probability, it is all caused by someone who is in a confused state of mind, mostly a frustrated child whose spirit is searching for a way out in a violent manner or screams for attention. Wolf has something to do with this disgraceful quality, it seems. Beyond that, however, there are no more comparisons with the poltergeists. Here, in this room, I am away from his direct sphere of influence, and I flatly refuse to believe that he is able to pop up here just like that—without using the stairs first, as we have done!"

Abraham had seated himself in one of the chairs. The doctor seated himself in the other. He put on a self-confident face, took off his glasses, and started to clean them with the corner of his jacket. Then he put them on again and produced his pocket watch.

"We'll have to wait a couple of minutes more, Abraham."

The men kept silent now. The doctor remained staring at his watch. At a given moment he raised a forefinger and looked at Abraham from under his eyebrows.

Then, all of a sudden, Wolf was there!

He stood there near the fireplace and blinked his eyes. There was an expression of amazement on his face. The doctor and the secretary sat rigid with fear in their chairs. It was as if the air in the room had become even colder. An unexplainable gust of wind made the ashes in the fireplace fly up. Wolf rubbed his chin and seemed to be looking for words. Then he looked at the doctor and said in a loud voice:

"Your wife's maiden name is Schwartz."

He made a wooden bow, and the next moment he had disappeared again.

A period of absolute silence followed.

It was the doctor who finally spoke:

"I asked my wife to think up a question for him. He had to tell her maiden name. Schwartz. And that's right. Her name is Michaela Schwartz. I never wrote that to you, did I?"

"No. You didn't. I'm absolutely sure of that."

They stood up with a feeling as if they were dreaming, left the room, went downstairs.

There they found Wolf sitting in his armchair. Michaela massaged his temples and brought him back from his hypnotic state.

"We saw him disappear," said Johan.

"We saw him appear," said Krohn. "He has answered your question perfectly, Michaela, he told me the name. Is the power of the human mind that big, and does it reach so far? I would have sworn that it was a man of flesh and blood who was standing there in the room."

"I think it was really Wolf himself and not an apparition," said Abraham.

The voice of Wolf sounded tired:

"Yes, yes . . . I was there. In the room. I saw the doctor, I saw you, Abraham."

Dr. Krohn slapped his hand on his forehead.

"I should have done more to make the test complete! I should have touched Wolf. But on the other hand, who could have told me if what I felt then was real or suggestion? No, I should have done something else. But what . . ." He snapped his fingers. "I should have given him another task. I should have given something to take along with him. An ashtray, a small sculpture, a glass. He should have brought something here from the room above. Wolf! Are you prepared to go under hypnosis for the third time?"

"No," said Wolf decidedly. "Not a third time. It tires me too much. I think that I have furnished enough proof to convince you that I am not playing games."

"No, you don't play games. That is to say, not knowingly. From now on I will always be interested in everything you go through. It must be possible to find an explanation for your apparently magical behavior. I . . . I am totally upset. You are right, we'd better do this another time. I've already seen too much to deal within a short time."

Wolf stood up.

"We'll go back to the hotel. To be quite on the safe side, we'll ask for other rooms and order the hotel staff not to tell anyone where we sleep."

The doctor invited Abraham to spend the night at his house.

"Then we'll have time to talk. Tomorrow morning you can pick up your suitcases at the hotel and go to the station from there."

Abraham agreed.

Wolf and Johan said goodbye and left the house.

"Are we going to look for Joachim Vulpe?" asked Johan, as soon as they were standing on the snow-covered sidewalk.

"Another time," answered Wolf. "I'm really tired. We'd better go to sleep."

 # 24

Next morning, on their way to the restaurant to have breakfast, Wolf and Johan came across the hotel manager. The man wished them a good morning and then asked Wolf, "How long are you planning to stay?"

Wolf looked at him in surprise.

"This was our last night here, I guess. Why do you ask?"

The manager, a slender man in a spotless white suit, nodded and said, "All right, Mr. Wolf. Then I have no further questions. Yesterday evening you asked for another room. We're always only too happy to meet the wishes of our guests. Now, something has happened. Someone burst through the door of your old suite last night. Inside they wreaked havoc. Of course, I am not blaming you for that at all, but it's just that I wonder..."

"Thanks very much for the information," said Wolf. "I will pay for the damage. If you make out the bill for me, then I'll leave right after breakfast."

The manager swallowed a remark and mumbled a thank-you. Wolf turned his attention from the man and walked on with long strides.

"The sooner you leave the better," said Johan, who could hardly keep up with him. "There's someone here in Munich who will do anything to lay hands on you."

Wolf was due for another surprise when he entered the restaurant. A man stood up from a table and hurried up to him. It was Abraham de Wild.

"Once more I have to be a messenger of misfortune," he sighed, looking at Wolf. "In Amsterdam, I brought you the sad news about Jacob van Beek; now it is about Dr. Krohn..."

Wolf put a hand on his shoulder and pushed him back to the table.

"Sit down, Abraham. What is the matter? Is he dead?"

"No, it's not that bad. He was beaten up, and at the moment he's on the verge of a nervous breakdown. I couldn't help him. Look..." He shoved down the collar of his shirt and revealed a small red stripe on his neck. "They put a knife to my throat and threatened to cut my throat if I dared to stir a muscle. Another man with a knife threatened Michaela."

"Whom are you talking about? And how come I hear this only now? How long have you been sitting here waiting for me?"

"A couple of hours. But that's no problem. I would even say that it is fine, for no one was willing to tell me in which room you slept; the hotel people kept their promise."

"Yes. I know. It has saved me from a brutal kidnapping. But I will inform you about that later. Now go on..."

"It was so good, so interesting to sit face to face with Hans-Erich after so many years of correspondence. We talked about many things till late at night. First, we talked about you, of course. Then about all the other inexplicable affairs from our archives and about things he had investigated by himself. We were sitting in the living room. Michaela was just about to go to bed. The door was kicked in. Michaela and I were overpowered immediately and held with knives at our throats.

The doctor flew into a blind rage! He grabbed a stone ashtray from a table and tried to throw it at his attacker. But he had no chance, no chance at all. Hard fists hit him, big boots kicked him. He got such a thrashing that he lost consciousness. Michaela started to cry, thinking that he was dead. His attacker brought Krohn around and made him answer questions. It was all about you. They knew you had been there—no, they suspected that you were still somewhere in the house. Krohn said that you had left, that you had gone to your hotel. The man dragged Krohn along with him, all through the house, looking for you. In the meantime he made Krohn tell him what had happened during your visit. That's what the doctor did. He was scared to death and talked and talked. Then he was pushed back into the living room again. The knife was taken away from my throat. They let go of Michaela. The men disappeared. Soon we found out that they had managed to enter the house from the back. Krohn went to his consulting room and took a sedative. We didn't sleep a wink, as you can imagine. Early this morning I came to the hotel. Since then I've been sitting here waiting."

"And now? Will Krohn go to the police?"

"No. He says that he would have done so if it was a daring burglary. But how would he be able to explain that there were three men who came looking for a guest from Amsterdam who can disappear before your very eyes as if by magic and then come back again as if he falls right out of the sky? He says that the police would say that he had gone crazy. In other words, he believes that making a statement will injure his reputation."

"What a situation!" sighed Wolf. "This is going too far. No matter what is going on, the doctor has nothing to do with it. I will go to him right away and tell him how sorry I am—"

"He asked me emphatically to tell you to stay away from him. For the time being it seems better to let him be." Abraham heaved a deep sigh. "Michaela wishes you strength and hopes you'll find out one day what's exactly the matter with you.'

"And the doctor?"

"He does not give a damn about what is going to happen with you, and one more time—you're better off staying out of his way. Or, no . . . I'd better be honest. He thinks that it's best for all of us if you go back to where you came from."

"Back to Amsterdam? With you?"

"He didn't mention Amsterdam. He was talking about hell!"

25

They had no appetite for breakfast. Wolf paid the bill. The baggage was loaded up a coach. They got in and drove to the station. From there the three men went separate ways.

Abraham boarded the train.

Johan followed a porter, who brought the baggage outside again and loaded it on another coach. After having convinced himself that no one was watching him, he got in and had himself driven to another hotel. After having arranged everything there, he would spend the rest of the day roaming through Munich, in search of a man by the name of Joachim Vulpe.

Wolf stayed behind at the busy station.

He had no particular plans; he just had thought it better that Johan made his investigations all by himself.

Now Wolf pushed his way through the mass of people and felt just as anonymous as all these hurried travelers. He was lost in the crowd and thus untraceable to anyone who might have followed him.

He began to get hungry and was dying for a cup of coffee.

In a big, crowded station cafeteria he looked for a vacant seat at the bar or a chair at a little table.

Someone standing nearby waved at him with an umbrella. It was a fragile figure, a lady in a long fur coat. A big hat balanced on her piled-up hair.

"Wolf!"

It was Michaela Krohn. She rushed up to him and took him by his arm.

"I'd already given up hope of seeing you again. First I went to Der Bayerische Hof, but you'd already left. Because I knew that Abraham would go home by train, I came searching for you here at the station."

"Michaela, I'm so sorry for what happened. Those three men broke into your house and then they battered your husband..."

"It was horrible. You really are a very special man, and someone is obviously willing to do anything to get you. Oh, look over there—those people are leaving. Let's sit down there before someone else does."

He followed her quickly to a little round table in a corner. A waiter was already clearing the table. Wolf ordered coffee for two and breakfast for himself. He felt rather uncomfortable; if Michaela had been able to find him, others could find him as well.

"Why have you taken so much trouble to find me?" he wanted to know.

"I know only too well now how deeply in trouble you are. When my man was talking with Abraham last night, before we had to deal with those brute intruders, I heard them mention a certain name over and over again. Wera Keller."

He looked up in surprise. In a flash he could see Wera Keller, in all her overwhelming beauty, standing in front of him, and his wooden chair creaked when he shrank back with fear. Seldom before had he had such a clear vision.

"Are you all right?" asked Michaela.

He managed to recover himself quickly. The vision had gone.

"Please, go on..."

"Well, I understood that it was important for you to find out more about her. I knew her. As far as I know, there was only one Wera Keller in Munich, and when I tell you that she was young and very beautiful…"

Wolf nodded enthusiastically. What he did not like, however, was the fact that Michaela talked about her in the past tense. He said, "What do you mean with 'was'? She 'was' young and beautiful and…"

Michaela started to say something but kept silence while the waiter served coffee.

"Your breakfast will be served in a minute, sir."

He turned around and walked away.

Michaela said,

"You know that my husband is interested in everything that has to do with the human mind. He makes a convincing study of psychology. He is in correspondence with Abraham about paranormal affairs. Searching for solutions for the most puzzling and sometimes even frightening phenomena is a passion that we share, my husband and I. We met for the first time when we both attended a séance. After we got married and he had less time to visit mediums, I often went on my own. Just like every town, Munich swarms with mediums, from charlatans to the most talented persons. But I guess I don't have to tell you. Wera Keller was a woman of great talents. She was a very sensitive and gifted medium…"

Wolf moved his head forward and spread his hands, to let her know that she must go on.

"More than often her prophecies came true. When she had gone into a trance and made sad statements, you could see the tears run down her cheeks."

"Yes, all right… But where is she now? Is she still alive?"

"Oh yes, she is alive. Only the circumstances . . . I feel so sorry for her…"

The waiter brought Wolf's breakfast. Suddenly Wolf wasn't hungry anymore, but he forced himself to eat.

"Perhaps it was her oversensitivity that finally brought her so much misfortune," he heard Michaela say. "She got ill. Mentally ill, that is. One could say she even became insane. When in hysterical fits, she wounded herself. Therefore it was decided to put her in a private institution. They locked her up—"

"Where? Do you know where?"

"I have heard different things from people who visited her séances and knew her better than I did. According to what they said, she still should be in Germany. In a mental home in the Odenwald. Is this useful information for you?" She shuddered. "I mean, I came all the way to the station and hope it wasn't for nothing..."

"Oh yes, this is useful information indeed," Wolf reassured her. "I thank you very much for it, and of course I am very happy that you came looking for me—although this was the last I expected after what happened."

Michaela took some time to think. Then she said:

"That's the reason why I went searching for you. You have problems, and someone is chasing you as if you were some kind of a wild animal. One way or the other I feel sorry for you. Promise me to come and visit Hans-Erich and me! After you have managed to solve all these problems, my husband will no longer be angry with you, I guess..."

She smiled at him and rose to her feet. He started to get up, too, but she said, "Remain seated." She rubbed her fingers through his hair. "Keep your eyes wide open and don't do reckless things. See you again someday!"

"See you," said Wolf.

Michaela walked past the little tables and waved at him one more time after she had reached the door.

The next moment she had disappeared.

Wolf ordered another cup of coffee.

Michaela had given him useful information. He was glad that she had come to the station and found him. Wera Keller actually existed, she was a human being of flesh and blood and not some kind of phantom.

After ten minutes he left the station as well, and outside he stepped into a coach.

Gasthof der Steinbock was about two miles away from Der Bayerische Hof; it was a much smaller and cheaper hotel, mainly frequented by traveling salesmen.

Along the way, Wolf had asked the coachman to stop and had bought himself a bottle of brandy.

Many a time he had looked around to see if he were followed.

Now he sat on a chair by the fireside in his room, drinking, staring into the flames, thinking about his next steps, waiting patiently for the arrival of Johan.

He leaned forward to throw a log of wood in the fire.

Suddenly he had a bizarre spiritual experience.

He sat upright with a start and took a deep breath. He needed time to figure out what exactly had happened.

Something had left his mind, and strangely enough, he only knew that it had been there because it was gone now.

That was very confusing, or at least odd, but he felt there was something that vanished from his mind. He was convinced of the fact that he was no longer able to make objects move, that he couldn't make windows rattle anymore nor break them with the power of his mind, that he could not make chairs scoot over the floor any longer nor overturn cupboards. Something had changed. He concentrated, and in his mind's eye, he saw a big hand appear that pushed on his head and then disappeared again.

It was a symbol—but a symbol of what?

"Someone has washed his hands of me," he said aloud. He took a sip of his brandy. "Yes, that's what it looks like. But there is more..."

Then the truth came home to him in a shock.

The collective! The collective has washed its hands of me. I have been under their influence, from the moment they started to concentrate on what would happen in the harbor of Lindau. That's it! I'm sure of it.

He felt as if he just had awakened from a deep sleep. His mind was sharp. There was another thing he began to understand.

Abraham already came up with the idea, when he was at home with me and looked at the map of Europe with the seventy-nine pins connected with the red woolen threads. The web of the seventy-nine mediums. Abraham wondered where the pins would be that symbolized the mediums of Wera Keller's collective. He said that a number of my mediums and those of Wera Keller probably would be the same persons. Her web is my web...

He picked up another log and threw it into the fire with such strength that the sparks flew up high.

He started to swear heartily.

"I've been sold," he said aloud. "I have traveled from one to the other with their letters of recommendation. They all have fathomed me and found me appropriate to—to what? What kind of a game is this?"

He shoved up the sleeve of his jacket and touched the golden bracelet.

Her web is my web, he repeated in his thoughts. *The power of the collective is enormous. And I'm probably the only one who knows which people are members of the collective. There's a chance that Wera Keller knows it, too, but she's locked up in a mental home. I must try to find her. And who can Gerardus Klijn be, that white larva?*

The long waiting was making him drowsy.

Wolf fell asleep in his chair.

It was already late in the afternoon when he woke up again. He left the room and went to the bar. He ordered a big glass of beer and a hot meal. Every time he heard someone stamping the snow off his shoes in the hallway, he hoped that it was Johan coming back from his search.

Traveling salesmen came in, warmed themselves by the fireplace, discussed their day, and sat down at the tables to have a drink and something to eat. Wolf sat there listening. He drank another beer and then went back to his room.

Johan still hadn't shown up.

Now Wolf began to get worried.

26

Johan felt in Munich like an ant in the wrong nest; everyone around him was a potential enemy, and he must do his utmost not to attract attention. As soon as he opened his mouth, he would give away that he wasn't a German. He was looking for Joachim Vulpe, which was a tricky venture because Joachim Vulpe was also looking for him. If Vulpe's henchmen got hold of him, they would work him over until he told them where they could find Wolf.

With his hands in his pockets, the collar of his coat turned up, he strolled through the Augustinerstrasse, reached the Frauenplatz, and stopped near the big church. He looked around. No one seemed to have followed him. Several coaches stood in front of the Frauenkirche, and he addressed a coachman who sat on the box waiting for fares.

"Could you tell me where I can find a certain Mr. Joachim Vulpe?"

The man looked down and bared yellowed teeth when he smiled.

"Do you have any idea of the size of this city? If I knew everyone by name and also was able to tell the right address, I would be a genius, a mind reader, or a fool with only one amazing talent."

Other coachmen gave answers of the same tenor.

He went through the Sporenstrasse and the Weinstrasse and finally reached the Marienplatz, which had become familiar to him by now. In the meantime, he had asked more than three dozen men about Vulpe, all in vain. He left the center of the city and wandered around. In a busy market, on a snow-free spot under the arcades, he bought himself to bread and fish and drank hot wine. A man in a worn-out coat stood next to him and stared forward He spoke in a soft voice.

"I hear you're looking for someone..."

"That might be so," responded Johan. "You must be someone with big ears."

The man grinned.

"This afternoon at five o'clock you can find Joachim Vulpe in his favorite beer house, Der Landjunker. He'll have time for anyone who has anything meaningful to say."

"Where can I find Der Landjunker?"

The man turned his head, gave him a questioning look, and kept silent.

Johan got the message.

"What do you ask for your information?"

"I saw you standing here, eating and drinking. Bread, fish, hot wine."

"You'll get the same."

"Plus a few coins, so that I can buy myself the same tomorrow."

"All right!"

The man got what he had asked for, and then he gave Johan the information.

Not much later Johan went to another district by coach and got out on a busy street. There he entered a beer house not far from Der Landjunker, where he used his time to consider the best way to approach Vulpe. The beerhouse was packed. All the seats were taken. People crowded around the fireplace to warm themselves. Johan noticed that they were all poor - dressed in worn-out clothes, who temporarily escaped the cold of the street; they stamped their feet and blew on their numbed fingers. A fat publican walked up and down, looking around with asperity, throwing everybody out who couldn't show any money.

"Outside you can scoop up as much snow as you want; that's eating and drinking together!" he shouted as he pushed someone in the direction of the door.

A few steps from Johan stood a man who shivered with cold, keeping his ice-cold hands pressed under his armpits.

He wore an old, brilliant red jacket, with gold-colored adornments and copper buttons. He was of small stature and broad-shouldered like Johan himself and also had the same clear blue eyes. Johan suspected that he was a circus hand who had to wait until spring to get started again. The publican came back and went up straight to the man.

"Hello, my good old friend!" shouted Johan.

He jumped to his feet, walked up to the circus hand, and shook his hand.

"Good old friend!" he repeated, and turning to the publican, he said, "Beer for the both of us, and later on we'll want a bite to eat as well."

He dragged the man along with him by the sleeve of his red jacket.

"Do we know each other?" asked the man in surprise.

"Not yet," smiled Johan, as he reached out his hand for the second time. "Johan Simons, from Amsterdam."

"Karl Holm, without a fixed address," laughed the man.

"You see? Now we know each other. Well, just a little bit... Do you work for a circus?"

"I once passed by a circus," said Karl, still grinning. "And suddenly I was wearing this jacket and had a nice pair of boots on my feet as well."

"Too many people leave their things lying around."

"Others pick them up."

"Right. Listen. I'll give you plenty to eat and to drink. Then I'll even do a swap: my thick, warm coat for that red jacket of yours. There's also something you can do for me, and I will pay you well for it."

"I'm all ears," said Karl, struggling out of his jacket.

The publican brought beer. Johan paid him and ordered bread, sausages, and soup.

"I'll see to it that you get a seat," promised the publican.

Around half past five, they left the beer house and walked through the dark street to Der Landjunker. Johan took some snow from a window frame and rubbed it through his hair. He combed his wet hair backward. He was wearing a red jacket now and began to feel cold. He also wore a pair of low-heeled boots.

It wasn't as crowded in Der Landjunker as in the other beer house. Karl walked up to the bar and asked in a loud voice for Joachim Vulpe, making use of a strange accent.

"Who wants to know?" sounded from a table in the darkest corner.

"Johan Simons. From Amsterdam," answered Karl, turning around. "I am here on behalf of my employer, Mr. Willem Hendrik Wolf."

"Then come to me. I am Joachim Vulpe."

Karl walked carefully toward the table.

A tall man pushed back his chair and rose to his feet. He was handsome and wore a brown tailor-made suit and a brown hat. He reached out his hand.

"Well, well, all the way from Amsterdam. Take a seat and tell me what I can do for you."

When Karl arrived at the table, three other men stood up. Karl stiffened. Someone put a hand on his shoulder.

"Keep calm. Sit down, as Herr Vulpe asked you to do. And answer all his questions."

"Keep your hand away from me," said Karl. "I don't like being touched. I'm a free man."

Scornful laughter sounded. Vulpe sat down again and said in a loud voice:

"You'll be my guest tonight. You're going to tell me quite some things. And yes, you're a free man indeed. Till I decide to ask one of my men to break your neck. I will only make that request, by the way, if I suspect that you're not telling me the truth. Now tell me, what are you having?"

"A beer, please," said Karl.

He remained standing. Two of the men tried to force him to sit down. He attempted to slip away but was caught by the third man. A fight started. No one interfered. Karl proved to be a tough man. He received punches unblinkingly and dealt hard blows himself. Suddenly he let himself fall to the floor, rolled underneath the table, jumped to his feet, and started to run.

"Stop him!" shouted Vulpe, but it was already too late.

An ice-cold wind blew snow inside as Karl opened the door. Without bothering to close it again, he disappeared into the dark street.

Silence fell.

Someone closed the door.

Then Vulpe spoke.

"You there! In the red jacket!"

Johan turned around and raised his eyebrows.

"Didn't I see you come in together with the Dutchman?"

Johan nodded.

"Yes, that's right."

He also used a strong accent, which was difficult to place.

"Come over here. Sit down. Eat and drink on my expense."

Johan went to the table and sat down near to Joachim Vulpe.

"I'm not hungry, a glass of beer will do."

Vulpe looked at him searchingly.

"Who are you and what about your relation to the Dutchman?"

"My name is Karl. I'm from Norway." Johan could only hope that there was no one present in Der Landjunker who spoke a word of Norwegian. "I work for the circus. I travel from one country to the other. At the moment there's nothing for me to do..."

"The Dutchman," urged Vulpe.

"Ah, yes. Well, I met him in another beer house." Johan pointed to a window at the side of the street. "That's why I'm not hungry anymore. He offered me a good meal. I think that he just needed some company. There were certain things he wanted to tell. I think it gave him a feeling of relief and..."

"Do you have money?"

Johan shook his head. Vulpe reached into his pocket and produced a handful of change.

"For you. Keep it. And now you're going to tell me exactly what that Dutchman told you."

"It is such an unbelievable story," said Johan, slowly shaking his head. "He mentioned his name to you as well—Johan. And he works for a certain Wolf. Now that Wolf has to be a very odd person. Possessed by the devil, if you ask me. Too scary for the circus, and that is saying quite a lot. He asked me to come with him to Der Landjunker. He wanted to meet you, Joachim Vulpe. It's too bad you scared him away. I believe he wanted to talk with you."

"Tell me what you know about his boss."

"As I said, he must be a strange person with special gifts. And...excuse me, I have to search for the right word. Ah, yes. A magician, that's what I meant to say. He's very much like a magician. His boss, that Mr. Wolf, has the power to..." Again Johan seemed to need time to think. "...to pluck valuable objects from the air." He raised his hand and gestured as though he were reaching for something. "Ornaments. Made of pure gold. Now isn't that peculiar?"

Johan leaned backward, shook his head slowly, and reached for the big glass of beer that had been put in front of him.

Vulpe stroke his chin.

"So that's what makes him so interesting. Strange, very strange indeed. Go on..."

Johan took some deep drafts, to win time to think.

He'd already become much wiser. Vulpe was not fully in possession of the facts, and he could actually be a middleman—someone who would be paid off after he had managed to kidnap Wolf. Now Johan must try to find out who he was working for.

He put his glass down calmly and wiped his mouth with the back of his hand.

"There's not much more to tell, actually. I hardly know the man, I've just met him. Oh yes, he knew for sure that you must be a man of influence here in Munich and that you were intending to hand Wolf over to another important person. He was talking about the highest circles and even mentioned a name..."

He snapped his fingers to indicate that he couldn't bring it to mind immediately. Vulpe leaned over to him.

"Well?"

"A man of learning ..." guessed Johan; noticing a sudden sparkle in Vulpe's eyes, he knew that he probably had made a good guess.

"How could he know a thing like that?"

"They were surprised in their hotel room. This Johan and his employer Wolf. There was a fight. The intruders were overpowered and were forced to talk..."

"I don't think so," sounded a voice right behind Johan.

He turned around on his chair and looked up to the blond man whom he had knocked down in Der Bayerische Hof.

"Don't buy that nonsense, Herr Vulpe. This is Wolf's servant. That funny jacket is a bad disguise. I recognized him the moment I stepped inside."

Johan jumped up. His chair shot backward with force, and the top of the back hit the blond man's chest. Johan punched his fist on the right arm of the man, remembering that he had hurt him there before, in the hotel, with the cane. The man winced with pain, and Johan scooted past him. But three other men blocked Johan's way to the door. Vulpe came and stood behind Johan.

"You have nowhere to turn, rat. Tell me where I can find Wolf. Speak the truth this time, for every new lie is good for a couple of broken bones."

"In Der Bayerische Hof," said Johan. "He is still there. He never sleeps in the same room, nor on the same floor."

Vulpe shrugged his shoulders.

"Suit yourself, rat," he said and raised his hand.

A hard blow hit Johan in the neck. He made a gurgling sound and fell forward. He had already lost consciousness when he was caught by one of the three men.

 # 27

Wolf sat at a table in an office of the police station not far from the Marienplatz.

Opposite to him sat Joachim Vulpe.

Markus Krause, a police officer, stood there with them, both hands leaning on the tabletop.

His main reason in sending for Vulpe was to frustrate him: Everyone knew that he was a very important man in the Munich underworld, but Vulpe was a sly fox who never had been caught red-handed. The policeman only believed half of what Wolf had come to tell him, and even if it turned out to be true after all, no one would be able to prove it.

Vulpe leaned easily backward and grinned.

"Now listen to me, Krause," he said in a familiar voice, "if this man here says that he got surprised in a room in Der Bayerische Hof, then why didn't he report that to the police earlier? And besides, what do I have to do with it?"

"Mr. Wolf says that they mentioned your name. That they acted under orders. And these orders came from you," said Krause, as he sat down at the table. "And now the man who traveled in Mr. Wolf's company has disappeared—after he went out looking for you. Does the name Johan Simons really mean nothing to you?"

"No. Nothing at all," said Vulpe, and then he burst out laughing. "I don't have to tell you how many people disappear just like that in a city like Munich, to turn up again after having enjoyed themselves for several days or even weeks. Anyway, it was nice talking to you, and I was happy to see the police station from the inside one more time. Since you and I have become such good friends in the course of time, I will make inquiries after this Johan Simons. People often come to whisper secrets in my ear; you know that just as well as I. That's all I can do for you and Mr. Wolf."

"I asked Johan to send for you," said Wolf. "Yes, you're right, it would have been wiser to go to the police earlier and report about what happened in Der Bayerische Hof. But my story happens to be rather complicated. That's why I let the matter rest. It is all different now since my friend disappeared. I know for sure that someone gave orders to you to kidnap me."

"Who would dare to give me orders?" asked Vulpe with a smile. "Kidnap you? And what would I have done with you then?"

"You're the only one who is able to answer these questions."

"I'm sorry. I'm really sorry. I cannot help you."

Wolf considered whether he should tell Krause about the three men who had broken into the house of Dr. Krohn, but changed his mind when he remembered that the doctor hadn't gone to the police himself. He knew exactly what Abraham de Wild had said about that: "How would he be able to explain that there were three men who came looking for a guest from Amsterdam who can disappear before your very eyes as if by magic and then come back again as if he falls right out of the sky? The police will say that he has gone crazy. He believes that making a statement will injure his reputation." He heaved a deep sigh and looked at the police officer.

Krause asked, "Why don't you try, Mr. Wolf, to tell us your complicated and unbelievable story? Maybe one of us will understand..."

"I already informed you thoroughly when I first came to you. It has all to do with very special affairs. As you know, I am a person who makes long journeys to meet mediums and magicians. I try to unmask them or if they seem to be real, to examine their true talents and to describe the way they work wonders. I've had certain experiences myself, and it has turned out that I also have special talents at my disposal. I don't want to go further into that matter now. It is just a fact that someone wants to know more about what I know and what I am able to do. Someone who will do anything to kidnap me by Joachim Vulpe and his henchmen."

"I don't like to be accused of things that have absolutely nothing to do with me," remarked Vulpe.

The discussion went on without yielding any results. Krause promised that the police would look out for Johan Simons.

"I'm sorry, but that's all I can do for you."

"I would ask you for a favor," said Wolf. "Please allow me to talk with Vulpe in private."

"No problem. Without any objection," said the police officer, after which he got up and left the office.

This was the moment Wolf had been waiting for.

This was the only way to meet Vulpe and have a chance to talk with him without incurring risks: at a police station.

The atmosphere in the office had changed the moment Krause had closed the door behind him.

Vulpe looked at Wolf like a hungry predator that saw no way to catch its prey, and Wolf had difficulty holding himself back.

"Listen to me, Vulpe. I am a rich man. I can cough up a great deal of money right away. Bring Johan to me, or tell me where I can find him. Just name your price."

Vulpe whispered:

"It is very possible that the walls have ears here. Please keep that in mind."

"Make me a proposal," said Wolf, lowering his voice. "I am sure that a rotten bastard like you will have no scruples about playing a dirty trick on his former client."

"There is nothing I can do for you."

"Of course you can. Give it a thought."

"First let me make clear to you that I don't know any person by the name of Johan Simons. But if I understand the story you just told, it all revolves around you. If there is someone who holds Johan prisoner, I would advise him to exchange him for you."

"Understood. That's all right. Arrange it for me."

Vulpe shook his head.

"That would be too risky for me, assuming that I would be able to do a thing like that. You could play a dirty trick on me and keep the police involved."

"Then bring Johan back and earn a lot of money."

"We'd better stop this discussion," said Vulpe loudly. "I'm going home." Then he continued in a whisper, "If I'd only known that you were so rich, I would have been on your side—no doubt about that!" Before Wolf could react on this, he shouted, "Herr Krause! Do we shake hands before I leave?"

Wolf left the station a few minutes later. He was in low spirits. It was clear to him that Johan had fallen into Vulpe's hands, and he also knew that he was not able to prove it. He roamed through the city, stepped into different coaches, went into department stores and pubs, and was on the alert all the time for pursuers.

Tired and cold, he reached Der Steinbock.

In the bar, he sat down close to the fireplace and ordered food and drink.

He wondered what he had to do now.

Back in his room he took a map of Germany from a suitcase and unfolded it on the small writing desk near the window. It took him some time before he found the Odenwald, which Michaela had mentioned. It was a mountainous region between the rivers Neckar and Main. He had the feeling that he had been in that neighborhood. With his index finger, he followed the course of the river Neckar until he found the city of Heidelberg.

He pronounced the word slowly

"Heidelberg..."

Immediately he remembered—yes, he had been there before. And not so long ago.

Viktor Blum. The doctor, the medium, the magician, the psychologist, the hypnotist, the man with the unorthodox working methods and the brilliant ideas. Has practice in Heidelberg... Wolf snapped his fingers. "Manages a clinic in the forest! Or a private institution, as Michaela called it. A mental home! Somewhere in the Odenwald..."

28

"The police will not understand a thing of this," said Hans-Erich Krohn. "There is nothing they can do with information about extrasensory perception or paranormal events. Anyway, you knew that yourself as well, didn't you? You were out for a confrontation with Joachim Vulpe. That was the most important to you. Nonetheless, it pleases me that you mustered the courage to come knocking on my door again, Wolf."

Wolf had gone to see the Krohns. Michaela had let him in and led him into the living room, where Hans-Erich sat reading a book.

He had looked up in surprise and then gave Wolf a hearty welcome.

"So you're no longer angry with me?"

"Perhaps I've never been angry at all. Shocked. That seems to be the right word."

"I told him that you were angry," said Michaela. "When I met Wolf in the station cafeteria."

"A natural reaction," said her husband. "It is simply horrible when three men break into your house and attack you, hurt you, make demands... But let's forget about that. I began to realize that something extremely special must be going on. Michaela already understood that earlier, and she said that she felt sorry for you and compared you with a hunted, wild animal. I have done the most strange experiments with you right here in this house, which I still have no logical explanation for. Under hypnosis, you seemed to be able to disappear and—oh well, I'd better stop about it. Creepy phenomena like that can make a man crazy. I must concentrate on something quite different. What really interests me is the fact that someone will do everything possible to get you. Please! Sit and tell me why you are here now."

Wolf sat and filled the doctor and his wife in on the recent events.

"So," the doctor said when Wolf had finished. "You say you have lost your magical powers, and you think that the collective, if it actually exists, no longer concentrates on you. My wife went looking for you and found you at the station, and there she told you about Wera Keller. You searched for the Odenwald mountain range on the map and noticed the city of Heidelberg. As for Viktor Blum . . . I've not only heard a lot about him, I once attended one of his lectures! In fact, it was more than just a lecture. He made an entire show out of it. Now you tell me first about your meeting with this man . . ."

"I went to Heidelberg with Johan. Viktor Blum is considered a great medium, and his séances are spectacular. But I had no chance to have a word with him. I wasn't able to ask him my three most important questions while he was in trance."

"What questions?" Michaela wanted to know.

" 'Who is Wera Keller? Is there a union of mediums? Do you have a message for me?' We didn't visit him in his house either. There was a restaurant on the bank of the Neckar, and Blum received between fifty and sixty guests there at a time, in a big hall. He gave a lecture, there was a complete dinner, and then there was that unforgettable entertainment..."

Krohn nodded.

"I know the restaurant and I have paid a substantial sum as well to get in and listen to Blum and see him perform."

"We went there together," said Michaela. "It was a fascinating evening."

"Then I don't have to tell you any more about it," laughed Wolf.

"On the contrary," said Krohn. "Maybe all kinds of other things happened when you were there with Johan."

"He started with a story about the new developments in psychology, in which he gave the individual a central place. When every person is unique, the mentally ill should be given a unique treatment. He mentioned different theories and then indicated how small adaptations changed them into personal care. Wealthy guests were reminded of the fact that financial contributions for his examinations were always welcome. After his lecture, he introduced his audience to a great number of extraordinary people. I remember a boy, withdrawn into himself, who totally revived when he was allowed to multiply numbers of six to ten figures and even more. He never made a mistake and was always faster than a man of learning in the audience who worked it out using a slate and a piece of chalk. Someone who could hardly be described as musical was hypnotized by Blum and then played a beautiful, moving piano concerto. The entire of human ability and human imperfection, genius and stupidity passed in review, and the whole time we sat there eating and drinking... It was mainly Blum himself who drew everyone's attention. He placed himself on a pedestal and seemed to tower above us all; in my eyes, he was a pedantic, conceited man. Besides that, he was unreachable to his audience; I think he only spoke with people who made donations."

Krohn agreed with him.

"Yes. He thinks highly of himself. But I have to admit that I became interested in his way of thinking after having read several publications from his hand about the interplay of spirit and body."

"I can imagine that; when I visited you for the first time, you mentioned the fact that many physical complaints find their origin in mental problems."

"Exactly. I saw Blum as congenial. Especially because he is a doctor just like me. He studied on and became a psychiatrist as well. In fact, he does tower above a man like me, but that should be no reason for him to behave so detached and haughty."

"Maybe he does so on purpose. After dinner, there was that spectacular séance, and no one dared to suspect a man of his stature of trickery. No one made comments. He talked with the dead, predicted stunning events, and embarrassed different people by confronting them with their strongest desires."

"Most of the time we have to deal with deceit," said Michaela. "And then, unexpectedly, there are experiences you can only believe were real. As far as that is concerned, your experiment here is very comparable with the wonders that Blum performed. You disappeared, and when you came back again, you could tell in great detail about the little house in Bavaria, near Vohenstrauss. A thing like that is simply incredible!"

"Maybe Blum and I draw from the same well," said Wolf.

Krohn was surprised. He clapped his hands.

"Just imagine... Go on! What is your idea?"

"If the collective exists, Dr. Blum must be one of the most important members. I have visited countless mediums to ask them about the collective. Of course, some of them didn't commit themselves. While I had the feeling that I was manipulating them, they manipulated me and tried to find out if they could use me. We all know the result..." He shoved up his sleeve and showed the bracelet. "Blum didn't even take the trouble to invite me for a talk. He obviously knew already that I was an eligible candidate for spiritual experiments. I have the strong impression that he is the man who ordered Vulpe to kidnap me and bring me to him. For now, he may need me for something. I will have to go to Heidelberg not only to find out if Wera Keller is locked up in the clinic of Blum but I want to know if Johan is there, too!"

"How will you set about it?"

Wolf rubbed his chin.

"Well, I've thought that over. I will cut my hair short and put on other clothes. I could play the servant of a traveling medical man and have a look together with him in Heidelberg and the Odenwald."

Krohn clapped his hands for the second time.

"Ha! And what do you expect me to do? Cut my beard?"

Michaela burst out laughing.

"Not a bad idea. And buy yourself another pair of glasses as well."

Wolf remained serious.

"There's only a small chance that Blum would recognize you. Vulpe probably didn't bother telling him about what his henchmen did to you, because it was an ineffective action."

"Wolf, I've been hard on you, and you haven't flinched. Because I still have no idea about what's going on—and you yourself have no idea either—I'm inclined to give you the benefit of the doubt. And to be honest—I really like the idea of taking a holiday for a couple of weeks. It is a long time since I have been on vacation."

"That goes for me as well," remarked Michaela.

"It has little to do with vacation..." said Wolf and then abruptly fell silent when he saw how the man and woman looked at each other with raised eyebrows.

"Would you come along with us, then?" he heard the doctor say.

"But of course!" said Michaela. "I'm interested in all these affairs as well. We can make plans together. We must examine this down to the last detail. If you go, I will come with you."

Krohn got up, put his hands in his pockets, and started to pace up and down.

"After those three men attacked me right here in my own house, I never stopped thinking about what Wolf had shown to us. What he did is far beyond what illusionists, charlatans, or even the best magicians can do. It passes our understanding. All of our new psychological knowledge is useless here. It seems that the human mind is a much more powerful instrument than we ever dared to believe. I throw doubts upon the tricks of all mediums, fortune-tellers, and people who practice black magic. Oh, I have written good old Abraham de Wild countless letters about that. I sweep this swindle all in a heap and set fire to it. But what's happening with Wolf, that's quite something else! This goes far. This is unique. Yes, let's go to Heidelberg. The three of us. Let's drink a good glass of wine to it and talk things over. I suppose you already have some ideas, haven't you, Wolf?"

"Yes, I do."

Krohn opened a bottle of wine and put glasses on the table.

Wolf raised his hand.

"No wine for me. Water will do."

The doctor raised his eyebrows.

"I will not drink another drop of alcohol before I have found Johan."

"Then I will see to it that you will not break your word," said the doctor and filled the glasses for Michaela and himself.

He sat down again and asked Wolf to fire away.

"Well," said Wolf. "We assume that Viktor Blum actually is the man I'm looking for and in charge of the clinic where Wera Keller stays, and that he is one of the many members of the collective."

"Wait a minute," interrupted Krohn. "Did Blum belong to the seventy-nine mediums you picked out yourself for your experiment?"

"No. But that means nothing. He might as well be number eighty, and it is very well possible that more people belong to the collective than I suspect."

"All right. Understood. Go on."

"We'll leave for Heidelberg. If I am not mistaking, I'll find the solution there to all riddles. I want to meet Wera Keller. And above all, I want to get Johan back."

They stayed up until late that night, making plans.

Wolf slept for a few hours on a bed in a guest room, and early next morning he went back to Gasthof der Steinbock to pick up his belongings. There he found out that he had escaped from a great danger. The door of his room had been kicked in. His trunks were missing. He paid the bill and once again made good the damage generously. He did not care about having lost his clothes and other personal belongings. Now he worried even more about Johan; the fact that Vulpe's henchmen—whom else could it have been—had found the room in Der Steinbock meant that Johan had given away the relevant information. He tried not to think of what they had done to his friend before he made this confession.

He left the hotel without baggage.

Making a complex detour, plowing through snow-covered streets, he reached a post office. There he wrote a long letter to Abraham de Wild, giving an account of the events.

He sent the letter in a parcel, together with the golden bracelet; he had enough confidence in the German and Dutch postal services and felt greatly relieved now that he had gotten rid of the heavy ornament.

29

Heidelberg, in the valley of the Neckar, now was a town under white roofs, watched over by a castle of red sandstone. The bare deciduous trees on the surrounding mountains, the Heiligenberg, and the Königstuhl, were covered with frozen snow. The leaden sky brought more snow and grew darker quickly in the late afternoon.

Instead of putting up at a hotel, Wolf and the Krohns had rented a furnished house in the Hauptstrasse right after their arrival. It was a big and comfortable house, but it had been unoccupied for a long time and they had lit fires to heat it and chase away the damp. The three tired, hungry travelers, not wanting to wait until it finally would become more pleasant, decided to go out in search of a place at the fireside in an inn. They wouldn't have to go far for that. The Hauptstrasse is Germany's oldest college town full of pubs and inns.

When they stepped outside, they noticed that the silent street had undergone a total metamorphosis.

They remained standing in the doorway, all three of them flabbergasted.

It was dark now.

The street was lit by lanterns hanging from curved, cast-iron posts. Drummers appeared around a corner and made a noise as if they were busy casting out evil spirits. Behind them came a roaring crowd. Everyone was masked. Most of them held big mugs of wine or beer in their hands, and no one appeared able to walk with a firm step anymore. It was a noisy, reeling row that passed along and quickly grew smaller as they entered the beer houses by the dozen.

"Drunken students?" Krohn asked aloud.

"Probably..." said Michaela.

Right at that moment a couple of men and women passed by.

Most of them had gray hair.

Krohn tapped a long, thin man on the shoulder.

"Tell me ... what's going on here?"

The man stopped. He put his thumb under his cardboard nose and pushed up his mask as if it were the visor of a knight's helmet. With little, searching, bloodshot eyes, the man, who looked to be in his fifties, looked down on Krohn and said:

"Oh, you're such spoilsports! And why? You can get your masks for free. Everywhere!"

He moved on again, dancing with light feet through the slippery street, in the direction of an open door, where the warmth of a beer house beckoned.

Wolf stood there rooted to the spot. He considered himself fortunate for changing his looks before he left for Heidelberg. He had close-cropped hair now and had bought himself simply, nondescript clothes in place of the wardrobe that had been stolen from his hotel room. The half-drunk man hadn't recognized him, but Wolf knew immediately who the man was.

Doors closed everywhere. It became quiet again in the street. Wolf didn't have to raise his voice when he said in surprise.

"That was Armand Montet, a medium from Belgium! I visited him recently and was impressed by his true talents. He touches objects from people he never met and spontaneously sketches their life story with all possible details. Well, he's far from home now, and I refuse to accept that it is just by pure accident that I see him here in Heidelberg."

"How can this be possible!" reacted Krohn. "Are you sure?"

"Very sure, indeed."

"We'd better go after him," said Michaela.

They walked up to the beer house Montet had entered and gone inside. A doorman stopped them. His face was hidden behind a cardboard owl's head.

"Just a moment," he said, as he looked at them one by one.

He bent down to a small wooden table.

"A dragon for the lady, a fox and a wolf for the gentlemen," he said. He handed them three masks.

"The fox's head is mine," grinned Krohn, taking one of the masks and putting it on. "Only one of us is entitled to wear the wolf's mask."

It was so crowded in the beer house that all the tables and chairs had been pushed to the edges of the room, and everyone had to stand. Musicians played acoustic guitars and zithers. The people sang along at the tops of their voices.

"As soon as you see another acquaintance who might belong to the collective, we'll know that there's something very special going on here," said Krohn in Wolf's ear.

Wolf pushed his way through the crowd. At the moment the music stopped, he stood not far from a person who attracted attention by his down-hearted attitude in the midst of all cheerfulness. He was of medium height and rather stout. His chin rested on his breast as if his head was heavy from depressing thoughts. It was funny to see how his head sank even deeper when he wanted to take a sip from his beer, toward which his lips appeared through an oval hole in his monstrous mask. Long, gray, greasy hair stood to all sides.

Wolf knew immediately who he was, and now he also remembered his gold signet ring; the man had become fatter and fatter in the course of time and the ring, originally meant for his middle finger, had moved to his little finger.

"Reinhard Arntz from Vienna," said Wolf to Michaela, who had come standing next to him. "An illusionist who is able to do more than makeup tricks and perform them. He is able to set everyone off laughing with unexplainable actions—and in the meantime, he's actually a gloomy man. He suffers from heavy depressions. He's a melancholic..."

"Did you visit him as well?"

"Yes, I did. He's a phenomenon! I have seen how he made monstrosities that belong in the deepest hell. They were not dressed up men or women. They were not misshapen animals either. I felt their warmth, smelled their stench, heard the rattling in their throats—"

"So they were real?" asked Michaela in surprise.

"Probably not. The man has the odd gift of showing you and letting you experience something that is actually not there. I simply cannot explain it."

It still made his flesh creep.

The music started again. A choir of drunken singers joined in. Wolf elbowed his way to the bar, with the Krohns following in his wake. Only when the song had ended and the musicians took a break were Wolf and Dr. Krohn able to make themselves heard without having to shout.

Michaela walked away from them and went looking for the Austrian.

She saw him standing in a dark corner, leaning against the wall and staring into his beer mug. Watery eyes lit up behind his mask when she came standing in front of him.

"Hello," said Michaela. "What a special experience this is! The whole town seems to be in movement tonight, and everyone wears a mask. I arrived in Heidelberg only a couple of hours ago and don't know anything about such a custom. Are you from here? Can you explain to me what exactly is going on?"

"I'm a stranger here as well," answered the man, as he extended his hand. "My name is Reinhard Arntz.

"Michaela," she introduced herself. "Are you on a journey?" she asked.

Arntz shrugged his shoulders slowly. "Isn't the world just one huge hotel?"

"I never looked at it that way. Which feast is celebrated here?"

"What does it matter? We join in, we laugh, we get drunk, and tomorrow we'll find ourselves somewhere else and then there will be another party going on."

She understood that the man didn't want to give anything away; no matter what she asked him, he would never give her the true reason for his presence in Heidelberg. Still, she tried to keep the conversation going, but the man only gave evasive or puzzling answers.

The moment she decided to turn around and go back to her husband and Wolf, she felt something move past her foot.

She looked down and gave a scream. Her glass fell from her hand.

A rat the size of a cat was gnawing at the leather of her shoe.

She kicked at it with her other foot, and the animal disappeared immediately.

Looking up at Arntz, she noticed how his shoulders shook. He was laughing behind his mask.

He laughed at her. She understood. Wolf had been right. This man was able to make something appear that actually did not exist.

No one had paid attention to her startled cry. The reason for that became clear to her soon enough. On another spot in the big taproom, a fight had started up. There was a confused noise, voices scolding and shouting, the sounds of breaking glass and hard blows. The people shrank back, and Michaela also had to take some steps to one side.

Then she stood with her back against the wall, next to the Austrian. The man paid no more attention to her, and the noise didn't seem to bother him. He'd had his bit of fun and stood there staring at the bottom of his beer mug again. Someone bumped up against her, and she stumbled to one side. From a dark corner came the cracking sound of breaking wood.

I'm going stir crazy here, she thought and looked down to see if the rat had actually disappeared.

The crowd pushed forward again, and she heaved a heavy sigh.

The fight went on.

And then, unexpectedly, it was silent.

The musicians quickly picked up their instruments and started to play. Soon everyone was singing along again as if nothing had happened.

The people standing in front of Michaela stepped to the left and the right, making way for someone who urgently wanted to go outside. To her surprise, she recognized her own husband and Wolf, who together half-carried, half-dragged a man who seemed to have lost consciousness. It was a young man, and there was blood trickling down from his neck. His legs hung down, his heels dragged over the floor.

"Out of the way!" she heard her husband shout. "Out of the way there!"

She followed them.

Once on the street she took the victim by the ankles and helped the men carry the victim to their rented house. Being a doctor's wife she knew how to react in a situation like this. In front of the door of the house, Krohn threw off his fox's mask. Wolf and Michaela did the same with their masks. Krohn searched for the key, found it, and put it in the keyhole. The door swung open.

"Michaela!" shouted Krohn. "My bag!"

The temperature in the house was pleasant now.

After they had laid the young man on the couch and the Krohns started to examine him, Wolf could think of nothing better to do than to throw some logs on the fire and then to take a seat.

The young man's mask, bloody on the inside, lay on the floor. Jacket and shirt had been removed. Krohn stitched a cut in the neck and at the breast. Soon the boy recovered consciousness, sat up, and looked around in surprise. His face twisted with pain.

"It isn't as bad as it looked, with all that blood," said Krohn. "The cuts are not very deep."

"My headaches," sighed the boy. "I was hit on the back of my head, right above my neck. Someone used a club."

Krohn felt with his fingers under the hair of the boy.

"I can feel it. That's quite some swelling. What's your name?"

"Jürgen Löhndorff. One of the three chairmen of the students' union."

"Take your time. Come to yourself first. Then tell us what happened. We saw how you received some telling blows. The club was a table leg. Suddenly a knife was flickering. You had a hard time of it. Well... my name is Hans-Erich Krohn. I'm a doctor."

"Yeah, you must be," Jürgen said, looking down at the stitches on his breast.

"This is my wife Michaela. Over there is our servant, coachman, faithful helper..."

Silence fell.

Jürgen stared into the flames of the hearth.

Krohn brought his hand to his face, from force of habit, in order to touch the hairs of his short beard and remembered he had shaved it off.

"Yes, what has happened?" Jürgen suddenly asked himself aloud. He shrugged his shoulders and winced as he felt the pain go through his breast. "I cannot explain it all. I mean, where should I begin? It is all a matter of behavior, doctor. Or, better said, with the changing of behavior."

Krohn gave him an encouraging nod.

"I happen to know one or two things about the human psyche . . ."

"I've been beaten up, stabbed with a knife . . . by my best friends. Uwe and Horst."

"The two other chairmen of the students' union?" guessed Krohn.

"Yes! We'd go through hell for each other. The evil is haunting Heidelberg, invisible but perceptible like the wind. People abuse each other, begrudging each other everything. Every now and then it results in a fight. Especially in the students' pubs, they're at it all the time, and this time I became a victim. Attacked by my own friends." He heaved a deep sigh. "I'm happy to know that all misery will come to an end this very night."

"What do you mean?"

"Tonight all evil spirits will be chased away. All students will lend their assistance. Prior to the event is the feast of the masked, which started this evening."

Krohn had sat down in an armchair. Now he leaned forward, his elbows on his knees.

"All right, all right. Negative changes in Heidelberg. A feast for the masked. Chasing the spirits away. Who organizes the feast? Who chases the spirits away?"

"We all rely on a colleague of yours. The honorable citizen Dr. Viktor Blum."

"Right."

Krohn exchanged a look of mutual understanding with Wolf. Then he concentrated on the student again and looked him deep in the eyes.

It was obvious to him that Jürgen hadn't had too much to drink.

There was something in his eyes that expressed something other than drunkenness. It was as if a certain mist covered the irises and the pupils. Suddenly he knew what it was, and he felt an impulse to snap his fingers and say out loud what he thought. But he managed to restrain himself and didn't speak a word.

It may be compared to hypnosis, he thought. *Some kind of a trance. He is under someone's spell. Viktor Blum. The collective. Wolf's theories are beginning to take shape.*

 30

For some hours Jürgen hovered between sleeping and waking; sometimes his eyes were closed, sometimes he stared out in front of him with a glazed expression.

The three others exchanged their thoughts in whispers.

Krohn admitted that he had been too skeptical of Wolf's assertions.

Michaela expressed her feelings candidly and said that she was afraid. The huge rat that had shown up at her feet so unexpectedly had especially given her the creeps. "Someone who is able to show you a thing like that..."

"I think that every member of the collective will have his own specialty," whispered her husband. "And what are they up to tonight? What does this all mean?"

It was almost midnight when Jürgen suddenly jumped to his feet. He seemed to be in a hurry, and his stitched wounds didn't seem to bother him at all.

"I have to go," he said. "Thanks. Thank you very much for all your kind help."

Wolf got up, too.

"I'll come along with you."

Krohn decided to accompany them. Michaela felt too tired.

"It has been a long journey. I'm dead sleepy. Please, be careful!"

Wolf and Krohn followed the student outside.

The weather had changed. The sky was clear now and showed an impressive number of bright stars. It was freezing. The street was covered with a layer of fresh snow. People left the pubs and staggered home.

"Your mask. Give me your mask," said Jürgen to a passenger.

Wolf and Krohn decided to do the same.

For a moment the street was deserted. Then sounded, the same as earlier that evening, the roll of drums. A group of men and women came into the street.

"The collective!" said Krohn in Wolf's ear.

The doors of the beer houses swung open. Students stepped outside and joined the group. When they passed by, Jürgen, Wolf, and Krohn followed them. The instruments made so much noise and everyone was screaming so loud that it was no longer possible to talk to each other. The procession marched out of the town. Dancing and yelling, they went over a small path that at first apparently led to the high castle, but soon curved away to a dark wood of bare trunks.

The moon, almost full, shone through the tangle of branches.

Krohn started to pant as the path began to incline more steeply. The journey had tired him as well, and he felt sleepy. He had difficulty keeping up with the crowd of light-footed dancers. Wolf was not much better off and stayed close to him. Jürgen had already disappeared from view.

The drums fell silent.

The dancers quieted down.

Soon there was only the muffled sound of footsteps in the snow.

"Maybe we'd better stay behind some more," suggested Krohn. "We're not under the spell of the collective like the rest. That might make us conspicuous. I am masked like everyone else, but still one could tell that I am much older than the students."

For a while they walked slower than the procession, in silence, staring out in front of themselves to the white, moonlit path under the chaos of black branches.

Wolf put his hand on Krohn's arm.

"I can hear sounds behind us. Newcomers." He looked up and saw something move in the yellow light. "And someone's coming back!"

Wolf jumped to the right side of the path and hid behind a tree. Krohn did the same on the right side.

Not much later a big, masked man appeared, wearing a long fur coat. In one hand he held a big club, with which he slowly tapped the flat of his other hand.

He stopped and listened.

Loud voices echoed through the forest. More people were coming uphill.

The big man made odd, long-drawn-out guttural sounds.

Six women came back from above. They lined up and stretched their arms. Waving with their fingers they began to hiss. The newcomers, a group of Heidelbergers who had followed the procession inquisitively, came up to them about twenty paces. There they stopped as if there was something that scared them. Yet it seemed as if they didn't notice the women, who still were making gestures. Suddenly they turned around and ran back down, slipping on the frozen snow. They seemed to be in a big hurry as if the devil himself was close on their heels.

The man with the club greeted the women.

"Almost Nibelung, sisters. Good work."

The women answered in the same way and in chorus:

"Almost Nibelung, brother. Thank you."

All seven of them hurried back toward the head of the procession.

Only after considerable time did Krohn dare to come out of hiding. Immediately he heard Wolf say in a soft, warning tone:

"There he is again!"

The man with the club came down for the second time. With his free hand, he felt around him as if he were able to detect if someone was touching the air. Muttering unintelligible words, he made two steps to one side and banged his club against the tree behind which Krohn was concealed.

He remained standing there, listening, turning his head to the left and to the right. After letting out a deep, loud sigh, he went on again.

Krohn waited until Wolf came out from behind his tree.

"Would he have hit me with that club if he had discovered me?" he wondered.

"Oh yes," said Wolf. "I'm very sure of that. Besides, the students want no one to follow them. So much is clear to me by now. Come, let's go on."

While the path did not become any steeper, they had more and more trouble getting up, as if an invisible power tried to stop them. It also seemed to get colder. A wind rose suddenly and whistled through the branches. A crow flew up, for a short moment visible in the almost perfect circle of the moon.

The path ended on top of the mountain.

There was a round open spot with a huge oak tree in its center.

All the students were sitting down in the snow and looking up with open mouths at a rope that hung down from one of the side branches. Wolf and Krohn hid behind another oak tree at the edge of the open spot.

Masked men and women had gathered around the tree in the center. They linked hands and began to walk past the tree. Their steps became faster and faster. Soon they were dancing, and they started to sing a song. The words sounded loud and clear through the night, but Wolf and Krohn didn't understand it.

The dance was executed with wild, stamping feet, while everyone straightened their backs and kept looking at the oak tree. The rope swung to and fro in the wind.

"Are they going to hang someone?" Wolf asked himself aloud.

"That's what it looks like," said Krohn. "And if so, we're not able to do anything against it. Going back and ask for help in Heidelberg takes up too much time, and we cannot attempt a confrontation with so many people. The students are under their spell—the hypnotic influence of the collective. But maybe it is all no more than a ritual. Jürgen was talking about chasing away evil spirits..."

The dance, which was not accompanied by the drums, stopped abruptly. The men of the group came standing behind the rope, while the women lined up in front of the sitting students.

A soft singing floated through the night.

The students shivered.

A woman spread her arms forward and pointed with trembling fingers along the rows.

"A victim for the hangman: someone must sacrifice to the highest power," she said. "A victim to satisfy the highest power . . . I'm looking for a volunteer. We'll tie your hands behind your back. We will lift you up. We'll put the rope around your neck. Your throat will be squeezed by your own weight. Don't kick your feet. That will only tighten the rope even more. A volunteer. Quick, otherwise, I will pick and choose someone myself..."

The students searched for each other's support, fell into each other's arms, bit their lips, closed their eyes, shook their heads in despair.

"No! Please, no!" shouted someone.

The supplication was taken over by others.

"No! No! Please, no!"

No one seemed to be able to stand up and run away.

"A volunteer!" the voice sounded, commanding. "I've already seen a few candidates who will beg the god for mercy when they are dangling up there."

She pointed behind her with her thumb. Then she made a beckoning gesture with that same hand. The men stepped forward, now all armed with clubs. With threatening expressions on their faces, they walked past the front row of students. As they stepped between the rows, they bent forward every now and then to look at someone searchingly.

Wolf clenched his fists.

"What can we do?"

"Nothing. I've already said so. When you step forward and show yourself to them, you'll be the first one who'll get a rope around his neck. This is a ritual of the old Germanic tribes. A victim for the gods; the hanged person will go straight up to Valhalla to enjoy battle, drink, and very attractive company. Look, Wolf, look—"

The students gave cries of distress. Two men stooped. Together they made movements as if they were lifting up a heavy load.

The voice of the woman was loud.

"Brothers, sisters, feel their fear. Learn from their agony of terror; let their feelings penetrate deep into your mind. Bring yourself up to a higher plane! Almost Nibelung!"

"Almost Nibelung!" responded the men and women.

The sitting spectators panicked. Many of them cried. Everyone reacted according to his nature—from indignant rebelliousness to resignation, from soft sobbing to hysterical screaming.

The two men stood there under the rope and lifted up their invisible load.

"Learn from their fear, feel their emotions!" shouted the woman.

The rope swung to and fro and then, suddenly, it hung down straight.

Some of the students fainted.

The men and women took each other by the hands and danced around the oak tree. A storm was rising. The rope remained hanging down straight, but every now and then it seemed to tremble.

Some men left the dancing group and picked up drums from the ground. They started to beat on them with their clubs. Some of them started singing again.

The students rose slowly to their feet, wiped their almost-frozen tears from their eyes, and started to walk back to the path. They looked depressed and full of fear, broken in spirit, close to insanity. They knew no better than that they had been a witness a horrible execution.

But the moment they passed the tree behind which Wolf and Krohn were standing, and had set a foot on the path, they looked up with bright eyes and smiles passed over their faces.

Further down the sloping pat, they began to sing a students' song full of merry double ambiguities.

Wolf heaved a sigh of relief. Tears welled in his eyes.

"If I only knew the text, I would sing along with them at the top of my voice."

Jürgen passed by. Krohn hardly recovered from his shocking emotions, walked up to him with uncertain steps.

Jürgen smiled, looked up to the starry sky, and started singing. Krohn stood in front of him.

"Tell me... How are you? Don't you feel any pain?"

The student looked at him as if he saw him for the very first time.

"What do you mean?"

"Your wounds. I stitched them, remember? Knife stabs. Your neck. Your breast."

"Who would have done such a thing to me? What do you think has happened?"

"Your best friends became your temporary enemies. Uwe and Horst. You fought with them."

Jürgen burst out laughing, shook his head, and walked away. Krohn tried to stop him.

"Don't you remember me? It's me, Dr. Hans-Erich Krohn!"

"You must be drunk," concluded Jürgen. "Well, who cares? We all have had a bit too much, and it's already late..."

He took off his cardboard mask and threw it away. Then he walked on. After the last students had gone down the path, Wolf and Krohn followed them.

There were thrown-off masks everywhere. They threw their own masks on the ground as well.

Seldom if ever had they felt so tired; like sleepwalkers, they followed the singing students. Every now and then they saw, far away, in the depth, a few lights of Heidelberg. They slipped, fell, scrambled to their feet, joined the students, and sang along with them. The singing gave them a feeling of relief. It chased all anxious fears and horrible memories away.

But the fear came back when they stood together in front of the door of the house in the dark, silent Hauptstrasse, where Krohn searched his pockets for the key...

31

What had happened on top of the Königstuhl, the mountain above Heidelberg, remained a mystery. What remained of the festivities were the masks, frozen in the snow. What had happened on the open spot after the students had left it, no one would ever know.

Wolf had gone back there to look around.

The rope had been taken away.

All the men and women who had danced there and made the students believe that actually someone was hanged there had left Heidelberg by coach or train.

Together with Michaela, Wolf visited Heidelberg University. It was established in the year 1386, and through the ages, it had built up an impressive library containing more than one million books. They went there looking for information about the saga of the Nibelung and made notes of everything that seemed to be important. In the meantime, Krohn had managed to make an appointment with the magical Dr. Viktor Blum. He had pretended to have given up his practice to go deeply into psychology—it had come to his ears that Blum managed a mental home somewhere; perhaps there was a task for him as a doctor, being able that way to experience all psychological aspects of the recovery processes. He had also hinted that he was a man of substance who had often donated money to special institutions—as far as this was concerned, he knew that Wolf would pay anything necessary to help him reach his goal.

While Michaela and Wolf devoted their attention to the books in the university library, Krohn paid a visit to the famous doctor of Heidelberg...

32

On the imposing desk of Viktor Blum stood a stone tobacco jar in the form of a man's head with long sideburns and a mustache. Blum himself, big, self-confident, and gray-haired, had risen to his feet and lifted the lid from the jar. He plucked out some fine tobacco and began to fill his pipe. He nodded into the direction of the jar:

"How I love it, in a symbolical way, to open the human skull. Knead under the crown. Squeeze out all that's in it. We're all the same, but still so endlessly different. The working of the brain, the seat of the soul of personality . . ." He lit his pipe with a match and blew a thick cloud of smoke at the ceiling. "The human mind . . . until recently elusive as smoke in the air. A new era is dawning. Slowly but surely we begin to understand what's biting the individual human being."

Krohn, who was sitting opposite to him in a leather armchair, nodded.

"Psychological discoveries move with the speed of a steam locomotive."

"Nothing, absolutely nothing in this world is as marvelous as the human being. The possibilities of the mind seem to be unlimited. The best way to study human behavior is to work with people who enlarge certain talents to the extreme. The brilliant piano player, the morbid kleptomaniac: the one who has developed himself in a positive way, the other who has acquired negative qualities. The riotous hedonist, the destructive personality." Blum put the lid back on the jar. "I study my patients while I am trying to help them. Some of them remain close tongued, withdrawn into themselves, others are more easily approached. Sometimes I can help by prescribing a treatment, sometimes a wise word will do the trick. And with that, I come to an important point, my dear Krohn, and that is the interplay of body and mind—and you just told me that you are interested in that as well. These days there are many doctors who go deeply into psychology. We both are good examples of that. Someone like you could be very useful in my clinic. By the way, how did you find me?"

He sat down and put his pipe in his mouth.

"My wife and I were in Heidelberg once before, to enjoy your lecture and the following show. It was an interesting evening and also unforgettably entertaining. I was impressed by your wisdom. I am a practical man. My years of study are far behind me. I would be simply terrific if I was able to make myself useful as a doctor and could gain experience in psychiatry at the same time. Don't misunderstand me; I'm not looking for a job for the rest of my life. For a certain time, I would like to learn as much as possible about the human mind, and I hope that we can come to an agreement. How I would like to take a look in your clinic first!"

"That can be arranged. This week I'm going there myself. There is space enough in my coach for you and your wife. I heartily invite you to come with me."

"Thank you. That would be great."

"On our way, we can talk about everything that happens in the clinic. It is quite a long ride. We'll go to the Odenwald, to a building deep in the woods. It costs me a fortune to keep everything there running. You said something about a donation, didn't you ... ?"

"Yes, I did. As I said, I'm eager to learn everything about the present psychology and psychiatry. I don't ask any payment in return, and if I like the clinic, I will be happy to make a large donation. We live in an exciting period in which we finally are able to learn something about ourselves. This is the age of the individual! We escape from our gray background, and everyone gets his own, personal color!"

"Well spoken," remarked Blum. "My compliments to you, Krohn. It wouldn't surprise me if you turn out to be the man for whom I've been looking, for a long, long time!"

The men talked for some time about new developments in psychology and exchanged ideas.

All of a sudden Blum seemed to be tired. He rubbed his thumb and forefinger down his nose. He used the same fingers to brush past his eyebrows, while he gave Krohn a piercing look. Then he rose to his feet and reached out his hand.

"I have many things to do. Thursday morning, around half-past six, I will come with my coach to your house in the Hauptstrasse."

"Thank you," said Krohn. "I really look forward to that."

33

The staggering blow Johan had received in Der Landjunker had put him out of commission him for a long time. When he finally regained consciousness again, he noticed that he was swinging to and fro. He found himself lying in darkness. His hands were tied. There was a monotonous roaring and bumping. It took a while before he remembered what had happened. Then it dawned on him where he was.

A wagon, he thought. *A freight train is taking me out of Munich.*

It took him much trouble to sit up. As soon as he had, a voice sounded in the darkness:

"You'd better try to sleep some more. It's a long journey."

"Who are you?" asked Johan.

There was no answer.

Heavy, shuffling footsteps approached over the shaking wooden floor. Someone lit a match. For a moment he thought he could see a face. The match fell and extinguished itself. Strong hands took hold of him, and he was pushed forward. A stab of pain went through his neck when he bowed his head. A knife cut through the thin material of his red uniform jacket sleeve and the shirt beneath.

"Now don't move," sounded next to his ear. "Otherwise the needle might break."

Something pricked in the bared skin of his arm.

It was as if the darkness had weight and pushed him down. Feeling and sound disappeared. His head touched the floor. He didn't feel a thing.

❀ ❀ ❀

When he woke up again, he had a splitting headache, and he was hungry and thirsty. Now he found himself in a cell of ten by ten feet. He lay on a wooden bed. The walls were whitewashed. There was an iron door. A cold wind blew inside through a high-placed, barred window that also let in somber daylight.

Johan found that his hands were no longer tied behind his back.

Only with great difficulty, he managed to get up; he began to walk up and down to limber up. His neck and back hurt. He knew he wasn't in a condition to jump up to the high window, catch hold of the bars, and pull himself up so that he could take a look outside and possibly discover where he was.

Besides the wooden bed, the cell contained no furniture. There was no food, nothing to drink.

Just when he had sat down on the bed again to ponder on his situation, a little hatch opened in the metal door. He saw an eye, a nose, and a mouth, too little to form an idea of the entire face, although he saw enough to understand that there was a man standing at the other side of the door.

"Welcome," said a flat voice. "I bring you a meal. In a moment I will open the slide at the bottom of the door and push your plate inside. You just stay where you are."

"Welcome to where?" asked Johan.

"What does it matter? You have no business being here anyway."

"Then why am I here?"

"Consider yourself as a temporary guest. As far as I know, it depends on the arrival of a certain Willem Hendrik Wolf when you are going to leave us again. Wolf will stay, you will go. One seems to need you, and therefore you'll have to eat. If you're dead, you're useless to us."

There was the sound of iron scraping over the stone floor, and an opening appeared at the bottom of the door. A plate was pushed over the floor, and behind it rolled a corked bottle. The slide was closed again.

"Enjoy your meal," said the man, and then he also closed the little hatch.

"Wait a minute!" cried Johan.

The hatch opened again.

"What if it takes years before the man you call Wolf finds out that I am here?"

The man reacted with a cheerful laugh.

"Don't be so vague about Wolf. He is your friend and your employer as well. How long it takes entirely depends on you. Or, better said, it depends on your stamina. For you're going to tell us where Wolf is, and if it turns out that you really don't know, you're going to tell us how we can find him. So make up your mind. I think you will decide to cooperate. That saves us effort, and that saves you a lot of pain."

The hatch closed again, and no matter how Johan begged, it was silent on the other side of the door.

Suddenly he didn't feel hungry anymore and in his sad circumstances, food didn't seem to be of any importance at all. He pondered his situation and understood that he found himself in deep waters. He feared the moment that the door would open and someone would step inside to grill him.

The twilight began to gather.

Johan gave a start when the window suddenly slammed shut. He jumped to his feet and looked up, just in time to see a part of a stick with an iron hook at the end. Someone was walking around to close the windows against the cold night.

As long as Johan was able to see, he used his time to investigate the small room. He felt along the walls, pushed against the little hatch, and knelt down to see if he was able to open the slide. Soon it was clear to him that there was no possibility of escape. He heaved a deep sigh, took the bottle, and uncorked it. After the first swig, he realized how thirsty he was; it had been a long time since he'd anything to drink.

The bottle contained cool water. He drank it all.

Then he also decided to eat. The plate was filled with beans and a piece of fatty meat.

In the meantime, it had become dark.

He lay down on the bed and covered himself with a thin, old blanket.

Although he felt exhausted, he couldn't sleep. Too many thoughts kept him busy. And no matter what he was thinking of, again and again, there was that scene in his mind of someone torturing him to make him tell where Wolf could be found.

Hours went by. It was cold and quiet.

Johan found himself in the twilight zone between waking and sleeping.

Something sneaked into his mind, knocked on the door of his consciousness.

He turned on his side, pulled up his knees, and opened his mind to his spiritual visitor.

A voice sounded in his brain. At first, he couldn't understand a word of it. But soon the voice sounded so clear that it was as if someone were sitting near the bed who bent forward to his ear.

But if someone had come in that moment and had asked him what happened, he wouldn't have been able to tell in which language the voice had spoken.

"I don't know you. You must be new here. Your presence is strongly perceptible. I am in the room next to yours."

Johan couldn't think clearly. It vaguely occurred to him that he might be in contact with a medium who was going to suck all information necessary out of him to find Wolf.

"Don't you worry," he heard. "I bear you no enmity at all. I think that your name is Johan. Am I right?"

Yes, answered Johan, replying without making use of his voice.

"You are a sensitive young man, although you do everything you can not to show that to anyone. Can it be that you have had quite a bit to do with businesses of spiritual nature?"

Yes, he reacted again.

"That explains a lot. Unconsciously you learned to open your mind to others. Can we have a talk together? I cannot reach you when you are wide awake, and I will lose contact with you when you fall asleep. I hope you will remain in this half-slumbering state."

Johan didn't react.

There was a pleasant aspect to this strange circumstance—a salutary warmth radiated from his head to the rest of his body. He got a feeling as if he was lying on a soft bed near a burning fireplace. The pain in his neck abated quickly and finally disappeared.

The voice continued:

"Talk to me. Tell me about yourself. About your problems . . ."

Johan ignored warning stimuli in his brain. He sent his thoughts through the silent darkness, and his lips formed a constant smile.

His story told a cold gust of wind went through the room like a long-drawn-out sigh that ended in a sob.

"You move me, Johan. Sometimes, unexpectedly, fortune smiles on us! I'm floating on the very edge of death and did not expect to hear such a story again. As long as I'm still alive, I will do my utmost to protect you against the people who want to do you harm.

Unfortunately, I'm not able to open doors for you; I don't master magic like that. Wolf seems an honest man to me. He little knows how important he is. But I know! Once I was at the head of the group you and Wolf have to deal with now. Let me tell you my name. Eckart. And let me explain to you what it is all about..."

A rain of words descended on Johan.

Soon he realized that Eckart actually wanted to help him and had no sinister plans for the information he had given him about Wolf and himself.

 # 34

Next morning Johan sat quiet and relaxed on his wooden bed, while it slowly became light in the little room. The window was opened again from the outside. Snow fell inside. Johan didn't feel cold, and he also wasn't hungry or thirsty. He remained staring out in front of him with a smile when the iron door opened and two men stepped inside.

"You're going to tell us one thing and another," one of the men said to him.

But Johan told nothing at all—not even when they started to beat and kick him.

"He is in another world," finally panted one of them. "His spirit is far away. Someone has taken care of him and put a spell on him. He is under the influence of magical powers—or maybe he's been hypnotized."

"Even a knife cut through his heart will not make the smile disappear from his face," said the other. "Someone must take his spirit back. Someone must bring him back into the present."

"There's only one man who can do that. Dr. Blum."

Nonetheless, they came to look in on him every day.

And one afternoon it seemed that they didn't have to wait for the arrival of Viktor Blum at all; Johan lay on his bed shivering with cold and looked up at them with fear in his eyes.

"Isn't that an odd coincidence! Eckart passed away, and our honorable guest here suddenly sees the gravity of his situation."

Still, it took a while before Johan moved his bleeding lips and whispered the name of a Munich hotel:

"Gasthof der Steinbock…"

They let go of him.

He lay full length on the floor and did not move, hoping they would let him be now, praying that Wolf had already left Gasthof der Steinbock.

35

Wolf sat on the box of the coach, his hands deep in his pockets, his mouth covered by a wool scarf. Staring at four stampings, steaming, snorting horses, he faced the cold and listened to the coachman, who constantly shouted in his ear. Every time the coachman finally stopped talking for a while, Wolf came up with the urgent question:

"Are we almost there?"

And just as he began to think that this was a never-ending journey, he heard:

"Oh yes, we're almost there..."

Before they left, Michaela had tried to give him a place on one of the comfortable, soft benches inside, but Blum had refused her request abruptly:

"A servant's place is outside, on the box."

They had crossed one of the bridges over the Neckar and followed the river for quite some time. Then they had gone uphill, over slippery, small paths, along bare limestone rocks, and snow-covered vineyards, and eventually through deep deciduous forests. They stopped at an inn to have a meal and quench their thirst. The horses could take a rest and didn't have to be changed.

After finally having left a big oak forest behind them, where not a single living creature had shown itself and where the paths were made dangerous by the thick layer of frozen leaves under the snow, the coachman slowed the horses to a walking pace. Now the road went down abruptly.

"The Mansion of the Madmen!" he shouted in Wolf's ear. "Stable your horses there for the night, and in the morning they'll be turned into donkeys!"

This remark was followed by his roaring laughter.

Wolf did not respond and looked out in front of him with surprise.

A brook, undoubtedly leading the mountain water to the Neckar, traversed a valley that widened on this spot. Here the human hand had interfered in a drastic way. In a park, surrounded by high fences, stood a gigantic gray stone building. The square main building had two side wings. There were houses, stables, barns, and pigsties.

The coach went down slowly, sped up in the valley, and crossed the clean-swept wooden bridge with rattling wheels. Then through a gate that was opened by two men who rushed up hastily. They both doffed their caps and made a bow as the coach passed them. The gate was closed again immediately.

On the left side, in the back of the park, behind thorn bushes, tens of persons had gathered around a freshly dug grave; a heap of earth and a rectangular, dark hole formed a sharp contrast with the snow-covered ground. Gray stones with a layer of snow on top indicated the place of other final resting places. Four men bent forward and eased off the ropes to let the coffin down.

The coachman looked as though he intended to make a joke about it, but changed his mind; he pulled the reins with one hand and took off his hat with the other.

"Maybe Dr. Blum wants to get out and go there," he mumbled.

But a window opened and the voice of Blum snapped:

"Drive on! To the main entrance!"

The horses started walking again and brought the coach around a well to a snow-free square in front of the building.

Blum and the Krohn stepped out.

Wolf took his hands out of his pockets, stood up, turned around, and started to undo the leather straps that had kept the trunks and suitcases in place. His fingers felt stiff. Men rushed out of the building to lend a hand.

But first, they greeted Blum with a bow.

"Who has passed away?" Blum wanted to know.

"The old master Eckart. He departed in peace, during his sleep."

Blum's face remained impassive, but there was a glance in his eyes betrayed an indefinable emotion.

"Then it's all right," he said—a remark that could be interpreted in many ways.

With short steps, still stiff from the long ride over the bumpy roads, he showed his guests the way to the open doors.

The imposing hall had a shining scrubbed floor of black and white flagstones. Above the oak wood paneling, the walls were covered with white tiles. To the left and to the right were deep corridors. Wooden benches stood against the back wall. Broad staircases led to the upper stories. There was a strong smell of cleaning products.

It became dim when the high front doors were closed and the daylight only shone inside through stained-glass windows.

"We will warm ourselves by the fire," said Blum, and the echo of his voice came from different sides. "Then we can finally take off our coats."

A servant opened a door that gave entry to a soberly decorated room. When Wolf moved to go inside as well, Blum looked at him with raised eyebrows.

"You'd better go with the servant," he said. "You can take the baggage to the guestrooms."

The servant, a gray, middle-aged man with a crooked back and calloused hands that stuck out of the too-short sleeves of a white jacket, had a different idea.

"You just follow me. He is not the only one who can afford himself the warmth of a fire."

He shuffled over the flagstones and turned into a corridor. "My name is Fritz. Where are you from?"

"From everywhere and nowhere," was Wolf's vague answer. "I work for Dr. Krohn and his wife. On his journey, he stopped in Heidelberg and made contact with Dr. Blum. Maybe he will stay here for some time and get cracking. Or maybe not..."

"Hmm. And you? Do you have a name?"

Fritz hadn't told him his family name and Wolf used the first given name that came up in his mind.

"Rudolf."

Blum had never troubled to ask him his name.

"You talk with an accent."

"You're not the only one who notices that."

Fritz shrugged his crooked shoulders and went into another corridor.

In the left wing of the building was an enormous kitchen where it was pleasantly warm and where a dozen men and women were up and about. Fritz poured out hot tea and held up a bottle of liquor.

"Would you like to have some?"

"No, thank you. I don't drink alcohol."

"Then I'll have yours as well," grinned Fritz. "We'll also get ourselves a bite to eat, and then I'll take you to the guestrooms. There are no other visitors yet, so I can give the doctor and his wife the best rooms. Do you prefer to stay close to them, or would you like a small room in the staff's department?"

"The farther I'm away from them, the less they can order me about," responded Wolf, who was eager to meet people who were able to give him answers to urgent questions.

After a nutritious meal, they went back to the big hall of the main building to pick up the trunks and suitcases. They went up a number of stairs, and Fritz showed Wolf a well-furnished suite.

"I think the doctor and his wife will feel at home here. They'll find all sorts of luxury here. Blum always reserves these rooms for his best friends."

"Do you know Blum well?"

Fritz nodded.

"I arrived here years ago. Well, to be honest, I was brought here. Put in irons, as a matter of fact. I was an aggressive, mentally-disordered barbarian. Blum himself took care of me, and after a long time, I was fully cured. Now I live and work here. The borders of my world are formed by the high fences of the park."

"Have you never left the clinic?"

"No. Never."

"Aren't you free to go?"

"I need permission for that. I never asked for it. You cannot just walk into the park and go through the gate. And no one just leaves here like that."

"The guests do, don't they?"

Fritz started to grin.

"You can always give it a try. There's that pack of hungry dogs prowling round out there. About twenty of them. They all have some wolf's blood running through their veins. Fast as the wind. Bloodthirsty like vampires. They always know how to find you, and then they tear you to pieces. Now let me tell you this ... "

He fell silent.

Krohn stood in the doorway.

"Ah! There you are. Blum explained to me where I could find the guestrooms. So here we'll spend the night. Look at all this luxury..."

Fritz made a stiff bow. When he passed Wolf, he said,

"I will wait for you outside, in the corridor."

As soon as he left, Krohn began to speak.

"This does not look good at all. Michaela is very nervous. I'm afraid that she'll be unable to cope with the situation."

"What do you mean?"

Blum has made it clear to us that he will stay here for seven days and that he takes it for granted that we will do the same. We cannot leave. In fact, we are prisoners here, and that's something that sticks in her throat. Of our own accord, we might stay here probably for several months, and she wouldn't complain about it. But the feeling of being locked in ... "

"I just had a talk with the servant. Anyone who tries to get out of here will be caught by a pack of bastard wolves. Once they run you down, you're no more than dog food."

"What a situation! I told Blum that I wanted to change my clothes. I have to go back as quickly as possible; I can't leave Michaela in the company of Blum for too long. But I just had to talk to you. Good to find you here. What are you intending to do now?"

"I'm going to make some inquiries. Johan must be here somewhere. And Wera Keller ... "

"Please be very careful. Blum will show us the rest of the building in a while. possible that we'll meet again..."

They shook hands and wished each other strength.

Wolf stepped into the corridor, and together with Fritz, he went down the stairs and then back to the left wing.

Unasked for, Fritz showed him different departments of the clinic. In big, fully equipped workshops male and female patients carried out repairs and produced all kinds of little objects.

KOOS VERKAIK

"Every person who is not aggressive to other persons has to fulfill a duty," explained Fritz. "Making yourself useful gives you a feeling of satisfaction, and it is much better than being bored. It is an important part of the recovering process—at least that's the way Dr. Blum sees it. Here they make wooden toys. The advanced people make figures and animals for nativity scenes. We have cabinetmakers, coachbuilders, painters, a blacksmith... We are miles away from civilization here, and we form a community that is thrown back on its own resources. Responsibility is the key to recovery, is what Dr. Blum always says."

"Do patients ever leave here? I mean, when they are fully cured like you?"

"Yes, some do. Sometimes. In my case, it was simply wiser to stay." They found themselves in a spacious bay with high windows. Fritz pointed outside. "I had nothing out there. No family, no future. So I stayed right here. Seriously mentally disordered patients stay here forever. They are outcasts. No one wants them to return into society. Finally, they'll die here."

"Like the man who was buried today. His name was Eckart if my memory serves me well..."

"A man from the right wing," said Fritz.

Wolf gave him a questioning look.

"Now let me ask you something," said Fritz. "Suppose that the doctor whom you're working for decides to stay here for a while. What about your plans, then? Are you going away? Or do you prefer to stay as well? How about your 'capabilities'?"

"I would stay here," said Wolf in a decided tone, hoping his answer would go down well. "I am a versatile man. I can work in the kitchen, in the stables, anywhere..."

"The reason I asked you this is that I don't want to give information to someone who's intending to leave us again before long. If you stay here, we'll run across each other more than once—we're all inside the same walls, aren't we?—and then I want to be able to greet you as a good friend. Well," and suddenly he lowered his voice, "in the right wing are performed all kinds of experiments."

He looked meaningfully at Wolf and tapped a finger against his temple.

"In the mental sphere. Dr. Blum gets hold of your spirit, and then he does odd things with it. And it's not just so that he knows how to get fools back to normal persons again. Maybe he doesn't want to do that at all. Blum uses people, that much is certain. Oh yes, he's been a great help to me. I was a mining engineer! Yes, that surprises you, doesn't it? But that was all before I . . ." He stared out in front of him as though he recalled vague memories that belonged to another personality. "Now I'm only a servant who can carry things and repair things. But I'm healthy, and I would never use a knife again to change things for once and for all..."

His eyes lit up; now his words were ahead of his thoughts and he pictured things to himself in that he would rather forget. Slowly he shook his gray head. He stretched his arms and stared at his wrists.

Wolf looked at the wrists and saw scars.

"Dr. Blum is a dangerous, ruthless man," said Fritz, quickly putting his hands in his pockets. "Don't ever tell anyone that I've said that..."

"Of course not," promised Wolf. "This remains between you and me. You know, I would like to have a look in the right wing."

"Most of it is forbidden territory for everyone from the left wing."

"All right, all right. But I think you know the right people and the right way to get in there anyhow."

"Possibly. But I have no business there."

He stepped out of the bay and walked along through a high, long corridor. Wolf decided not to press the point and followed him in silence.

 **36**

While Viktor Blum entertained Hans-Erich and Michaela Krohn at dinner, Wolf was sitting at a long trestle table in a crowded canteen where the domestic and nursing staff and patients had supper together.

A nutritious stew was served.

Wolf talked to different people of the staff and soon found out that Blum had the reputation of a dictator in the clinic.

Everyone seemed to have a different opinion about what happened in the right wing. One whispered speculation was even more spectacular than the other. Mysterious guests arrived and left in closed coaches. There were patients in the crazy wards who were used for unknown experiments. Blum was a man of genius—and all his bizarre plans were executed. It all had to do with a secret society.

"He tore someone's heart out of his body and let it beat on for another three days, only by the power of his mind," whispered a patient who had listened in.

And above all, Blum was the boss and wouldn't be contradicted. No one dared meddle in his business.

And it was better to keep silent about everything:

"Ears are listening everywhere, mouths tell in the right wing what eyes saw in the left wing."

Wolf didn't throw this warning to the winds. He concentrated on his stew.

❀ ❀ ❀

Later that evening he pondered on his situation in a little room under the roof that was assigned to him. There was a knock on the door, and Fritz stepped inside. He held a metal pocket flask in his hand and uncorked it.

"Cognac. Are you sure you don't want some?"

Wolf shook his head.

"I just cannot do without it. And every day I manage to find more or less enough of this stuff. But often I go out in the middle of the night to look for more to quench my thirst. That's how I learned to find my way here. No one knows the way as well as I do, that's for sure!"

He took a good swig, put the flask away, and sat down on a chair. Wolf sat on the only other chair; the rest of the room held only a table, a closet, and a bed.

"Now you tell me, Rudolf, why are you willing to go to the right wing?"

"We can be honest with each other, can't we?"

"You know that."

"Very well, then. I'll take my chances with you. I am looking for somebody. A man of my own age. His name is Johan. Johan Simons."

Fritz stood up again immediately.

"I'll make inquiries about it. In a very careful way, of course. And I'll be back within an hour."

❀ ❀ ❀

Fritz kept his word. An hour later he knocked on the door again and stumbled inside. It was obvious that he hadn't used this time only to make inquiries. He heaved a deep sigh and let himself down on the chair. He gave Wolf a kind-hearted nod.

"Hello, my dear friend. How are you?"

"I'm fine," said Wolf. "And how about you? Do you have any news for me?"

"First a little drop," said Fritz and took out a small bottle. After taking a pull and wiping his mouth with the back of his hand, he started to whisper: "When you've been here as long as I, you know to whom you can go safely to get some interesting information. There is a man here, whose name is—"

"Johan Simons?" asked Wolf hopefully.

"Johan Simons, indeed. He arrived just a couple of days ago. There is a man who is willing to bring you to him."

"Introduce me to him."

"He's sitting right in front of you."

Fritz started to grin softly, and Wolf grinned along with him. After Fritz had taken another sip and had put the bottle in his pocket, he rose to his feet and pointed at the door.

"Are you ready to go, Rudolf? We're going to make a trip. To the forbidden right wing."

Wolf stood up too.

"Just a minute, Fritz. Is it safe?"

Fritz looked at him in astonishment.

"Safe? Certainly not! Nothing ventured, nothing gained. But you won't have to worry, nobody knows the way in this building as good as I do. And I have friends. Nothing in life is more important than having some reliable friends. Come on, let's go. Stay right behind me and always do as I say. If I smell a rat, you'll be the first to know."

They left Wolf's little garret and went down a stair. Fritz stopped in a dark niche, took the bottle from his pocket and emptied it.

"Listen," he said in a soft voice, "We don't have to go all the way back to the ground floor of the main building to reach the right wing. There are also doors and corridors on the different stories. It's just that one seldom makes use of them. In a while, we will enter the main building. The higher stories there are forbidden territory for me. If they find us, they'll throw us in the isolation cell for a week or so."

"And still you're helping me..."

"Once I lost my fear," whispered Fritz. "There is only one drawback where the isolation cell is concerned—they don't serve alcohol there..."

He had to chuckle over his own joke.

Together they went on, through dark corridors and rooms, over parquet and thick carpet.

"These are mainly guestrooms," explained Fritz. "At times it can be very crowded here. But there's no one here now, which makes it the safest route to the right wing."

"Do we have to go past the rooms of Dr. Krohn?"

"No. These rooms are mainly meant for the true friends of Dr. Blum. They come from everywhere, from different countries. One story down is the enormous library, and there's also a room where séances are held. Another story down is the private rooms of Blum. Let me show you... We must be silent now."

They tiptoed down two flights of stairs. Wolf felt the temperature rising. They came upon a wooden landing that was built along a wall. Opposite to the wall was a balustrade of oak wood bars.

Voices sounded from below. Wolf looked carefully over the balustrade. Deep underneath him, he saw two men and a woman sitting in comfortable leather armchairs around the fireplace. He recognized Hans-Erich and Michaela and Dr. Blum. It was a strange sensation to look down at them in the knowledge that he could not greet or address them. Fritz pulled his sleeve. He stepped back into the darkness and followed Fritz to the other side of the landing, where they slipped through a door and entered an empty room. Inside, Fritz lit a match.

"Ah, I know where this is. I've been here once before. This is my chance..."

The flame flickered in the direction of a closet. A key creaked in a lock. Just before the flame extinguished, Wolf caught a glimpse of the contents of the closet: bottles.

"We did not come here for that," he hissed.

"That goes for you, not for me," said Fritz. He lit another match, snatched a bottle from a shelf, and put it in his pocket.

Wolf's heart sank.

Fritz took another bottle.

Next to the closet was a showcase. Wolf saw a gun rack behind the glass.

Just before the match burned his fingers, Fritz blew it out.

The next moment his voice sounded some steps away from Wolf:

"Are you going to stay there forever? Come along with me!"

Another door opened. Wolf could not see his hand in front of his face and carefully shuffled in the direction of the sound. Fritz pulled him through the doorway. Again there were stairs and then a dark corridor.

"Welcome in the right wing," said Fritz.

Cries of distress sounded.

"Lunatics," explained Fritz.

A light appeared in the depths; a male nurse, like a ghost in his long white coat, made his round.

Wolf followed Fritz. They reached a wooden staircase and went down to the ground floor. They tiptoed past an open door. A lamp was burning inside. Voices sounded. Wolf caught a glimpse of four or five men and women dressed in white, who sat down at a table and had a drink. Their voices faded away as Wolf and Fritz went on.

Finally, they reached a dimly lighted, broad corridor at the back of the wing.

It was ice-cold.

There were high metal doors.

"Here we are," whispered the old man. "No one has seen us, and we did it fast and without making a sound. I have no idea which people live here, I don't know any of them. There is a big white figure painted on each door. If everything is all right, we will be able to open door number nine. Inside you will find the man who's called Johan."

"Maybe he already escaped," speculated Wolf, as he walked through the corridor and looked at the figures on the doors.

"That's impossible. From the inside, the doors only open with a key."

Door number nine opened easily.

Wolf stepped into the cold cell.

 **37**

"Johan?"

Immediately there was moaning.

Carefully he went in the direction of the sound.

"Strike a match, Fritz."

"Wolf? Wolf? Is that you? Is that really you? My God, I hope I'm not hallucinating," said a thin voice.

A match flamed up.

For some seconds only, Wolf was able to see what he didn't want to see at all. Big, fearful eyes in a pale face. Swollen lips. Clotted blood in hair. A shivering body on a wooden bed.

The match fell on the floor.

Then, suddenly, light shone inside from the corridor.

Two big men with lanterns in their hands came inside; one stepped to the left and the other stepped to the right to give way to a third person.

Wolf recognized the man in the middle at once.

It was Dr. Blum, whom he had seen just a moment ago, sitting by the fireplace, in conversation with Hans-Erich and Michaela Krohn.

"Well, Wolf," said Blum in a calm voice. "You'll probably ask yourself forever how you came to be here. Did you ride along on the box of that coach out of your own free will, or were you forced by a thought that had lodged itself in your mind? Would you also have ended up here if your friend Johan Simons had been somewhere else? Anyway, you'll have more than enough time to think things like this over, for the door will be closed again in a moment. Don't level your anger at me. Soon I will ask you to help me. I want to make friends with you and work together with you. But first, it has to become very clear to you that only one of us can run the show. As soon as you fully understand that it is best for you to cooperate on a voluntary base, we'll meet again. In better circumstances, I can promise you that."

Blum gestured at the man who stood behind him at the left; the man made a step forward and put the lantern on the floor.

"See you later, Wolf. I'm glad that you finally are here. Welcome."

Blum made a courteous bow and stepped backward into the corridor, followed by the two men. The metal door slammed shut. Wolf sank down on the cold floor and turned down the flame of the lantern.

"We must save the oil," he sighed, at the same time surprised about the fact that he was able to think in such a practical way.

Fritz came and sat next to him, produced a bottle, opened it, and started to drink.

Wolf and Johan looked at each other, and they both asked a question.

"What have they done to you?"

"Where am I?"

They both had to grin. Johan's smile became a painful grimace when his torn lips threatened to burst open. Wolf shoved up closer to the wooden bed and put a hand on the shoulder of his friend.

"You were taken away. Probably by Vulpe and his henchmen."

"That's right."

"It is so good to see you again. They've brought you here from Munich—to a mental home in the Odenwald, not too far from Heidelberg."

"Heidelberg . . ." whispered Johan. "But of course. We went there once to see Dr. Viktor Blum. That man who just came in—that was Blum, wasn't it?"

"Yes."

"And who has accompanied you?"

"Fritz." Wolf turned himself to the man who was sitting next to him. "And I don't know if he wanted to help me or frame me."

Fritz wiped his mouth with the back of his hand and closed the bottle again.

"I swear, Rudolf—I mean, Wolf... I would never—"

"All right, all right. We won't talk about it anymore." Then he turned himself again to the young man on the bed. "Tell me your story, and then I'll tell you mine. Short and to the point; I am dead tired and will try to sleep as soon as possible."

"Understood," said Johan. "There is something you should know for sure. Allow me the time to come to myself. I am totally confused, as you can understand. Here you are... I didn't expect you at all. You're a prisoner now. Just like me. I understand that it all revolves around you. It's you whom Blum seems to need..."

Wolf nodded, and then there was a silence for a long time, during which everyone was occupied with his own thoughts—staring into the motionless flame, red and yellow, of the lantern.

When Wolf finally looked up, he saw that there were tears in Johan's eyes.

"What's the matter?"

"I have betrayed you. I'm so sorry about that. I could hold out for a long time, but they came back again and again and beat me to a jelly. I told them you had moved to Der Steinbock."

"And they did it for nothing. I'm sure I'd been gone from Der Steinbock already for a long time when the men of Vulpe came looking there for me. You don't have to blame yourself for anything. I am very proud of you. Now tell me everything I should know..."

"I had special experiences right here in this cell. Of paranormal, telepathic origin. If it were only possible to find out if it was all real. A man with immensely strong willpower managed to penetrate into my mind. He was old and sick. He helped me to endure the cruelty of my warders. But his efforts exhausted him, and he passed away. He was lying in the cell next to mine."

"Wait a minute," said Wolf. "Today someone was buried here. His name was Eckart."

"That's him!" Johan cried out in surprise. "He told me his name."

Wolf turned himself to Fritz.

"Did you know someone by the name of Eckart?"

"Oh yes, I did. That is to say, I've never seen him myself, but I have heard a lot about him. There was something between him and the doctor. Blum must have hated him. There was a special name for Eckart's cell, and one only said it in a whisper: the forget pit; like the medieval pits where prisoners were put to die of hunger and thirst... And it was true; often Eckart was forgotten on purpose when food and water were brought round. Doctor's orders. For Eckart was a magician, and magicians can easily live on air only. A downright shame, if you ask me. It was said that this old man once stood high above Blum and that his wisdom was far beyond that of the doctor. Now he is dead. The snow must have covered his grave by now..."

"So it wasn't imagination after all," sighed Johan. "There were moments I thought I would go crazy. Solitary confinement in an ice-cold, bare room, plus the knowledge that someone could come in at any time to beat the hell out of me, make the ideal circumstances to get someone hallucinating. Fear isn't a pleasant companion. Anyway,

Eckart managed to confide his secrets to me. It was a surprising experience. Listen to me, Wolf, and many a thing will become clear to you. You know very well that I'm no more than a street urchin and that my knowledge has its limitations; all I can do is tell what was whispered to me in a magical way. Eckart searched his way back into history. Back into the deep, dark past."

Johan sat up straight on his bed and stared out in front of him as if he were in a trance.

"The Celts had their druids, the magical priests, the seers. The druids formed a special brotherhood. Every year they came together to exchange experiences, to consolidate the position of their high priest or elect another one. Eckart told me this and then asked if it sounded familiar to me. That was a fact, I could admit it. I think everyone has heard one thing or another about the Celtic druids. In this way, Eckart brought me into a special mood. I could see the old priests until Eckart made them fade away. He took me with him, in thoughts, to holy oak wood. Again I saw priests, and I was supposing that they were Celtic druids. I hadn't only made a leap into the past, I also had bridged the distance—now I found myself to the north of the Celts; I had reached the immense territory where the Germanic tribes ruled. The priests had come together and sacrificed to the god Tyr. Thereupon they chose themselves a new leader.

"For that purpose, they seemed to fathom each other's minds and penetrate into each other's realms of thought. While they were sitting around the fire in silence and in peace, they made war in their head!

"In that way, they elected someone from their midst, whom Eckart called the central brain. The most important priest, the man with the most special mental power, enabled the group of priests to bring about great wonders. The high priest was judged by the special powers of his brain, not by his character—which therefore might be good or bad. Eckart discovered the old rituals and their magical effects. He became the high priest of his own circle, in his own time. Till he got discarded. By Blum. And then all good intentions were washed away by waves of greed and hatred."

Johan shook his head slowly and looked around as if he had just awakened from a state of hypnosis.

"I . . . I know that I started to tell you about the things Eckart showed me. But I drifted away, and I cannot remember what all I have told you. Was I talking stuff and nonsense? Was I raving?"

"By no means," said Wolf. "I'm afraid, however, that I'm just too tired at the moment to interpret things right." He stretched his length on the floor. "I really need some rest now. I'm at an end."

In spite of his uncomfortable position on the cold stones, he managed to sleep for a while. He woke up with a start from loud sounds. The slide at the bottom of the door had opened. A bottle of water rolled inside and plates were pushed over the floor. A loud voice sounded:

"I have a message for someone by the name of Wolf. Dr. Blum counts on your cooperation. He has ambitious plans with you. Keep in mind that it is impossible to escape from this building. And something might happen to your dear friend Johan. Also, something could happen to Hans-Erich and Michaela Krohn. Don't let it all go that far—do everything Dr. Blum asks you to do."

The slide closed.

Behind the high, closed window sounded the howling of dogs or wolves. Then it was quiet again. Wolf sat down and looked up to the window. It was still dark behind it. He took out his pocket watch and turned up the wick of the lantern.

"It will take a while before it gets light," he said. "What a strange hour to bring us food."

Johan took a deep breath through his nose.

"Someone wants you to be favorably disposed towards him, don't you think? Hmm, this smells good. They've cooked an excellent meal for us! I'm famished!"

"You can have my plate as well," offered Wolf.

"And mine too," said Fritz. "Once I started drinking, I don't need any food at all."

Wolf turned up the wick a bit more and looked at Fritz.

"How many bottles did you steal, actually?"

Fritz shrugged his shoulders and started to empty his pockets.

"Three. The first one is almost empty, the other two are still full."

"Give me one."

"You don't drink, do you? That's what you said yourself."

"I have kept my promise. No more booze till I had found Johan. And now I need a good swig." He opened the bottle and drank with long drafts. "To become who I was," he said, upon which the others gave him an uncomprehending look.

He held out the bottle to Johan.

"No, thank you," said Johan decidedly. "The alcohol will burn my torn lips. I'll stick to the food and drink some water with it. Now tell me … what are you up to?"

Wolf didn't speak another word.

He drank and drank.

And steadily he built up unbridled aggression.

Johan nodded when the metal door started to rattle and sounds of splintering wood came from the corridor.

"That terrifying talent," whispered Johan. "It's still inside of you, and now you're using it again."

Voices sounded.

Somewhere glass burst apart.

The door shook on its hinges.

The hatch opened.

An angry face popped up.

"What are you doing? Are you kicking against the door?"

An invisible power pushed the warder against the door. His face was pressed through the square opening of the hatch. His mouth opened, and his eyes partly disappeared behind his squeezed-together cheeks.

Wolf took another good swig from the bottle. Johan jumped up from the wooden bed and went to the door.

"Do you have the keys?" he said to the twisted face.

"Yes, yes..." panted the man.

"Open the door."

The man, stuck to the iron like a magnet, had to exert himself to the utmost to get the bunch of keys from his belt.

A key got turned around in the lock.

The door swung open, and the warder fell to the floor.

 # 38

Wolf jumped up and went into the dimly lighted corridor. Johan was right behind him. Fritz first picked up the bottle from the floor, and then he followed them.

Shadowy figures moved to and fro. From behind the closed cell, doors sounded cries of distress. Wooden girders creaked on the high ceiling. Tiles snapped from the walls and fell into pieces on the stone floor.

Someone bumped up against Johan. It was a tall male nurse, dressed in white. Johan prepared for an attack and clenched his fists, but the man fell down on his knees, raised his hands, and started to shout:

"Now we'll be punished! All of us! The revenge of Eckart!"

Johan bent down, took the man by the shoulders, and gave him a shaking.

"Eckart? What kind of nonsense is this? What are you talking about?"

The man looked up at him with protruding eyes.

"Have you heard the dogs howling?"

"Yes. A moment ago..."

"Edgar Klatt was outside making his round. The dogs went with him. He saw the grave of Eckart. It was open! It was wide open, you hear? Eckart has disappeared. The dogs barked, howled . . . and then they fell silent as if they received an order that could be registered by dogs' ears only. Eckart takes revenge for his bad treatment..."

Johan let go of the man.

He didn't know someone by the name of Edgar Klatt, but he understood that he had to be a member of the guard and that he probably had rushed inside to cry out his horrible discovery—and in that way, the pandemonium caused by Wolf had been imputed to the wrath of Eckart.

Wolf had forced the warder to stand up. He held him tight and pushed him through the corridor.

"Wera Keller," he said. "Do you know that name? Is she here?"

He twisted the man's arm.

"Yes. Wera Keller. I know her."

"Bring me to her. Right now!"

Now a noise sounded from all side as if the entire right wing could come down at any moment. The walls rattled, windows burst and broke and splintered, even the floor was trembling. There was a banging on countless doors and screams for help. From a dark niche sounded a strangled voice:

"Eckart! Oh God, it is Eckart!"

The warder opened a cell door. "Let me go now. Please!"

Wolf pushed him away. He stepped into the cell. There was a stale atmosphere inside. The dim light from the corridor was blocked by the size of his own figure. In front of him, in the darkness, someone stood up from a bed.

"Wolf?"

He recognized the voice immediately.

"Wera?"

The person came up to him.

Two arms wrapped around him, a warm body pushed against him.

He knew that it was her.

He long hair hung loose and felt dry and stiff when he stroked a hand over her head.

"Come with me," he said; his hand slid down over her shoulder and arm and took her by the wrist. "Quick."

As he took her along with him to the corridor, rage and frustration spun around in his fuddled mind and set free new powers. The walls shook, and somewhere high above the floor was a sound like rolling thunder. Wolf beckoned to Johan. He pushed Fritz out in front of him.

"Where to?" asked Fritz.

"To the closet where you stole the bottles!"

Fritz quickened his pace, and the others followed him.

No one attempted to stop them; everyone was on the run from what they thought was the revenge of Eckart.

A door opened. Men and women pushed their way outside, where a gray light heralded the morning. Immediately there was the barking and the howling of dogs.

The small group went up to different stairs, through corridors, and finally reached the main building.

Fritz, heavily panting, stopped in front of the closet in the half-dark room.

"How many bottles do you need?"

Wolf didn't react but concentrated on the showcase. He screwed up his eyes. The glass burst and fell with a swishing noise to fragments on the floor. Together with Johan, he took a large number of rifles from the rack. In a drawer, they found wooden boxes with ammo.

"Let's go!" said Wolf. "Fritz! Where are the rooms of the Krohns?"

"Not so far from here," replied Fritz, who sadly dropped two bottles when Wolf handed him some rifles. "Only one story down."

They went down a staircase.

Men walking through the corridor—guards or male nurses—immediately took to their heels when Wolf aimed a gun on them and made to walk up to them. Someone opened a door. Hans-Erich Krohn looked into the corridor.

"Wolf! Wolf! This way!"

The small group went inside. Krohn closed the door. Wolf flopped into an armchair and gasped for breath.

Soon it became quiet in the building.

Wolf's spirit calmed down.

"Michaela, take care of Wera," he said. "I think she would like to have a good wash. Maybe you can give her some of your own clothes."

Johan loaded the rifles and put them in line against a wall. Krohn, who had locked the doors, looked at Johan and said, "You look bad. Allow me to examine you."

He took Johan with him to another room. Fritz had found himself a place by the fireplace, where he stared into the flames and swigged from a bottle.

Wolf closed his eyes.

He smiled, fancying himself to be a winner who had freed two prisoners and himself from a cold cell. But right after that he realized that he had brought the others and himself into desperate straits because he had acted without any strategic plan—well-armed as they were, they would be able to defend themselves in the suite for a long time, but when they were almost dying of hunger and thirst, their rifles and bullets would be of little use.

All Dr. Blum had to do was to wait for a couple of days; then he could get the door kicked in and step inside without any fear, to make his demands.

# 39

But things went quite differently.

Wolf woke up with a start when there was a knock on the door.

He had slept for a couple of hours. He reached for his rifle and looked around. Fritz stood ready to open the door, and Johan and Krohn stood at both sides of him with their weapons in their hands.

All three of them looked at Wolf.

He nodded.

Fritz twisted the key and turned the knob. He opened the door carefully. A cheerful voice sounded:

"A good morning to every one of you. A late breakfast, together with the good wishes of Dr. Blum, the owner of this clinic. None of us is intending to come inside—you can push in the trolley with foods and drinks yourself. As long as you prefer to remain in this situation, you will want for nothing. Tomorrow I would like to ask Mr. Wolf if he is willing to exchange thoughts with Dr. Blum. Enjoy your meal."

Footsteps sounded and faded away. Fritz stepped into the corridor and pulled a wooden trolley inside. Krohn checked everything carefully.

"It looks perfect to me."

"What's Blum up to?" wondered Michaela, as she walked up to her husband. "Is this some kind of a psychological move? Did he poison the food? Or is this just the way things go in a madhouse like this?"

Wolf wanted to say something, but suddenly his attention was caught by someone who sat down in an armchair opposite to him. It was Wera Keller, who gave him a grateful look. She wore one of Michaela's splendid dresses. He noticed the complex plaiting of her thick, almost black hair, the same hairdo she'd had when he first met her in Amsterdam. But he noticed that she had changed. She was still as beautiful and attractive as then, but now her beauty was earthly instead of heavenly as if she had been an angel who had become human again.

He stood up and moved toward her. But Krohn stepped in front of him, put a hand on his shoulder, and gestured with his other hand.

"Please, come with me."

They walked through the room and stopped in front of a window.

It had stopped snowing.

Looking outside, Wolf could make out the grave of Eckart. It looked like a grotesque molehill in the white park.

It made his flesh creep.

"I take you aside for a while to inform you about what's been said while you were asleep. You had drunk a lot, you needed that sleep," said Krohn. "I am in the possession of the facts now. I know what happened between the man who was called Eckart and Johan."

Wolf and Krohn talked in soft voices. Their conversation complete, they decided that Wolf would go to Wera now to ask her some questions. They walked back to the armchairs and the couch by the fireplace. Fritz was sitting there eating. He had poured himself a cup of tea and mixed it with cognac.

"The question of whether anything is poisoned seems to have been answered," said Krohn. "If Fritz is willing to drink a bit less today, he'll undoubtedly stay alive."

Everyone burst out laughing. And it felt good to do so.

Then Krohn said, "There is a second door to the corridor in the bedroom. Johan and I have placed a heavy closet against it. We are relatively safe in our suite. But I still wonder what Blum is going to do now."

He took a plate from the trolley and started to pick out food. Wolf did the same. The only one who didn't want to eat was Wera. She looked at Wolf constantly and seemed to search for words—time and time again she opened her mouth, to close it again after a little while. Then she shook her head slowly, heaved a deep sigh and said:

"Thank you, Wolf. Thank you so very much. I asked for your help, and you actually showed up. You freed me from my cell, but now you're trapped like a rat yourself... I'm so sorry about that."

Wolf stared into her big eyes.

"I'm glad to see you. And of course, I am very curious about everything you have to tell me."

"Ask me questions, Wolf. I will answer them all in the most honest way. I didn't spend all my time here in that cell. I have been in contact with other persons, and I am well informed about the events here. Dr. Blum allowed me a certain freedom and didn't seem to have a problem with the fact that I became familiar with all kinds of affairs—he took it for granted that I would never get a chance to leave here."

"And maybe he was right about that," remarked Michaela.

Wolf was used to asking questions in a professional way and finding out the truth where paranormal matters were concerned. Now he tried not to be distracted by Wera's beauty.

"You showed up at Jacob van Beek's funeral. You asked me for help. Later, when I was at home, I saw a little man in a white suit and a woman in a long, flowered dress in a rowboat on the river Vecht. A man who called himself Gerardus Klijn, whom I had met before in a train. That woman was you. You had come into my garden with a picnic hamper filled with all kinds of food, wine—you name it. Again you asked me to help you. 'They're taking me back,' you said, and all of a sudden you had disappeared. This encounter shocked me in such a heavy way, that the most horrible powers broke loose in me. The same powers I made use of yesterday—hopefully for the very last time! Wera, that hamper and its contents were really the same as the rowboat and the parasol."

"They were not real materializations," said Wera. "They were incorporeal. They were illusions. After some time they'll all have disappeared."

"And how about you? Were you there yourself? Were you real?"

"No, I wasn't. Michaela knows that I have certain talents. But Dr. Blum raised it all to a much higher level. I learned to draw from a collective well, brought about by the doctor and members of his society. That gave me unknown powers. Oh, Wolf, you little know what all is happening!"

Krohn leaned backward and looked at her in a dazed sort of way.

"The collective!" he whispered. "A well of spiritual energy . . ."

Wolf ignored him.

"Who is Gerardus Klijn?"

"A man with special paranormal powers. He belonged to the select group of the doctor's confidants. Till he rose against the cruel methods of Blum. Soon he became a prisoner in this clinic, just like me and so many others. We had long, long talks together, before he . . . well, one day he was found him on his wooden bed, as someone told me, and he lay there staring up at the ceiling with dead eyes."

"He died the way Jacob van Beek died as well, by the will of the collective."

"Yes."

"He appeared on the train when I was traveling from Prague to Munich. He was talking about the Nibelung and—"

"The Nibelung. I'll tell you about that later," said Wera.

"All right. All right. He knew everything about the death of Jacob. He talked about a whispering of the collective. Jacob had gone outside. According to Klijn, he did so to take his leave of Amsterdam, of life. For death had already crossed the threshold. I touched Gerardus Klijn, I even lifted him up... He seemed so real..."

He fell silent for a while, with difficulty swallowing his fury.

Then he continued:

"Jacob van Beek was like a father to me. He meant everything to me. If Dr. Blum is responsible for his death, in any way, I will shoot a bullet through his head! Why did Jacob have to die?"

"Sometimes Blum and his people aim their mental poison arrow at someone without special reason, just to stay sharp by practicing. Hans-Erich told me about the nightly gathering in an oak wood near Heidelberg. That was a meeting in the tradition of the old German priests and priestesses who wanted to share each other's thoughts and feelings. You have witnessed how they drove the students to mortal fear. Believe me, they sucked in all that fear of the students and made themselves stronger that way. It is a psychological process that we don't know anymore, but that has been found again by Dr. Blum. But what happened to Jacob van Beek is different. Here these processes become more incomprehensible, more mysterious... In the first place, one obviously thought that he had gathered too much information about mediums and magicians. He meddled too much with affairs that should remain concealed."

"I did exactly the same."

"It had to do with you all the time! They fathomed your mind and found out that you might be a likely candidate for their evil practices. Your mind had to get kneaded—I have no other words at the moment to explain it to you. You would have to deal with death and sorrow. You had to travel all over Europe. You visited so many people in so many countries. You met members of the collective. Without realizing it, you came under their influence. Special powers came up in you. You went through a magical process and then, at a certain moment, you were ready to go to Lindau."

Wolf jumped up and clutched his rifle with both hands. He rushed to the door.

"I'm going to kill Viktor Blum! I'll find him!"

Johan ran after him and took up a position in front of the door.

"Now calm down, Wolf. You get far this way. Don't think that Blum will allow himself to be shot down just like that. Sit down again, please, and go on talking with Wera."

Wolf gasped for breath. It took some time before he came to his senses again.

"And how about you?" he asked after he had sat down face to face with Wera again. "How real were you, when you visited Jacob in Amsterdam?"

"Oh, very real! I was there in person! Never before had I felt as I did then. My spirit was fed by a powerful, external energy, and I was able to work wonders—well, you saw that with your own eyes. I nullified gravity and made a thousand guilders by making a die fly around. But as soon as the attention of the collective slackened, fear rose up. An almost unbearable fear it was! Fear of Dr. Blum, who had made me come to this desolated place under false pretenses and kept me under mental pressure constantly. He manipulated me, did all kinds of experiments with me, kept me in his power the way he turned out to do with so many other people. In my terror, I made use of the external energy in a totally different way. You saw me lying there on the floor like a wounded, repugnant creature. I asked you for help, I asked you to save me. And I did want you for the collective—"

"Don't forget about the collective—that's what you said."

"I wasn't able to make any more clear to you. Oh, I wanted to tell you so much, already, but the words stuck in my throat. All my efforts changed me into something that must have looked like a monster. There was nothing I could do against it. Rebelliousness against the collective got punished that awful way."

"Why did you come to me to ask for help, why did you warn me?"

"I will try to explain it to you. First, you have to understand that what Blum is doing is still in a stage of development. He is the first one to experiment with long-forgotten methods. Many a thing goes wrong. There are unexpected effects, side effects, possibilities create other possibilities. The influence that was exerted on me changed me in different ways. Slumbering clairvoyance became very strong, mind reading was no problem for me all of a sudden, and there were more phenomena that appeared unexpectedly. I heard your name sing round in my head. I knew something was going to happen with you. And I knew instinctively that you had to be someone who was able to help me."

Wera stood up and went to the fireplace to throw in some logs of wood. She remained standing in front of the fireplace and continued:

"I hope you understood what I just said."

"Most of it is clear to me," responded Wolf.

"I hope you'll understand what I'm going to say now as well. In Amsterdam, you were surprised by the fact that I was able to speak good Dutch. I said that I was also able to speak in other languages. Whereupon Jacob said, 'Then you just pluck the words out of the air,' remember? Everyone who occupies himself with paranormal affairs sooner or later discovers that there've always been people who were able to pluck something out of the air. Premonitions, truths, lies, facts, you name it. Not every spirit is open for things like that. One of Blum's most important theories is that you can actually pick everything out of the air. Everything that once happened or will happen in the future 'hangs,' so to speak, in the air. It depends on someone's mental condition what he is able to pluck out of the great nowhere. I have to add to this that most people don't receive any information this way, while others do nothing but listen with the ears of the mind. The old learning of the Germanic priests just came … blowing towards him!"

Johan raised his hand.

"Something odd came back to my mind. Look, this gesture was made clear to me by Eckart…"

First, he stroked his forefinger down over his nose. Then he used his thumb and forefinger to stroke over his eyebrows down to both sides of his head.

"Very odd indeed!" Krohn said in surprise. "I remember seeing Dr. Blum do the same when I paid him a visit in Heidelberg. After he had done so, he gave me a piercing look."

"Did Eckart also made clear to you what that gesture means?" Wera asked Johan.

"Has it something to do with the Germanic priests?"

"Not exactly," said Wera. "It is a gesture that was introduced by Blum himself. One recognizes the brothers and sisters from the collective that way. In fact, one is delineating an arrow that points upward. Doing that, one symbolizes the sky, supported by a pillar. But it is also the symbol of the spear of the old god Tyr. It is the *T*, the seventeenth letter in the runic alphabet."

For the second time, there was a knocking on the door. Wolf went to open it, while Johan and Krohn stood to the left and to the right of him.

A long, thin man was standing in the corridor, holding his white coat open to show that he was unarmed. Behind him stood a couple of girls holding wooden buckets filled with water.

"Clean water, so that you all can wash yourselves," said the man. "Are the girls allowed to come in and fill the jugs?"

Wolf nodded and stepped aside to let the girls pass through. Krohn inspected the contents of the buckets. The man looked inside and said, "Fritz needs to come with me. There's a lot of work waiting for him."

Fritz heaved a deep sigh, got up, and walked into the corridor. He gave Wolf a wry smile and came standing next to the man in the white coat.

"Duty calls," he muttered.

The girls came back. Wolf was already starting to close the door again when the man raised a finger and said:

"If there is anything more I can do for you, please don't hesitate to ask me. This night an extensive dinner will be served in your suite. And by the way, Dr. Blum has asked me to tell you another thing..."

"Which is?"

"I should tell you that you must understand that this is a mental home. And it would be rather strange to store weapons, ready for use, in places where everyone is able to get them. Well, the rifles are all right and well oiled. But please don't expect too much where the ammo's concerned... Goodbye for the present!"

The man turned around and walked through the corridor, followed by Fritz and the girls with the buckets.

Wolf leaned into the corridor, aimed his rifle at one of the buckets, and pulled the trigger.

All he heard was a dry click.

 # 40

Michaela had a nervous breakdown. Her husband gave her a tranquilizer and asked her to try and get some sleep. Johan sat down with his back against the wall, depressed, his elbows resting on his knees, his face hidden behind his hands. Wolf and Wera sat down close to the fire.

"What a horrible situation," she said in a soft voice. "If you only knew how I long to get away from here. During the day I often lend a helping hand in one of the kitchens and then I manage to hold out, but at night, in that unheated cell, without any comfort, on that hard bed, it is an ice-cold hell."

"Haven't you tried more often to ask for help? Didn't you make yourself appear in front of someone outside the clinic?"

She shook her head and looked at him dejectedly.

"When the people of the collective don't occupy themselves with you intensively any more when they stop concentrating on your mind, you lose that sort of talent. It is over and done with, my special gifts. They don't need me for anything anymore. But in the meantime, I know too much, and so I'll have to stay here. Forever. This place is swarming with experimental subjects who are no longer of use to

Blum." She took his hand. "Now tell me everything about what happened to you, Wolf..."

Wolf started to tell, and she listened to him without interrupting. After he had finished his story and looked up again, he noticed that Johan and the Krohns had sat down with them again.

"How are you doing? Couldn't you catch your sleep?" he asked Michaela.

She looked bad. Her face was pale, and there was fear in her eyes, but she nodded bravely and bit on her lower lip.

"I can't sleep, but I'm beginning to feel better."

"Still, she needs rest," said her husband. He looked at Wera. "And how are you doing?"

"All right," said Wera. "Now I know what Wolf has been through—and that's quite something! In your home, he disappeared right before your very eyes and materialized himself again in another room. He made long trips in a short time and told you where he had been."

"And his information was right," assented Krohn.

"That same way I appeared in front of Wolf. Then the collective saw to it that I was no longer able to do a miraculous thing like that."

"I am a skeptic," said Krohn. "Always have been a skeptic! I am very interested in paranormal affairs and always want to solve any riddle. Just like Wolf himself, I have seen much trickery. But this . . ." He shook his head slowly. "This is simply incredible!"

"Blum says that we find things like this incredible because we still don't understand all the laws of nature. He says that insects, like bees, also are able to act as a collective; that every bee feels what one bee feels, that one bee understands what all bees understand. Everything revolves around the queen. She is the central brain, the beginning of everything—and the end of everything when she dies. He sees himself as a king, who keeps his subjects together and makes it possible for them to work wonders."

"You are Dr. Blum's mouthpiece," remarked Krohn. "And maybe that isn't a coincidence at all."

She looked up at him with big, surprised eyes.

"No, no," he hurried to say, "Don't get me wrong, I don't mean to say that you are playing games with us because you're working together with Blum—what I think is the other way around; he himself is playing one of his games with you."

"Most people who live in this building are under his spell," said Wera. "We all are very aware of that. He always says to everyone, 'You cannot actually see the spirit, and I knead it with invisible fingers; but I gain visible results with it.' Which explains an important part of his working method."

Silence fell.

Then Krohn said to Wera:

"Now we must discuss the Nibelung. Different mediums have used the word when they were in a trance and Wolf asked them specific questions. Johan bought a book entitled *The Nibelung Treasure*. In the library of Heidelberg, my wife and Wolf found two different books, *The Nibelung Saga* and *The Nibelung Song*. I read these two books myself."

"Right. Gerardus Klijn talked about it after he had seen me reading *The Nibelung Treasure* in the train," said Wolf. "And in Heidelberg, we heard members of the collective saying to each other, 'Almost Nibelung,' as if it was some kind of a greeting."

"What do you know about it, Wera?" asked Krohn.

"The story of the Nibelung is often told here," said Wera. "It is rather odd, actually; everyone knows it. Siegfried searches for the gold treasure of the Nibelung, guarded by a dangerous dragon. I know that Dr. Blum is searching for gold..."

Wolf and Krohn looked at each other, and they both had to think of what had happened in Lindau, at Lake Constance.

"I know that expression, too. I've heard it more than once here, when Blum received important guests; 'Almost Nibelung...' If it is true that the finders of the gold treasure are allowed to call themselves Nibelung, as I've heard different times, Blum and the collective will become Nibelung as soon as they have found a certain treasure themselves. That seems to be the most plausible inference to me."

"I agree," said Krohn. "Blum is searching for a treasure. Considering the fact that he spares no pains at all, it has to be a treasure of immeasurable value!"

Wolf heaved a deep sigh.

"And you'll never guess who will have to find that treasure for him..."

"He has a madhouse filled with candidates who failed the tests," sneered Krohn, "but now, finally, he has managed to get the right person between these walls. You're here to search for the treasure of the Nibelung, Wolf."

 # 41

Dinner was served.

The suite was full of people.

Armed men walked up and down with much display of power. Servants brought wood for the fireplace. The stolen rifles were collected. Michaela hid her face behind her hands and waited until everyone had left again. She heaved a sigh when she heard the door close.

The food tasted good, although no one was very hungry.

The servants had also brought bottles of red and white wine.

Krohn opened a bottle. Wolf said no to a glass.

"The combination of frustration, rage, and alcohol takes me in a way we all know very well by now."

"I believed you'd already lost that doubtful talent," remarked Krohn. "I think that certain members of the collective still keep an eye on you and have a grip on your mind—you are making use of external energy, and that's what makes the outbursts so violent."

"What a horrible thought," sighed Wolf. "I'm beginning to wonder which of my feelings are real and which are forced on me unconsciously..."

That same thought also came to him when he lay in bed that night and listened to the calm breathing of Wera, who was lying next to him.

After a long discussion full of speculations about the collective, it had become late all of a sudden, and the Krohns retired to their bedroom. Johan slept on the couch. Wera could make use of a side room, where a big bed stood. She had coaxed Wolf along with her:

"I feel safe with you."

Wolf couldn't sleep.

He listened to the silence, interrupted two or three times by the howling of a dog.

 # 42

They all got up early in the morning and had breakfast at the fireside.

An hour later a man in a long white coat came in; he announced that he had been sent by Dr. Blum.

"I advise you not to leave the suite," he said. "The corridor is guarded by men who have received orders to shoot anyone who tries to escape. I would ask Mr. Krohn to come along with me."

Krohn stood up immediately and kissed Michaela.

"And where are we going?"

"To Dr. Blum."

"I'll come with you," said Wolf.

"You wouldn't get far," said the man in the white coat and gesticulated with both hands as if he were aiming a rifle and pulling the trigger.

"Well, I think differently about that," reacted Wolf. "I strongly believe that I am much too important to Blum to get shot down just like that."

The man shrugged his shoulders.

"Dr. Krohn is the only one who'll come with me."

Wolf flew at the man, grabbed him by the throat with both hands, and threw him off balance. They fell to the ground together. The man produced bizarre guttural sounds, and his eyes bulged in panic. He spread his arms to show that he didn't want to defend himself and knocked on the floor with the back of his hands to make clear that he accepted defeat. Wolf's fingers relaxed, but at the same time, he pumped his knee into the man's stomach.

"Listen to me. Listen carefully. You're going back to Blum right away and tell him that Krohn will not come all by himself. Now that I start thinking about it … tell him that we all want to have a talk with him. We'll stay together. He can come to us. If he is too cowardly to come here, he has to arrange something else. You just tell him that I actually do have plans to kill him, but don't know exactly how. I will try to keep calm and not fly at his bloody throat the way I did with you."

Only now did he let go of the man and stand up.

"Now hurry! Go to him. I expect you to be back here within ten minutes, understood?"

The man rolled on his stomach and then drew himself half up; bending forward, leaning on his hands like a monkey, he hurried to the door. There he hoisted himself up at the doorpost, and the next moment he had disappeared.

Wolf beat his left fist hard into the palm of his right hand.

"It is said that one kills the messenger if the message is bad. Well, I almost did so myself, didn't I? What does Blum expect to achieve? I want to get the answers to all my questions today. I want to leave this madhouse as soon as possible!"

It took more than ten minutes—the man returned only after half an hour. He knocked, opened the door, remained standing in the corridor, and looked inside with a fearful face.

"Will you follow me, please?"

The small group went on their way through the long complex of corridors. The man in the white coat stayed as far as possible from Wolf and walked in front together with Krohn.

"Dr. Blum planned to meet you in the library, here in the main building," he said to Krohn, "but now he has made another arrangement. We're going up to the upper story of the right wing."

They went over smooth marble, threadbare carpets, and creaking parquet.

Gray daylight shone inside through barred windows.

At the end of one corridor, a door opened, and two male nurses dragged a heavily resisting patient along with them.

"Here we'll take the stairs," said the man in white.

The wooden banisters were provided with splendid carvings. Dark paintings hung on the walls.

Upstairs they met up with two armed men who accompanied them to a corridor that connected the main building with the right wing.

The man in white led them into a big room.

A number of chairs and a small table were placed in the middle of the room. Dr. Blum sat on a chair near a wall, not far from an arched passage. To each side of him sat a man with a rifle. In a corner stood Fritz, head bowed, staring at his feet.

"A good morning to all of you," said Dr. Blum. "Please don't come any closer. Take a seat. The minute one of you comes towards me, I will disappear." He pointed with his thumb to the passage.

Everyone sat down.

Blum looked at Krohn.

"We had dinner together, Krohn. We've had nice talks together. I gave you and Michaela a warm welcome, didn't I? But you came here under false pretenses. It was never your intention to come and work here as a doctor. You never planned to make any donation either. But you did me a good turn by bringing Wolf here. I am most grateful to you. Now let's not talk about this anymore … "

Wolf had been struggling to keep his temper. He was ready to jump up and fly at Blum's throat.

"You killed Jacob van Beek!" he cried out. "One day you're going to pay for that, I swear!"

The men sitting next to Blum stroked their weapons and looked hard at Wolf.

"That is not entirely true," said Blum. "Listen, Wolf, I had planned to talk with Krohn today. With him only. That way I could have explained everything calmly, and after this conversation, he could have informed you. You already received lots of information from Wera Keller, so there are already several things I don't have to tell you. I'm not looking for a quarrel with you; on the contrary; I want to be friends with you."

"You're nothing but a murderer," said Wolf, pointing his finger at Blum.

"My candidates have to go through a long and hard process before they are ready for the specially developed proficiency tests," said Blum. "The kneading of the spirit is a difficult therapy. Mortal fear and sorrow are part of it, just like breaking off trusty relations, making long journeys, going—"

"That's all too vague for me," said Wolf. "I want to know what this is all about. What are you intending to do? What do you want from me?"

"Very well, then," said Blum. "Let's get down to business. I will speak freely. Look."

He stood up and took something from his pocket.

"Fritz, come over here. Show this to my guests."

Fritz took an object from him and walked with it to the middle of the room.

What he held in his hand was the golden necklace that Wolf had fetched out of the great nothing in Lindau and that was taken away from him immediately by his attackers.

"See how the fingers of Fritz tremble," sneered Blum. "It has nothing to do with the great value of the neck ring. Fritz is dying for a drink—

what he wants is alcohol. And if he steals another single sip from me, he'll spend the rest of his life in a cold cell. Now take a good look at the golden ornament, if you please. And try to imagine a treasure containing one thousand, no, ten thousand of these beautiful objects of the purest gold. That's what it's all about, that's what I'm after!"

"The Nibelung gold…" sighed Michaela.

Blum ordered Fritz back, took the ornament from him, and let it slip into his pocket again. Fritz went back to his corner and stared down at his toes.

"I am sure that Wera has told you that I am the central brain of my organization. I have breathed new life into ancient traditions, I have rediscovered almost-forgotten knowledge and gone deeply into it. The whole affair boils down to this: in the days when magic was still a part of every human life and one was able to do things that we would call wonders now, one worshipped the mighty god Tyr in northern Europe. The priests and priestesses formed an exclusive group of people who felt spiritually connected to each other. Their training was hard. It all depended on their spiritual abilities. They were able to combine their powers by electing the most capable leader—the man or woman whom we would now call the central brain—in those times it was the high priest or high priestess. In times of famine, a group like this was able to let different tribes survive."

Blum rose to his feet and began to pace up and down the room—but never going too far from the two armed guards.

There was a glint of enthusiasm in his eyes, and his voice sounded louder as he continued:

"They had developed a discipline, by practicing, suffering, patience, and accurate cooperation, that was unique for the human race—and at the same time human enough to be able to carry it into effect."

He snapped his fingers.

"All of a sudden there was plenty of food again. It rained grain when the fields were bare. At the same time, there was beef and pork when the stables were empty. There was beer and even that exquisite mead... But even magicians are not able to make something out of nothing. Something very special must have happened there. Short and to the point: supplies had to be stored up and replenished and should be within easy reach at any time. The priests of Tyr were able to combine their spiritual power, and they used it to bring food supplies in safety to places no one else could find."

He snapped his fingers for the second time.

"They made grain and meat disappear. To invisible places far out of reach of the uninitiated. A magic move, born out of necessity. To die or to work magic, that's what it was all about."

Now he eyeballed Wolf.

"A hard, hard road for everyone involved. Then ... and now! Need, death, horror, refusal, loneliness, patience ... the kneading of the sensitive mind. A forgotten discipline. That is to say, almost forgotten. Because I rediscovered the old traditions, I took my first careful steps on the Path of the Unknown, and slowly but surely it all became clear to me."

He sat down again, leaned backward, folded his hands behind his head, and stared up at the collar beams of the high ceiling. It was as if he were mainly talking to himself when he continued:

"I became an initiate ..."

Everyone had listened in silence. Now Krohn said in a loud voice:

"How can someone find out about facts that will remain a secret forever to everyone else?"

Still looking up, Blum shrugged his shoulders.

"Every destination can be reached in different ways. Straight on to it, via a side way, walking, by train... Please permit me to come up with another comparison. Maybe you all know the story about that experiment developed by medieval men to prove that life can originate spontaneously. They filled a wooden barrel with trash. They let it be for a couple of days. Then they searched through the trash, and guess what happened—in many cases, they caught a mouse in there. The rodent had, they were sure about that, risen from the trash. I am convinced that many of my theories don't fit, but still, I reached the intended result. The medieval people showed the mouse as a piece of evidence for their thesis. I have shown you the neck ring as a piece of evidence for my thesis..."

He stood up for the second time.

"A collection of spiritual powers round a central, coordinating brain, that's the beginning. That's the barrel, filled with trash. A golden bracelet and a golden necklace are the found mice. Oh, my organization has much power."

 43

Dr. Blum moved his forefinger over his nose and then stroked with thumb and forefinger down along his eyebrows.

"The *T* from Tyr," he said. "The uninitiated believe it's a way to recognize each other during a greeting. What utter nonsense! All members of my society know each other very well. The gesture activates that part of the brain that makes us susceptible to each other's thoughts. A telegraphic system without wires. Some members of the society, far away from here, have received an impulse now, and I'll ask them to help me with a little experiment. Pay attention please, for it's going to happen right now..."

There was silence.

Wera stood up and started walking with wooden steps over the parquet. Fritz did the same. For a moment they stood face to face with each other, then they took each other by the hands and started to dance. They stared out in front of them with glazed expressions in their eyes.

"Stop it!" cried Wolf. "I don't feel like being forced to look at the show of a mesmerist. Get down to business, Blum!"

"All right, all right," said Blum. "But don't forget—I'm not making use of any vulgar tricks here, I'm showing you the results of year-long cooperation with...kindred spirits!"

Wera sat down again, and Fritz went back to his corner.

"Magicians saved people from starvation. Times changed. Precious metals always had been unknown—amber was the most valuable product around. Trading and fighting, with Celts and Romans, brought riches in the shape of gold and silver! Weapons, ornaments, coins. In our days one finds much evidence of this. Excavations! One put big treasures into the ground, as an offering to the gods or to keep it hidden from the enemy. But the magicians knew another way to put their treasures in safety, out of reach of anyone who was not initiated. It was given to Tyr, or, better said, it was put into a heavenly safe."

He pointed up to the ceiling.

"There, where the human eye cannot see it, still lie the treasures that the magicians once brought there and never fetched back again."

Blum turned and strode out through the arched passage. The two guards remained in their seats.

Not much later some women came in. They brought tea and dishes with sweets, which they put on the table.

Everyone was whispering as if they found themselves on sacred ground.

Wera could not remember having danced with Fritz.

"Most of the time I can see through tricks," muttered Wolf. "And Johan has become a man of much experience as well and smells trickery from a great distance. But this time..."

No one drank from the tea, and no one touched the sweets.

 44

Blum was back. It was impossible that he had heard what Wolf said, but it seemed as if he had been able to read his mind when he said:

"It is of great importance that every member of the group has learned to concentrate, unconsciously, on all others. Every second of the day, every second of the night. A small part of the brain remains on the alert constantly for impulses from the others, no matter the distance between us. Not everyone is talented enough to be able to play that game. It's a matter of separating the wheat from the chaff. Now please, friends, drink, eat. I want you all to feel comfortable."

"I'm not your friend," sneered Wolf. "Just see how far you remain standing away from us!"

"Let me go on with my explanations," said Blum, ignoring Wolf's remark. Just as the priests of Tyr came together from all different regions to exchange experiences and cement relations, we also see each other every year. I know, Wolf, that you and Dr. Krohn followed us when we went up to the mountain with the students in the night, after the festivities. We kept up an ancient tradition. We sharpened our minds. This time it was other people's fear that we were after. We fed ourselves with external emotions. What might seem cruel to outsiders is an absolute necessity for us. Well then, back to the valuable treasures hidden by the priests of Tyr...I almost forgot to mention that the Celtic druids probably knew the secret of disappearing as well, which will only make the mountain of gold and silver that's for the taking out there much higher!"

With his hands on his back, he paced up and down between the armed guards.

"Ah! How much gets lost in the course of time! Who knows how many useful arts and sciences could be found again. But no, I must not wander from my subject. What we have is a group, under the leadership of a central brain, that is able, undoubtedly in an unorthodox way, to breathe new life into old rituals. It remains a riddle to me whether the old priests were able to make something disappear without an eligible middleman. Unfortunately—I repeat: unfortunately, I am dependent on a middleman. Nothing seems to be more difficult than finding someone who can be sent on this miraculous mission..."

He heaved a deep sigh.

Then he started to muse.

"Yes, oh yes, the ancient priests needed middlemen as well. This was revealed to me in many a dream. How did they call them? Messengers? Probably not. They could have been called sowers, the ones who brought the treasures away, and harvesters when they went to collect them again. Yes, that's very well possible. But more was revealed to me in my dreams. The sowers and harvesters had a pet name. One called them crows. Crows! Images in stone have been preserved of the old god riding the sky on his horse, and the crows are flying above his head!"

He looked around with the eyes of a madman. He licked his lips. Then he pointed at Fritz.

"See him standing there, unaware of my spiritual influence on him."

Then he pointed at the group.

"My power reaches far. Whom do I have in my power? Whom of you? Wera…Wolf…"

He gasped for breath as if he had become very tired all of a sudden. His eyebrows slid down.

"I have to admit that I have sacrificed lives for my case. There were no other possibilities. I had to do my tests. Every now and then you lose a subject. Just like that, men and women vanished into thin air and never came back again. Others went crazy. Crazy! They pass their days here, and I cannot help them anymore. They never became crows who flew to places where the gold and the silver are up for grabs. But now I have Wolf! A well-trained crow who has already proved his usefulness. The bracelet, the neck ring! What a splendid catch!"

He sat down on the floor and made a sad face.

His guards fidgeted in their chairs. For a moment it appeared that Blum would burst out crying. He rubbed his eyes and made a long face. After a while, he scrambled to his feet and started pacing up and down again.

"We searched everywhere for the perfect crow who could fly towards fortune on the wings of our combined thoughts. And there was Wolf. He got an idea—at least, he strongly believed that all his plans came to him spontaneously. He set out on a journey, visited the mediums and magicians of our time to test them—but in actuality he himself was the one who was tested over and over again."

While he said all this, he evaded Wolf's glance, but now he looked directly at him.

"Perhaps I should give furnish conclusive proof of this assertion. Go back in thought to Prague. You were riding a horse, following the Moldau. Something drew your attention. Something forced you to look round. You saw a coach stop at an inn, and you went there. Inside the inn, you met a fortune-teller who called herself Emma. She gave you a playing card, and later you would see how on one side a drawing of the harbor of Lindau came into being. When she left the inn, you followed her coach. How I would have loved to see your face when you discovered that the coach was empty!"

He put his hands on his hips and roared with laughter.

"To us, it was an important experiment. Would you actually go to Lindau? Then you sent everyone a watch with an inscription. The date. The place. Lindau. A golden watch! That was, without you realizing it, a symbol for everything I wanted. It was time to find gold... I do understand that it makes someone sad when he finds out that not all his acts were done out of free will. It must be hard to find out that another, external power is able to influence your life. If you think about that for a long time, you get a feeling as if someone had crept into your head. A little, invisible creature that doesn't want to get out any more."

His words made Wolf shudder. Besides his rage, another emotion had come up fear.

Wera, who was sitting next to him, searched for his hand with hers. Her fingers felt cold. The others sat there motionless as if they were posed for a painter - the little table with untouched sweets and tea was like a still life.

"We have tamed a crow," sounded the voice of Blum. "Now we'll let him fly again."

He looked at the company with a conceited smile.

"I'll leave you alone for another while," he said. "As soon as I come back, I will give you my demands."

He turned around, straightened his back, and strode like a king through the arched passage.

 **45**

Everyone leaned forward with a sigh, now that the Blum's absence had eased the tension. Michaela complained about a headache. The guards stood up to stretch their legs. Fritz remained standing in the corner like a statue.

"How wonderful would it be," sighed Krohn, "if we only had to state the fact that Blum himself is the merest fool in his own madhouse. Then we wouldn't have to feel so unbearably terrified."

The others reacted with a murmur of approval.

Wolf pushed Wera's hand aside and stood up. With slow steps, he went up to a window and observing from the corner of his eye how much leeway the armed men were willing to allow him.

They let him be.

Behind the barred window was a peaceful world. A blue sky, a white park, and in the distance wooded mountains.

He stood there for a long time, listening to his friends discuss things in low voices.

How he wished that he was able to knit his problems together into a monster, a visible, tangible creature to try to defeat. It was frustrating to have to admit that he had no grip on the situation and that his future could be determined by a man like Blum.

Suddenly he heard Blum's voice again, and he turned around.

There he stood. A serious-looking man, a doctor with a practice in Heidelberg. A man who sacrificed lives in pursuit of gain.

He is the visible monster, thought Wolf. *He is the one who must be destroyed.*

He walked back to his chair, and Blum began to speak.

"We'll be Nibelung, the owners of the treasure. Listen, for this is what I have decided to do. It is good to know that Wolf is not all by himself here, but is surrounded by good friends. It depends on him how long he'll still have these friends. First I'll address myself to Wera. My dear Wera, you've been a fine candidate—almost as good as Wolf himself! We nourished high hopes for you. Unfortunately, you couldn't fulfill our expectations. You were absolute putty in our hands, we could do with you as we pleased . . . except for one thing: we couldn't make you fly into the far distance like a crow, to behind the horizon of our perceptible existence, where the treasure of the Nibelung can be found. You heard me talking about Wolf with other people. You were disobedient and fled to Amsterdam. It wasn't to earn that thousand guilders. You wanted to escape from the will of our collective, and you knew you couldn't do that on your own. You hoped that a man like Wolf would be able to help you. We didn't lose contact with you, not for a single moment! We changed you into a monster when you were ready to ask him for help. We drowned your pleas in blood! But now you have become useful to us after all. Not our will, but fate, has decided that special feelings come into being between Wolf and you. I promise you solemnly, Wera, that you will be the last person to die if Wolf doesn't do his work well when he betrays us or lets us down."

Everyone was too dazed to react.

Only Wera made herself heard with a half-sob.

"I say it once again; it is good that Wolf didn't come here all by himself. He's here with his friends. And now he's going to work for us as soon as possible. He's going to fly! The divine crow is going to search for what's been hidden in the past. When something goes wrong, when there's obstruction from his side, or worse, when he simply refuses to co-operate, there will be an execution. According to old customs, someone will get hanged! The first victim will be Michaela Krohn."

Michaela sat up and immediately fell forward. Her husband caught her. He held her in his arms, limp as a rag.

"Dr. Hans-Erich Krohn will be the next one. Wolf's faithful companion Johan will be the third. Wera is number four. I don't think you'll have to worry about a thing, Wera. By the time it has come so far that Johan dangles down from a rope, Wolf will have understood that it is wiser to cooperate with us."

Wolf jumped to his feet.

"Enough, Blum, enough! If you know almost everything about me, you'll have heard about my riches. I have money, valuable property. Let my friends go, and I will pay you. As much as you want."

Blum shook his head and started to grin.

"Of course I know that you're a rich man. But everything you have pales into insignificance beside the treasures you will bring me soon. Be wise. Cooperate. And soon you'll be many times richer yourself."

"I cannot work together with a murderer."

"Murderer. It's only a word. All I did was following a winding path that led to my destination, as exactly as possible according to the indications of the priests of Tyr. Human sacrifices to the gods, Wolf, have always existed to bring a certain elite up to a higher level."

"How high is the level of gold and silver only?"

"Now you're mistaking. Think! Of course, there will be riches for me, for you, for your friends. But we'll also bring history to life, we'll bring back objects from ancient times. We'll find out together if the old Germanic trick is applicable to the Celtic traditions, to the Romans... It will all be so very easy for you to do. I am the one who made it all possible, and I know I've gone too far every now and then. But you are perfectly innocent, no blood taints your hands. If we get in trouble and you are called to account for your deeds, you can always claim that you were forced to work with me, that you did it to save the lives of your friends. That won't even be a lie, will it? Help me, cooperate with me, and be assured that Hans-Erich and Michaela Krohn, Johan Simons, and Wera Keller will stay alive."

Wolf was too shocked to react.

Krohn then spoke.

"Inside these walls all the power is yours, Blum—that can't be denied. We are doomed to listen to your horrible words. It is obvious that you attach no value at all to the lives of countless individuals. But maybe you are not as powerful as you think yourself."

Blum gave him a questioning look.

"What do you mean?"

"Who is the man called Eckart? The man that was being buried when we arrived here by coach and who seems to have risen from the dead?"

Blum moved his hands nervously to and fro as if groping for the right words. Then he raised both hands and shrugged his shoulders at the same time.

"Eckart," he said scornfully. "Who can tell who he is? Or better, who he was? Maybe he was nothing other than a product of my fantasy, of my power of the mind. Anyway, he wasn't someone you should worry about, and he wasn't a man who was able to limit my authority here."

Johan slowly stood up. With his eyes tightly shut he began to dance about. Soon he spun around like a dervish, holding his head to one side as if he listened to something only he himself could hear. As if hypnotized, he moved through the big room.

Only Wolf knew what he was up to when Johan started to sing in Dutch—words that no one else could understand.

"Don't you think I'm crazy, don't you think that I'm a fool. Now I'm going to make him scream. One hard blow on his temple ..."

Even the guards fell for it and remained sitting on their chairs with their mouths wide open. Johan moved closer to Blum. He spun around faster and faster. He stretched his arms and clenched his fists.

Suddenly he flew at Blum.

Blum was taller than Johan, and the shorter man let his fist come up with all his might. At the last moment, the doctor fell back but was still hit hard on the chin. The blow threw him out of balance and he stumbled backward and then sat abruptly on the ground. The guards jumped up. One of them called for assistance. Johan had to defend himself first against two, but soon against six men and more. Wolf ran up to help him. Michaela, not yet recovered from her breakdown, began to cry. Shots rang out. Johan gave a scream. Wolf caught one on the chin and was knocked down. Blum had scrambled to his feet again and shouted orders to his guards.

"No more shooting! Look out! I don't want Wolf hurt!"

Krohn dragged Michaela along with him and fled to the door. He managed to open the door and ran into the corridor. The guards tried to protect Blum and overpower Wolf. Johan limped around, his face twisted with pain, and blood dripped down into his left shoe.

The entire time, Fritz stood still as though hypnotized in his corner and stared out in front of himself with emotionless eyes.

Wolf wasn't afraid to receive hard blows and was standing on his feet again. He felt strong, knowing that no one would dare to shoot him down.

One thought suppressed all others: *If I manage to get me a gun, I'll blow the brains out of Blum's head!*

No one seemed to be able to stop him.

Now he that finally could get into action, a special state of tension came over him, and his fear lessened with every blow he received or dealt.

Two men had put their rifles on the floor and came to blows with him. Wolf hoped that his rage would rouse his formidable powers one more time and make the entire building shake and bring panic to all occupants. But it didn't work; he was no longer able to bring these powers into play.

"Go away!" roared Blum. "Away! All of you! This is absurd! Tomorrow, after everyone has calmed down, we will talk again. You all need time to come to your senses."

A fist hit Wolf on the chin, and he was caught by strong hands. But he managed to free himself again and struck back. Wera had come standing behind him and tried to pull him away. Johan came limping up to him. All three of them reached the door through which Hans-Erich and Michaela had fled and ran into the corridor. Five guards followed them.

The door closed.

"Backward, backward," whispered Vera. "Maybe they'll let us go."

Stepping backward, they went deeper into the corridor. Wolf and Wera supported Johan.

Johan's dragging left foot drew a trace of blood on the stone floor.

"This way!" Krohn shouted behind them.

A moment later they all stood in a niche, next to a high, barred window. The guards lined up in front of them, not knowing what to do now. Krohn sat down on his knees and rolled back Johan's left trouser leg.

"Consider yourself lucky," he said. "It's only a grazing shot. The bullet could easily have gone straight through the bone."

He produced a big handkerchief and used it to tie up the bloody ankle.

Wolf panted heavily and stood there with clenched fists; his fury still hadn't spent itself.

"What are you up to?" he asked the irresolute guards. "Are you going to stand around here all day? Bring us outside and use your weapons to keep the dogs away from us. We've stayed far too long here; it's high time to go back home. We need a coach. Do you hear me? Are you all deaf or something?"

The men looked at each other and started muttering amongst themselves, considering what they had to do.

After some time a guard made a step forward and spoke.

"One of us will go to Dr. Blum. He will tell us what is going to happen next."

But the moment one of the guards turned around and started to return to the big room, a shot rang out.

Everyone looked up in surprise. All of the guards wanted to go back, but they realized that someone should stay with Wolf and his company.

Then a second shot rang out.

All of a sudden there was an abrupt and clearly noticeable change in the atmosphere.

Everything had remained visibly the same, but perceptibly something had disappeared—just like a lasting headache one has become used to that has suddenly gone.

Wolf knew what had happened.

A spell had been broken.

He could also discern it by the change in the attitude of the guards; they looked around in surprise as if they didn't know where they found themselves.

"The central brain is put out of action," said Wolf.

"What are you trying to say?" asked Krohn, gasping for breath.

Wolf carefully stroked his painful chin.

"Dr. Viktor Blum is dead," he said, loud enough for everyone to hear him.

Everyone went back through the corridor. The guards went in front and didn't bother any longer about Wolf and his company; they held their rifles loosely in their hands, and it wouldn't have been difficult to take them away from them.

A guard prepared to knock on the door. Another one shook his head, pushed down the door handle, and stepped inside. At that same moment, other people entered the room via the arched passage.

Dr. Blum was lying on the floor.

A rifle rested on his breast. The doctor's mouth was wide open, his dead eyes staring up to the ceiling. His head lay in a still swelling pool of blood. There was a hole in his forehead. The back of the skull was blown away, and the ruined brains had partly come out.

Opposite to him, with his feet turned to his side, lay a guard who still held his rifle in his hands. A bullet had hit him in the chest.

"It is obvious that they have shot each other," said a male nurse dressed in white, who walked up and down along the two bodies. "There remains the question as to which of them was the first to use his weapon."

He looked around in bewilderment.

"What now? What are we supposed to do?"

It was Krohn who seemed to be the first to recover himself. He knelt down next to the guard and felt his pulse.

"He's dead as well," he said. "The bullet probably went through the heart. Take both bodies away. How many doctors do we have in this building?"

The male nurse slowly shrugged his shoulders and the corners of his mouth slid down.

"I don't know that anyone here is allowed to call himself a doctor, although many do act that way. There is the nursing staff. There are men and women who are trained by Dr. Blum and who mainly have specialized in psychiatry..." He fell silent for a while, searching for words. "That is to say, psychiatry according to the rules of Blum himself. And now he's dead! Oh, what has happened here?"

"Remain calm. I'll go back to my suite," said Krohn. "My wife needs my help—she's totally upset. Then I'll wash my face and pulses with cold water. I need some rest, and I would like to have a good swig of brandy. Gather the entire staff and all servants and guards somewhere in a big room and then come round for me. For anyone who doesn't know it yet, my name is Hans-Erich Krohn, and I am a doctor with a practice in Munich. From now on I am in charge here. I want to have a talk with everyone, and I want to be informed about the patients and their circumstances. Now, do as I say!"

"I'll take care of that, Dr. Krohn," said the nurse, who immediately turned to a couple of guards: "Bring Dr. Blum and your colleague Mildenberger to the mortuary."

The bodies were picked up and carried away.

Krohn pushed Michaela and Wera with him to the door and beckoned to Johan.

"You better come with me. I will disinfect the wound and put on a clean dressing."

Wolf stayed behind in the room.

 46

Wolf looked at all the blood on the smooth floor. Then he looked up at Fritz, who still stood there in his corner and stared out in front of him with glazed eyes.

Wolf smiled.

"There's much more going on here, Fritz," he said. "It's a matter of lining up the events. What happened? Two rifles lay on the floor. I remember that very well. One guard stayed behind with Blum. I heard just now that his name was Mildenberger. He's just as dead as Blum, and the nurse asked himself aloud who had shot first—in the meantime, he walked with his big shoes through that pool of blood and probably erased any traces by making red footprints on the floor. But I don't need traces. When the central brain was blown out of the head of the doctor, it didn't only mean the end of Dr. Victor Blum, but it was also the end of the collective. The mental power had faded away. We might say that a fresh breeze went through the building and blew all misery away. In your case, Fritz, this should mean that you felt relieved of a burden and should no longer stand in such a contorted posture. I see the veins in your neck pulsate with tension. There is blood on your fingers... Isn't that strange?"

Wolf straightened his back, stretched out his hands, and stared at his own trembling fingers.

"Go and get yourself a drink somewhere," said Wolf. "You know your way around here. Later we'll find some time to have a talk together. All I want to say to you now is that I think you're a brave man and that you rendered the world a perfect service by shooting down Dr. Blum."

Wolf turned on his heels and walked to the door.

"I think that poor Mildenberger wanted to protect the doctor. You shot him first. The bullet from the second rifle you picked up from the floor was meant for the man who humiliated you for such a long time and whom you hated so much. Take this advice: don't drink too much, my friend. I do not know as much about psychology as Krohn, but I can imagine that fear will pounce on you after having killed two persons, once you have reached the bottom of the bottle."

Right before he stepped into the corridor, he heard Fritz stammer:

"Wolf . . . will I be condemned? Will they find me guilty? Will I die as well, will they put me in front of a firing squad?"

He turned around and looked at the old man.

"No, I don't think so. On the other hand, I do know enough about psychology to explain to everyone that you found yourself in a special, hypnotic condition when you pulled the trigger. You are a psychiatric patient. Besides, I think this is something that should better remain between you and me. I'll be the last to blaze this abroad."

"Thank you, thank you very much. I'm very grateful for that. But . . . but how was I able to do a thing like this, when the doctor had me under his spell?"

Wolf had to laugh.

"Something else in your brain was probably stronger."

"What might that have been?"

Wolf laughed louder.

"You were thirsty, Fritz. You were craving for a drink."

He closed the door behind him and knew that Fritz would run through the arched passage now, to start his search for a full bottle.

 47

Wolf went back to Heidelberg with Michaela to return the key of the house they had rented there. They stayed not a moment longer than necessary in that place where Viktor Blum had lived and worked and where he had been buried recently in the presence of a large audience.

They traveled on to Munich.

Michaela would sell the house there and dispose of their practice to someone else.

"We know many young doctors who are waiting for a chance like this," Krohn had said, "and my offer is very generous."

Krohn had determined to make a clean sweep of the mental home and help the patients, who mainly were victims of the experiments of Dr. Blum.

Wolf had bought the building from Blum's heirs.

In Munich he bid Michaela farewell and went on to Amsterdam by train, mainly to arrange his financial affairs there and to inform Abraham de Wild about everything that had happened.

Johan, whose foot had healed enough to be able to walk around, remained at the mental home in the Odenwald to make himself useful there.

Wera Keller had gone into nursing.

The journey to Amsterdam brought about in Wolf a state of reflection. He hadn't had the time earlier to digest the events. He pictured the faces of all the people he had met during his long travels through Europe. Half-sleeping, moving to and fro with the beating rhythm of the metal wheels on the rails, he revived the events at steam-engine speed.

And like so many a traveler who had experienced this before them, he had the impression that his home town had changed during his absence until he realized that there had been a change in himself. The Wolf that arrived was different from the Wolf that had left.

For seven days he stayed with Abraham de Wild.

He feasted on the meals prepared by Maria Sterk and Hilde Hertog, and at night he sat by the fireside with Abraham in the same room where he and Jacob van Beek had found themselves when Wera Keller paid them a visit.

During the night he dreamt about Wera.

When he left Amsterdam again, he was wearing the golden bracelet.

He left a bewildered Abraham behind—what he had told him about the doctor and his collective went beyond his comprehension!

 48

In a small village in Luxembourg, he knocked on the door of a medium
to whom he had sent a golden watch. Her name was Arlette Gilbert,
and during his first visit, he hadn't been able to catch her out in a lie
when he attended her séance. Now she looked at him candidly when
she sat face to face with him in the sunroom at the back of her house.

"I am very pleased with your visit," she said. "I was hoping for a
message from you, for a letter... Are you intending to drop in on
everyone to tell about your experiment in Lindau? If you only knew
how curious I have been all this time."

Wolf pushed up the sleeve of his jacket and showed her the bracelet.

"This is the result."

"An ornament?" she asked surprised. "I don't understand. Please
explain it to me."

There was deep wisdom in her big, blue, innocent eyes. Arlette was
fragile, of short stature, but she was mentally strong. She paid much
attention to her outward appearance and looked very much like a noble
lady. Despite her age—she was in her late sixties—she still had a
smooth face.

Wolf posed a counter question.

"Have you been in Heidelberg lately?"

"Yes. At the invitation of Dr. Viktor Blum. Oh, I still love to travel. It was such an extraordinary experience to be there. Why do you ask?"

"I can imagine that you were exhausted after you had climbed that mountain. Did you enjoy the mortal fear of all those students?"

He passed his forefinger down along his nose and then he stroked his eyebrows with the thumb and forefinger of the same hand.

Arlette gave a thoughtful nod.

"I know that sign. But you don't belong to our group. I think there's something you need to tell me. I will listen to you, Wolf. But first, allow me to give you some information. The doctor from Heidelberg is dead. I'm told that he was shot down by his own bodyguard. A bullet straight through his noble heart."

"He had no noble heart," said Wolf. "That's exactly why the man shot his sick brain out of his head."

"This is going to be a difficult talk," predicted Arlette. "Promise me that you will remain calm and tell me why you have come to pay me a visit."

"I'll do that. But let's go back in thought to Heidelberg first, to the students. I was there, too. I saw what happened. Some of them became hysterical with fear."

"The entire happening was a part of the training of our spirit. I admit that we may have gone too far in that. But it makes us stronger. And the students have no bad memories at all of what happened there on that mountain. We are—no, we were followers of the doctrines of Viktor Blum. A genius with brilliant ideas. Therefore I don't understand why you are talking about a sick brain."

"The experiments of Blum have produced quite some victims. A madhouse full of them, to be more precise. Some people didn't get locked into a little cell in the Odenwald at all; they simply didn't survive the experiments."

Arlette's mouth fell open.

"Wolf, I ... no, this can't be true. Tell me everything you know!"

That was exactly what Wolf did, and he did not skip a single detail. Arlette listened and shivered; then she burst out into tears. She shook her head fiercely.

"No, Wolf, no!"

He waited until she had calmed down again, and then he ended his story.

It was not easy for her to digest all this information. Suddenly she said:

"So Mr. Jacob van Beek was a business partner of your father. To you, he was like a second father, and he was killed by—by us! You don't think I had anything to do with that, do you?"

"You've just told me, Arlette, that everything that happened in the oak wood in the mountains near Heidelberg was to make you all stronger. The death of Jacob was a necessity, according to Blum, to make me more susceptible to the collective."

"When you came to visit me at one of my séances, you were testing me, Wolf. You were very taken with my performance and asked me to join an illustrious group that would help you to perform certain wonders. After that you traveled on to other people, in other cities, in other countries, to judge them and ask them, if they seemed to you capable, for the same favor. Further contact was by letter only. Now then, about the contacts between what you call the collective—"

"The Nibelung ..."

"Right. The contact amongst the Nibelung was by correspondence as well, except for one meeting a year. We have received many men and women and tested them. We were instructed about that by Dr. Blum. The reason for that was the fact that we were searching constantly for people who were susceptible to a power that was roused by a concentration of our spirits. If I had only known that ..."

She fell silent and started to sob.

"So there's actually something like a central brain?"

"But of course! Wolf, allow me to explain some things to you, as far as it isn't already clear to you. You know very well, being an investigator, that many persons like me make much money by acting as an intermediary. The living want to speak to the dead. How many times have you been present at séances like that? Between you and me, Wolf, no living soul has ever made contact with someone from the hereafter. Dead is dead, that's what we say. But that's not the end of the story, for you know it's all quite something other than practicing deceit. Things are quite different..."

"Some people are able to read others' minds."

"So you know."

"You have to come to a conclusion like that after having attended so many séances."

"I am blessed with that talent myself. I concentrate, go into a trance, and look right into the depths of someone's soul. The thoughts of other persons well up into my own mind. All I have to do then is to transform these impulses into words. That is why people who come to visit me come to hear so often what they want to hear... Their wishful thinking reaches the sensitive ears of my mind. It is a gift that men and women have had throughout all ages. It was Dr. Blum who went deeper into this affair and started to dig into the past. I don't believe he developed these theories all by himself; he had help..."

"Eckart?" guessed Wolf.

Arlette shrugged her shoulders.

"That name doesn't ring a bell. However, Blum came up with his unique ideas. He said that the ancient priests and priestesses stood out from the rest by their special talents; they were telepathists, fortune-tellers, magicians. From their midst, they elected the man or woman who could lead them mentally. Yes, the central brain."

"The spider in the occult web."

"Or the puppeteer who pulls all strings—or, better, connects all strings! That is especially important: connecting the strings. A network like ours should be as old as mankind itself. We were brought together by Blum and formed a strong group that did experiments all the time. We were almost Nibelung... But that had nothing to do with a treasure of silver and gold. We were, according to Blum, on our way to reach a mental state of delight. Then we would be Nibelung, as he used to say. We drew strength from each other's existence, we pulled strength from the minds of outsiders—like students of Heidelberg. And maybe that wasn't so nice, but for the rest, I am unaware of any evil from our side."

"How did you learn that Blum had passed away?" asked Wolf suddenly. "You said that someone told you. Who was that?"

"I knew it the moment it happened. Let me be honest about that. It went through my brain as a shock. In thoughts, I saw Blum fall to the floor, and I heard a shot ring out. Later I received a death announcement. And then I had this talk with Armand Montet, a medium from—"

"From Belgium. I know him. I visited him at his home, and I saw him in Heidelberg."

"You know all of us. Armand confirmed to me that Blum had been shot.

"I think you've told me the truth, Arlette. But there are also things you conceal from me. I think you're all doing that. I know everything about the mental home in the Odenwald, where Blum wielded the scepter and where he locked up people who knew too much and were of no use to him any longer. I've bought the building and all the grounds around it. We help the people there and try to teach them how to deal with their horrible experiences and how to live on. I also know that Blum frequently received guests in the mental home. Have you ever been there? Were you ever invited? It would be hard for me to believe that—just as I can hardly believe that all of you murdered Jacob van

Beek without individuals like you feeling guilty about it. The group did it, the individual feels perfectly innocent..."

Arlette gave him a begging look.

"Please Wolf, don't say things like that. And no, I've never been in the Odenwald. There were important differences between the members of the group. Some of us stood closer to Blum than others."

Wolf nodded.

"Maybe I should pay Reinhard Arntz another visit to his house in Vienna. The melancholic who conjures up giant rats to scare other people. Maybe I should scare him by putting a knife at his throat to make him talk."

"Arntz belonged to Blum's confidants," said Arlette.

Wolf stood up.

"I should visit all seventy-nine of them to question them closely."

"You've already started—with me," said Arlette, making an effort to produce a smile. "But believe me, Wolf, you wouldn't become any wiser. You would hear the same over and over again. It might be better to listen to me for a while. I'll tell you about the rules Blum drew up to which we've all adhered."

"I'm listening."

"We were initiated via a stream of letters. We stuck to all agreements. At set hours, every day, early in the morning and late at night, we combined our mental powers. For what purpose? You seem to know more about that than I do. Our energy bridged great distances. The energy came together into the brain of Blum. What exactly he did with it, we'll never know. Murder, as you told me . . . a search for the treasure of the Nibelung. Not a mental treasure, but a tangible one! I've never heard that the worshippers of Tyr were able to hide their treasures in such a particular way."

Wolf shook hands with her.

"Take care of yourself, Arlette. Goodbye."

Then he used his thumb and forefinger to make the sign of Tyr along his nose and eyebrows.

"Almost Nibelung," he said.

"Almost Nibelung…" repeated Arlette.

 # 49

Wolf decided that he wouldn't visit anyone else from the group of seventy-nine. He preferred to be alone and take his time to think. In Luxembourg, he bought himself a horse and rode to Germany. From the border, it was still a long, long journey to the Odenwald, but he knew that one day he would stable the horse there.

And so, on a sunny summer's day, he reached the forest path that led to the mental home; the last time the trees had been bare, and he had sat on the box of a coach. Now the sunlight hardly filtered through the roof of dense foliage, and he rode through half-darkness.

The journey had made Wolf serious.

And silent as well, for there had been no one around to talk to.

He longed to see Wera Keller again, Johan Simons, and Hans-Erich and Michaela Krohn. The feeling that he belonged here became stronger and stronger, and at different times he had thought about selling his Dutch property on the river Vecht and settling down there.

Every now and then he had to lean down over the horse's neck to avoid the branches that, heavy with leaves, hung low above the narrow path.

Wolf finally emerged from the gorse. He pulled the reins.

He saw an old man with white hair and a white, stubbly beard. He wore a worn-out, frayed black suit. Wolf stepped down slowly from his horse, and with the reins, in his hand, he came standing in front of the animal and looked at the man.

"Good morning. Do you need help?"

"You must be Wolf," said the man in a firm, clear voice.

"Do you know me?"

"I know many things. And I know many a thing without actually having seen it. My name is Eckart."

Wolf shrank back and bumped against the breast of the horse.

"It's all right, Wolf," said Eckart. "There's nothing to be afraid of."

"You were the central brain before Dr. Blum changed everything and took control," said Wolf recovering. "You found yourself in a cell next to that of a friend of mine, Johan Simons. In the mental home ..."

"That's right."

Wolf shook his head.

"You were dying, the communication with Johan cost you your last energy. When I arrived here for the first time, you had passed away. They were burying you. Later there was a panic. It was said that you had risen from the grave! Which is a miracle in itself. But isn't it even stranger that the dogs didn't tear you to pieces and that you survived in the cold winter—outside, in this forest? Or was there someone who helped you and brought you to a warm and safe place? I ... "

Eckart smiled and raised his hand.

"Quiet, Wolf, quiet. We have all the time in the world. Most important is that I am standing here in front of you now. We'll become Nibelung and make the most spectacular discoveries. Believe me, that doesn't have to be attended with misery and death. There is another road! A longer road, that is true, but at the end of it, we'll find everything Blum was so eager to find. Come, let's go on together. We're almost there, Wolf. The path is already going down. Round the bend, you can already see the big building..."

Eckart turned around and started to walk. Wolf walked alongside him, leading his horse by the reins.

"This is past all belief," said Wolf, still not entirely himself. "You are alive! Does your knowledge go back to the ancient times when one worshipped the god Tyr?"

The old man smiled and stroked the nose of the horse.

"Take this from me, Wolf: the old Germanic priests could do more than retire to their oak forests and predict the future by listening to the snorting of their holy horses—which is about all most people know about them these days. But in every medium, in every clairvoyant, we can find something of the old magic. Bring enough of them together, under the inspiring leadership of a high priest, and the miracles will happen of themselves. Believe me, soon we'll be Nibelung!"

Down below them was the building, surrounded by a splendid, green garden. They went down the path. A dozen dogs ran up to Wolf, tails wagging, and he reached out his hand to stroke them. They looked like wild wolves, but someone had managed in a short time to tame them.

A servant, whom he had seen before, came up to him and took the horse from him.

"Mr. Wolf. Welcome, welcome!" he said. "I'll bring you the saddlebags later. Please, go inside quickly. No one is expecting you. Everyone will be so pleased to see you again."

Wolf nodded and walked on.

He went up the stone steps. The big doors opened. Fritz stared at him, took his hands, and smiled.

"Wolf! Wolf! Come in, oh, please come in! I will call the doctor and his wife. And Johan, of course. And Wera! They won't believe their eyes. What a surprise!"

Fritz ran up the staircase.

Wolf listened to the footsteps on the wooden steps, which went up higher, higher, and higher, as if Fritz would storm heaven.

All of a sudden he was seized with fear.

He didn't dare to look back.

He thought of the dogs.

They had all come up to him.

To him alone.

The servant had greeted him.

Him alone.

Fritz had talked to him.

To no one else.

Who had the mental capacities of a high priest?

He wondered if he would actually look in the eyes of Eckart when he finally had the guts to turn around.

THE END

The Author – Koos Verkaik

Koos, a 'Dutchy' with spunk and an inexhaustible drive and fathomless imagination, is one of the most prolific authors of sci-fi and children's books in The Netherlands. His novels, All-Father and Wolf Tears, earned him the moniker, the Dutch Stephen King.

He wrote his first sci-fi novel, Adolar, in one weekend when he was 18 years old and the manuscript was published shortly thereafter.

Koos has published over 60 books, both children's books and novels, hundreds of comic scripts, and he has worked as a copywriter. He is currently working on several screenplays and new novels.

To read more about Koos and his work visit his website at www.koosverkaik.com or follow him on Facebook at https,//www.facebook.com/koos.verkaik.5

Also by Koos Verkaik

Novels in Dutch

Adolar

Terug naar het Dorp

Conflict Afrika

Mana, en Toen Brak de Hel los

De Meesterparasiet

Grapstad

Psycho Park

Alvader

Wolfstranen

Neanderthaler Dromen

De Dans van de Nar

Children's Book Series

Saladin Series

Saladin het Wonderpaard

Saladin en Silver

Silver en het Spookpaard

De Nar van Nottingham

Slimmetje Series

Het Konijn uit de Hoed

De Boze Beer

Schipbreuk

De Hoge Hoed is weg

Ridder Joris

De Schat van Kabouter Bollewijn

Professor in Paniek

De Tovertrein

De Verdwaalde Walvis

Sneeuwmannen in Kabouterland

Otto de Otter

Krimpende Paddestoelen

Wolpertinger series

De Monsterherberg

De Onderlanden

Het Land van Franje

De Drakentuin

Roest IJzervreter

Drie Dolle Prinsen

Koning Leo Lawaai

Alex de Grote

Heros de Haas

Novels in English

The Nibelung Gold

All-Father

The Dance of the Jester

HIM, After the UFO Crash

Heavenly Vision

Children's Book Series

Wolpertinger Series

The Monster Inn

The Downhills

Uncle Balloon

The Land of Fringe

The Dragon Garden

Rusty Iron

Three Mad Princes

Saladin Series

Saladin the Wonder Horse

Saladin and Silver

Silver and the Ghost Horse

The Jester of Nottingham

www.ingramcontent.com/pod-product-compliance
Lightning Source LLC
Chambersburg PA
CBHW070637260626
47161CB00007B/2744